FIVE BONE ANTHOLOGY 5

FIVE BONE ANTHOLOGY 5

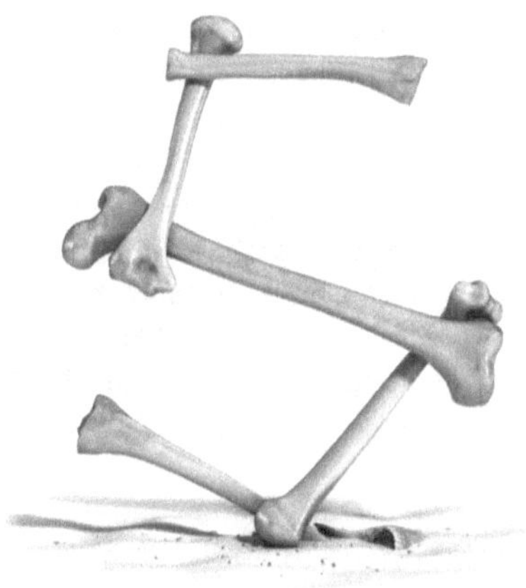

T.K. WRATHBONE

☠ Royal Star Publishing ☠

Skull & Bone is an imprint of Royal Star Publishing
www.royalstarpublishing.com.au

First edition paperback published in 2020

Trade Paperback ISBN: 978-1-922307-14-9
Large Print Paperback ISBN: 978-1-922307-15-6
Dust Jacket Hardcover ISBN: 978-1-922307-17-0
Case Laminate Hardcover ISBN: 978-1-922307-16-3
Trick Or Treat e-book ISBN: 978-0-6484864-5-9
All Hallows Possession e-book ISBN: 978-0-6484864-7-3
They Rise On A Blood Moon e-book ISBN: 978-0-6484864-9-7
The Bones of Wrath: Horrors e-book ISBN: 978-1-922307-13-2
A catalogue record for this book is available from the National Library
of Australia.

Cover design: Royal Star Publishing and Odyssey Books
Cover photos: istock.com/Koya79
Typesetting in Minion Pro by Royal Star Publishing

CONTENTS

TRICK OR TREAT

CHAPTER ONE

"Oh God, I feel sick," Robbie Colbert groaned to his fellow trick or treaters as they walked along the street in their neighbourhood. He and his friends weren't allowed more than a five street radius in any direction and they'd already done half of them.

"That's what you get for gutsing all of the Reese's chocolate you got." Pete Wells opened his bag and looked into it. They'd all exchanged their Reese's cups with Robbie for candy they wanted. And so far, Robbie had eaten a good fifteen to twenty pieces.

"Ugh, I know." Robbie's groaning continued and he clutched his stomach as if about to hurl. "But I love my chocolate. Ugh, hang on, guys." He bent over at the waist and, with hands on knees, breathed in.

"If you're going to hurl, Robbie Colbert, go and do it in the gutter." Jasmine Billings pointed to the side of the road. "I *do not* want you hurling all over me. This costume cost a lot of money." She glanced down at her Elsa costume with the long blonde braided wig. "My mother will kill you."

"Yeah, yeah." Robbie waved a dismissive hand

and fought the urge. He felt it fly up his insides and into his throat, and lunging for the gutter, he barely made it in time before all of the Reese's chocolate came back out.

"Ew…" the kids collectively complained. Besides Pete and Jasmine, there were Anna Gibson, who was dressed as Barbie, Bella Jessop, Jasmine's best friend, who was dressed as Anna, the other character from *Frozen*, and Kyle Richards who was Superman. All of the kids were in the same grade at *Richmond High*, and averaged twelve to thirteen years of age.

"Argh…dude…" Kyle pinched his nose between his forefinger and thumb and tried not to breathe. "Not cool, Robbie. So not cool."

"Ugh." Robbie rolled over and lay looking up at the early evening sky. "That's better. Anyone got any more Reese's?" He stared up at the five disappointing glares as they gathered around him. "What?"

"You just threw up what you ate and now you want to replace it with more?" Anna screwed up her nose. "You're such a pig, and make sure you don't have any spew on you because if you get it on me, I'll kill you." She glanced at her pretty pink ballgown-style Barbie dress and smoothed out the skirt. "It's gross and so are you."

"Come on, let's go," Pete told everyone. "We're only halfway done." Slipping his Batman mask over his eyes, he marched on to the next house and up to the porch, his friends following.

Robbie struggled up off the grassy kerb edge, checked his Robin costume, found some vomit, and flicked it off before hurrying after his friends. "Argh." His stomach churned and the pang in his side made him lurch to a stop at the fence.

"Trick or treat." The kids held up their bags to the home owner.

"Oh, well, would you look at that." The woman pretended to be surprised. "Who do we have here? Superheroes and princesses." She opened the screen door and held out a huge pumpkin bowl full of candy and chocolate. "Not too much now, just a handful each. Gotta save some for the other kids." She eyed Robin over her glasses. "Is he with you? He doesn't look too good."

They turned around to see Robbie leaning on her fence, looking green around the gills.

"Yeah," Pete muttered. "He's with us. Eaten too much already."

"Well, why don't you take a handful to him, to save him the trip, and from being sick on my lawn?" The lady held out the bowl to Pete. "Batman needs to help out Robin in his time of need." The twinkle in her eye gave her away.

Pete saw that twinkle and grinned. "Thank you." He grabbed a handful of candy, thanked her again, and rushed down the path to dump them into Robbie's bag. "There, don't say I never do anything for you."

Robbie glanced into his bag and saw a couple of Reese's cups. His stomach churned and he closed the bag. "I think I'll keep them for tomorrow. I don't feel so good."

"*Still!*" Kyle complained as they traipsed off down the road to the next house. "You may as well not bother with Halloween. Seriously, dude! This is the third year you've upchucked into the gutter from eating too much. You may as well just stop."

"*Stop!*" Robbie cried, horrified. "*Stop eating Reese's Peanut Butter Cups?*"

"*Stop trick or treating.*" Kyle rolled his eyes at Robbie's dramatic overtures. "It *clearly* doesn't agree with you."

"But I *love* trick or treating." Robbie fell into step beside him as they walked up the front path to the next house. "How can I give it up? It's the only way to get free candy."

"Is that all this is to you?" Pete asked before stepping onto the porch. "Free candy?"

"Ah…*yeah!*" Robbie put his hand up to stop their protest. "What do you think trick or treating is for, if not all the free candy?"

"The fun of the night," Pete said and stopped to ring the bell. "The thrill of the chase, the scaring of people, the wearing of cool costumes, the getting to hang out with friends. What else?" He turned to the door just as it opened. "Trick or treat…argh!" He jumped back and the others screamed and did the same, all staring at the werewolf lurking in the shadows.

"And what do you little kiddies want? A trick, or a treat?" the wolf asked, waving his clawed hands at them.

"Ah, ah, ah, treat," Kyle stuttered, knowing full

well it was just a man in a costume. But it was a very real-looking wolf costume that towered over him.

"And what sort of treat would you like?" The wolf stepped closer to the girls and waved his fingers under Jasmine's chin. "A good treat, or a baaaadddddd treat?" A deep, throaty sound came out with the last word.

"Ah…ah…" Pete gulped and stepped back, bumping into Robbie and Kyle. "Ah…ah…" He knew it was only a costume, but the homeowner was playing the part so well. "G-good," he managed.

"No!" Robbie scowled, finding his voice. "We want a *bad*. It's Halloween after all." He thrust his bag forward with both hands and opened it. "Bad please."

"All righty then." The wolf slunk back into the dark recess of the porch just as the light was flicked on.

"Oh, hello there, kids, my, don't you look good. Candy?" The middle-aged man stepped out the door with a bowl of goodies and saw them all gaping at the werewolf next to the door. "Ah, Waldo scared you, did he? Yes, he has the ability to do that. Not sure why, though. He's stuffed and just stands there. I keep him in my office for the rest of the year, and just bring him out at Halloween." He nudged his gold wire-framed glasses back up his nose with his knuckle. "I don't know why everyone's so scared of him. It's not as if he moves." He looked from Waldo, who stood tall on his hind legs, to the kids and held out the bowl. "Candy?" He eyed each of them as they one by one reached out a hand to grab some candy, their eyes never leaving the werewolf.

They managed to put the candy in their bags, thank the man, and slowly back down the path, their eyes never leaving the corner of the porch.

The man chuckled and patted Waldo on the shoulder. "Good boy. Heaven knows why they're so scared, though, it's not as if you talk, or move, or you're alive." Still chuckling, the man pushed his glasses up his nose, went inside, closed the door, and turned off the light.

Waldo's eyes glowed red and he waited for the next group of kids.

"*That. Was. Freaky!*" Kyle gasped in syllables, his heart pounding a mile a minute as they turned down the street. They all wanted to get as far away as possible from Waldo the Weirdo.

"*That* was scary." Jasmine placed her hand over her heart and felt the pounding under it. "*What was that?*"

"Maybe it was a mechanical thing," Pete suggested. "Like for a movie or something."

"*That was so cool!*" Robbie cried, shaking his fists and punching the air. "So cool!" He stopped when he saw his friends' expressions. "What? It *was* cool. A mechanical werewolf to scare kids at Halloween. How can that *not* be cool? All we need is a mechanical Dracula, zombie, Frankenstein—"

"Technically, it was Frankenstein's monster, not Frankenstein himself," Anna informed him. She loved to read and had seen multiple versions of the movie, as she didn't mind horror stories. But even this was a bit too much for her.

"Yeah, all right, know-it-all," Robbie complained. "You're draining all the fun out of Halloween for God's sake. I just hope other people have something just as cool."

"I don't," Jasmine muttered, and with a backward glance at the house they carried on down the street.

*****

"Children, bah!" the man exclaimed, throwing a hand in the air in exasperation. "Why do they have to come around? Why do they have to come…?" He moved the edge of the curtain aside with a crooked finger and peered out into the night, seeing bobbing torches and lanterns as the neighbourhood children went about hounding people for candy. "It's not what this night is about," he mumbled. "Not what Halloween is about. No, no, no." His head shook left to right with his words. "Not what Halloween's about at all. Bah! Children!"

He shuffled out of the room, across the hall, and into the room opposite to look out the window. "What do they want? *Candy*, the little gluttons. All the free candy they can get. Well, it's *not* free. No, no, no, not free at all since someone has to buy it. No, no, no. Someone has to buy it in order to give it out." He let the curtain fall and shuffled back into the hallway, glancing to his left into the dark expanse of the back of the house before glancing to his right. He stepped over to the door, lifted himself up on tiptoes, and peered through the frosted glass panel. "Little gluttons they all are. Wanting more and more and more."

He was glad the house was set back from the road and path and surrounded by dense bushes and trees. In the daytime, you could barely see it and no one bothered to come knocking because it looked abandoned. At night-time, it looked as if the house wasn't even there at all, and for those who knew it was, they didn't bother, just fearfully glanced up the path towards the blackness and raced on by. But come every Halloween, there was always a courageous one out there, needing to defy his friends or classmates and be the big man of the group. Every Halloween, there would be some idiot teenager who'd come running into the darkness of the lot, bang on the door, throw eggs, smash a window, and then go running back towards the safety of the road and their friends. Every damn year.

Shaking his head, he lowered himself and glanced over his shoulder into the blackness of the hall. Just another Halloween. Just like any other. "No, no, no," he muttered and shuffled back into the lounge room and looked around. The room was fairly bare, with only a small couch with two matching chairs, and a television that was his saviour. He didn't need knick-knacks, framed pictures, or photos on the wall. Didn't need shelves for books, didn't need rugs or carpet on the floor. But he did have curtains on all the windows, the ones facing the side, and front, of the house. He shuffled over and peered out of the one facing the street, seeing the sky was nearly black, the light was nearly gone.

The party was yet to begin.

CHAPTER TWO

"How many streets have we done now?" Bella asked, pulling her notebook out of her pocket and crossing off the street name on the list.

"You've got the list, you tell us," Kyle said and watched her count.

"Five streets left on the other side of Derbon Street, so six."

"Better get a move on then. I want more Reese's." Robbie barged ahead of them toward Derbon Street.

"Um…should we tell him…?" Bella murmured.

"That we weren't doing Derbon Street?" Jasmine finished. "I thought we had. Robbie," she yelled. "Robbie." They ran to catch up and caught him before he got halfway to the first house. Grabbing him, they swung him around.

"What!" he demanded with a growl.

"We weren't doing Derbon Street," Pete told him. "We never do."

"Why? Because of that old house?" Robbie frowned and tried to remember why. "Are we still bypassing a whole street of candy just because of one house?"

"It's not the house, just the kook inside," Jasmine reminded him. "Idiots have got lost in that place and never come out."

"That's just a myth," Robbie berated her. "We don't know that for a fact, and I personally don't know of anyone who's gone near it. Everyone gives the place a wide berth, but why should we keep missing out on the rest of the street for candy? We shouldn't. We can just bypass the house. And I, for one, am not the only one thinking that." He pointed and they saw multiple groups of children walking down Derbon Street.

They exchanged glances and Robbie said, "So, if they can do it, we can too. Let's go." Marching to the first house and up the path with the others following reluctantly, he waited for them before ringing the doorbell, and when the door was answered, they yelled out, "trick or treat." After being given candy, they went on their way with Robbie charging ahead.

"Does he *not know* that this is Derbon Street? *The* Derbon Street?" Kyle watched Robbie confidently stride down the path ahead of them.

"*Of course* he does, but he clearly doesn't care," Pete told him.

"He just wants candy." Anna rolled her eyes. "He's a glutton for punishment. And he'll end up being sick again if he eats all the Reese's cups we've ended up with."

They made it to the halfway point of the street and fearfully glanced across at the black abyss that was lot 666 before the chill in the air drove them towards the next house.

"Brains!" A zombie flipped up into a seated position from its place in a coffin in the front yard of the house.

"Cool! All we need is Dracula and Frankenstein," Robbie said.

"Frankenstein's monster," Anna corrected with a wave of her finger.

"*Whatever!*" Robbie objected. "*Argh!*" He jumped back as Dracula leered around the coffin on the other side of the path.

"I want to suck your blood," Dracula droned before retreating back into the dark so the mechanics could reset.

"*Awesome!*" Robbie fist pumped and noted the glowing pumpkins lining the path to the house. "This is one of the better set ups." He rang the doorbell.

"Yes." Frankenstein's monster turned on the porch light so they could see him standing in the doorway.

"*Double awesome!*" Robbie crowed and double fist pumped. "A Frankenstein—"

"Frankenstein's monster." Anna sighed.

"Trick or treat." Robbie held out his bag. "That is *one awesome costume*, dude." He noted the electrodes sticking out of the neck, the square head, the lopsided lips, and stitch marks.

"*Excuse me*, young man, but this is *no* costume," the man rumbled and left a handful of candy in each bag. "Unlike all of you, I don't get to take this off at night. It's the way I look permanently."

"Wait…what?" It dawned on Robbie and he flashed

a glance at the others who were just as surprised as him. "You really look like that? Like, *really* look like that, like, *in real* life?"

The laugh rumbled out of the man and he grabbed his stomach. "*Of course not*, lad. Had you all going there, didn't I. Hey, Sheila..." He walked into the house. "They actually believed me when I said I looked like this." His laugh continued as he shut the door.

"Brains!"

"Argh!" The kids jumped and spun around to see another group coming past the zombie coffin.

"Let's get out of here," Jasmine gasped. "I'm getting more freaked out by the second." They hurried past the group, along the street, and stopped to take a break.

"Blimey." Pete pulled off his Batman mask and swiped his forehead. "They get weirder and weirder every year. Did you actually think—?"

"*Of course not,*" Robbie boasted, puffing out his chest. "I knew he was having us on the whole time. I just went along with it to scare you lot." He looked from face to face to see scowls from the boys and raised eyebrows from the girls. "What?" He shrugged. "*Come on.* Like you really thought he was like that in real life. *Of course* it was a costume, it's Halloween. Come on, let's go."

They shuffled on down the road to house after house, calling out *trick or treat*, holding out their bags, which were filling up, and finally crossed the road and started down the other side.

"Cool, look at those!" Robbie pointed to the glowing carved pumpkins that lined the path to the front porch, and were placed all around the yard. Some even seemed to be floating in mid-air. "Ha, look at that one. That's so evil." Robbie stopped in front of the biggest pumpkin he'd seen. The face looked truly evil, and so well carved and lit up that it looked *very* real and alive.

"That...is *so* creepy." Bella's lips turned up in horror as she stared at it. "*So* creepy." She took a hold of Jasmine's arm and pushed her along the path. "Its eyes are following us," she whispered into her best friend's ear.

"Don't be silly, it doesn't have eyes," Jasmine chastised and then looked over her shoulder.

The pumpkin had turned around and was staring right at them. Its evil expression was haunting and chilling, almost as though it were laughing at them, which it was, since there was an evil cackling coming from its direction.

"Nope, I was wrong. It does have eyes and is freaking me out." She turned to her friends. "That pumpkin moved. It turned around to stare at us."

They glanced back at it to see it jiggling and the evil laugh emanated from its evil mouth.

"Whoa!" Robbie's eyes widened. "*That's so cool!* I gotta learn how to do that."

"Do what?" Pete asked, finally tearing his gaze away from their floating tormentor.

"Make one of those pumpkins," Robbie replied. "It's so cool." He stopped staring at it long enough to ring the doorbell, and when the door opened and the tenant stepped out, he looked up and up and up all the way to the pumpkin head on the top. "*Whoa, dude!* You've got a pumpkin for a head."

"Yes, young man, I do." The gentleman held out a pumpkin bowl of candy. "And so do all of my children. I see you've met them." He waved a long skinny arm above their heads to indicate all of the glowing pumpkins in the yard. "They all have names, you know."

The kids stared up into his pumpkin face, looked at his long, slender body, arms and legs, and realised he looked a lot like Jack Skellington from *The Nightmare Before Christmas.*

"Cool costume, dude." Robbie took a handful of candy and placed it in his bag. "You're the best so far."

"Costume?" The man's pumpkin face became puzzled. "What do you mean, costume? This is the way I always look. This is me, three sixty-five days of the year." He clicked his fingers and retreated inside, the door closed, the light turned off, and all six kids turned to see all of the pumpkins in the yard floating in mid-air and looking straight at them. Their evil grins were even more evil looking as they glowed bright reds and oranges, pinks and purples, blues and greens and yellows.

"*That. Is. So. Cool!*" Robbie bounced up and down in excitement. "*This* yard wins the best prize on Halloween." He ran over to one and waved his arms around it, over it, under it. "How is it doing that?" Puzzled, he bent over and looked underneath. Not finding anything, he stood up and scratched his head. "Seriously?" he asked the others. "How *are* they floating without strings or wires or sticks?"

"Dunno, but I say we get out of here." Pete moved the others down the path, onto the sidewalk, and heaved a sigh of relief. "Seriously, these people get weirder and weirder every year. I think they get into it even more than us kids." He waited for Robbie to join them before they moved on, and before long they came across the house they all tried to avoid.

Lot 666.

They stopped on the path while other groups veered out onto the street to avoid the place. Lot 666 had a reputation and neighbourhoods from all around knew it. Everyone avoided it, even the neighbours either side and across the road. No one looked at it or went near it. Everyone avoided lot 666 on Derbon Street like the plague.

So why were they all standing there, on the path, gawking at it now?

"Can we keep going?" Jasmine asked. Her stomach churned and quivered with nerves, and being there made her feel sick.

"We shouldn't be scared of a house," Robbie told them. "It's just a house." He waved a hand in frustration. "It's *just* a *house!* Why does it freak people out so much?"

"Because people have gone missing when they set foot on the property," Pete told him.

"Kids have disappeared at Halloween while trick or treating," Kyle added.

"Because they're stupid enough to go up to the front door and ring the bell," Bella chimed in. "Why take the chance on the stories *not* being true? We shouldn't go there. Period! Come on, let's go."

The girls started to move, but Robbie stopped them in their tracks. "Well, I'm going up there."

Everyone stopped and stared at him. "What?"

"I'm going up to the front door and I'm gonna knock." Robbie was staring intently into the dark black hole that filled the lot. He couldn't see the house from the street, and saw no lights illuminating the way, but he was determined to not believe the rumours. "I don't believe any of it. I think it's just stuff the adults made up to keep us away, and I'm not giving up the potential for more candy." The bravado he'd felt up till now was starting to wear off. "Who's with me?" Glancing over his shoulder at his friends, he saw their stunned and horrified expressions. "What?"

"Are you freakin' nuts?" Pete cried. "You'd risk life and limb just for candy?"

The bravado had nearly drained, but Robbie held on. "Yes. And I'm putting all of those rumours to bed." And with that, he opened the creaky old gate and marched into the blackness, leaving his friends behind.

CHAPTER THREE

They silently watched him go. Silently traded glances. Silently shrugged at each other, and silently moved to walk on. But they stopped after a couple of steps and traded another glance.

"There's no way I'm going in there," Jasmine declared. "*He* did this. *He* made the choice, and a stupid one at that." She crossed her arms defiantly. "You won't get me in there."

They watched as a group of kids detoured around them to bypass the house.

"See…even they don't want anything to do with it," Jasmine went on. "So why do we? Because our *stupid* friend had to go and be *stupid.*"

"And stupid or not," Pete cut in. "He's our friend and we need to go and get him. Who's with me?" He looked at each face hopefully and saw nothing but headshaking and frightened expressions. "Naw… come *on*, guys. We have to go and get him."

"*You* can," Anna told him. "*We* don't. He's *your* best friend."

"He's *your* neighbour," Pete shot back.

"But he's *your* best friend and a *stupid* one at that," Anna spat. "Just because we're classmates doesn't mean we're going to get him out of trouble all the time. And I mean, ALL.THE.TIME, because that's all he's *ever* in. *Trouble* with a capital T.R.O.U.B.L.E." She gasped in air and urged the girls on. "Come on, let Pete and Kyle go and get him."

"*Me!*" Kyle croaked. "I ain't walkin' up there." He pointed to the path leading to the house. "I ain't bein' caught dead in that thing. I'm going. Pete, you can go and get Robbie yourself, I'm with the girls." He walked after them, casting glances over his shoulder to see what Pete would do.

"Aw, *come on*, guys. I don't want to go after him alone." Pete stomped his foot. "Don't leave me… guys…" He watched them hurry past the property and frowned. How the hell was he going to find Robbie in that black hole, and had Robbie even found the house?

✳✳✳✳✳

Robbie's bravado had lost steam the moment he entered the property. He'd barely walked three feet along the path when he'd been swathed in black, the darkness enveloping him. All sounds had dulled. All lights had dimmed. And he was realising what a mistake it had been.

"I just wanted to look like the tough guy," he muttered under his breath. His eyes grew wide and took in everything around him, which wasn't much.

"I just wanted to be known as the kid who went into lot 666 and came back."

One foot in front of the other, he moved slowly, silently. A leaf crunched under his foot. "Bugger!" So much for silent. Maybe he should be louder? "Hey ho, hey ho," his voice faltered, "off to trick or treat I go…" *Why the hell would you start singing that?* he asked himself. "Hellooooo," he mumbled, hoping he was getting closer to the house. "Anybody there-ere…" His eyes moved rapidly from side to side. "Hellooooo."

The world was completely silent. Not a scream, not a cry, not a child getting excited over a piece of candy. Nothing. Absolutely nothing. A cool breeze ruffled his cape, causing the hairs on his arms to rise to attention, and he shivered as it sent a chill down his spine. *I must be absolutely bat shit crazy to think of doing this.*

His feet moved on, no longer controlled by him. He wanted to turn, to run back to the gate and his friends. To finish the last five streets off and go home and count how much candy he'd scored. But he couldn't. He'd be called a coward. A pathetic loser. Stupid. *Maybe I can say I rang the bell and no one answered. That no one lives here,* he thought. His gaze darted all over the place. *I could do that. Run back and say I'd done it when I actually hadn't. No one would know except for me. No one would be able to prove otherwise.* His foot hit something and he looked down. He tapped his foot against it, and felt the outline with it. *Is that a step? Have I reached the front porch?*

Gazing in front of him, he focussed on the small light on the floor. It was a pumpkin head, all aglow with the most evil expression he'd even seen. And he'd seen a few that night.

*****

"Oh, here we go," the man mumbled, heaving himself out of his lounge chair and over to the window. "One of them has dared to do it. One of them dared to set foot through the gateway and onto the path. Well, little does he know what he's in for." Silently shifting the curtain aside, he watched the boy tap the front step with his foot, look up and see the pumpkin, and slowly walk up the steps to the porch.

The man shuffled into the hallway and peered through the glass pane on the door. He knew no one could see him. Knew no one could see the house at night. It was all part of the problem. He could see them, but they couldn't see him or the house until they were standing on the porch, and by then, there wasn't anything he could, or *would*, do. And neither could they. He watched the boy slowly make his way forward, glance around at what little he could see of the house, scratch his head and clutch his candy bag for dear life. *He has no idea, the poor sod. But it's not my fault. I didn't do this. I don't make it happen. I just live this nightmare like all of the helpless souls who dare to cross the threshold.*

He lowered himself from his tiptoes, his old

withered hands almost flat against the door, and bowed his head. His lips murmured the Lord's Prayer, although no sound came from between them, and when he was done, he slowly glanced over his right shoulder into the black abyss of the hallway.

A low growl wafted in the still, dry air and a large pair of red eyes slowly opened to gaze at him. It only came alive each Halloween when it fed, waiting for him to find it prey so it could feast on All Hallow's Eve. And while the centuries had been long, it turned out that America had one of the best feeding grounds. Not only did they celebrate Halloween like other countries they'd lived in, but they trick or treated on that night. And with Americans being overweight, there were plenty of juicy fat kids around who wanted more and more and more and had no problem doing whatever it took to get more. Even if that meant stepping across the threshold.

*****

"Okay, I'm going to look for Robbie myself," Pete called out to the others. "Can you at least come back and stand guard?"

Kyle and the girls stopped, heaved a collective sigh, and turned around. They'd just gone past the premises and wanted to keep on going, but loyalty to their friend made them stop.

"What do we do?" Bella asked, watching everyone's faces for confirmation.

"We could stand guard," Kyle said. "That's all

Pete asked us to do. Easy enough."

"I guess we could." Jasmine nervously bit her lip while she thought about it. "As long as we don't go onto the property."

They traded glances and walked back to Pete.

Relief flooded through his body. "Thanks guys. I don't know how far in the house is, but I'll run in, grab Robbie, and run out. Sure you don't want to come with?" he asked hopefully, looking at each face.

"No way!"

"No how!"

"Nah-ah!"

"Are you crazy!" Anna said. "It's bad enough Robbie was stupid enough to go in there, and now you want to go in after him. Doesn't mean *we* have to."

"Okay, okay, I'll go on my own then," Pete placated them and tied the two handles of his candy bag into a knot. "Here, look after this and don't let anyone get it." He handed the bag to Kyle. "I'll be able to move faster without it, or worrying about dropping some, or losing it." Pulling off his cowl mask, he handed that over too. "Okay." He huffed in air a few times and jumped up and down on the spot to get the blood flowing.

"You're not running a marathon," Anna told him. "What *are* you doing?"

"Getting the blood flowing because I'm about to run." Pete took a couple of deep breaths, shook his arms, took another three breaths, and opened the gate. "Okay, here I go." He left the gate open and ran for it. He had no idea which way he was going, but felt a force directing him which way to go, until, finally, he came in view of the front porch and Robbie bending over to look at the glowing pumpkin beside the door. He saw Robbie jump back in surprise, wave a hand in front of his face, stumble, drop his candy bag, and slump to the floor. "Robbie!"

*****

Anna, Bella, Jasmine and Kyle had been waiting for a signal, or even for their friends to come back since Pete had gone rushing in like a bull at a gate. They watched groups of kids go past. They pointed and laughed, or shook their heads and moved on, giving lot 666 a wide berth. But one group of friends stopped to ask what they were doing.

"Idiot Robbie thought he'd risk life and limb by going and knocking on the door," Anna told them. "Pete went in after him, and now we're just waiting for them to come back."

"You *have* to be an idiot to consider that," Mark Beldair replied. He was in the same class as Pete and Robbie so knew exactly what both boys were like. "Do they *not* know what that place is about?" Just looking into the blackness gave him chills down the spine.

Jasmine rolled her eyes. "He did, he does, but didn't care."

"How long's he been gone?" Declan Pierce, another boy from their grade asked.

Kyle looked at his watch and was astonished to see so little time had passed. "Only five minutes or so, but it seems so much longer."

"If they don't come out soon, you'll have to go in there and get them," Lila August said. She was in class with Jasmine and Bella, but didn't hang out much after school and had different friends. She glanced over their costumes and then down at her own. She was Wonder Woman, and decided that was considerably better than being a princess.

"What are you going to do?" Trixie Power asked. She was friends with Lila as their elder sisters were best friends.

Kyle cast another glance at his watch and then the girls, who all shrugged. Only a minute had gone by since he'd last checked his watch, but he was wondering what was taking Pete and Robbie so long.

CHAPTER FOUR

"Robbie!"

They heard Pete yell out and immediately zeroed in on the spot the house would be. It was so dark they couldn't see a thing.

"Guess that's your cue to find them," Declan said. "Coz we ain't going in there. Good luck." He and his friends hurried on, but kept looking over their shoulders to see what their classmates would do.

"Do we have to go in?" Bella asked, nervously pulling on the drawstring of her candy bag. "I don't want to."

"Well…we don't know *why* he yelled out." Anna crossed her arms to ward off the chill permeating the air. "They *could* be coming."

*****

Pete saw Robbie fall and charged up the stairs, only to watch as the floor opened up beneath his friend. Robbie fell through, candy bag and all, and the porch floorboards settled back in place as if nothing had happened. "What the hell?" Pete stopped short and peered down. "Robbie?" He took a step closer and called a little louder. "Robbie?" Another step and he crouched down on all fours and felt around with his hands. "Robbie?" He inched forward, but found nothing. Not even by the faint glow the pumpkin was giving off could he see much, but he had seen enough to know his friend had gone. He sat back on his haunches and yelled. "Robbie… Robbie…" Banging his fists on the floor, he crawled towards the door where he banged some more, and climbing to his feet, he tried to look through the glass pane. "Hello! You've got my friend. I want my friend back. He fell through your porch." A cackling came from beside him and he looked down at the pumpkin.

"Trick or treat," it cackled. "Do you want a trick or treat?"

"I want my friend back." Pete moved over to it and bent down, the same action he'd seen Robbie do before stumbling backwards. "Where's my friend? What have you done with my friend?"

The pumpkin's laughter sounded like a witch's cackle that rose in decibels until it suddenly dropped to a deep growl. "He's been sacrificed." A mist spray released into Pete's face, making him stumble back the same way Robbie had.

"Hey, what is that? What have you done?" Pete waved at the air to get it away from his nose, but the effects of the spray included dizziness and he was falling fast. "Ugh." He slumped to the ground, his eyelids fluttering until they finally closed.

The porch floor flipped open and Pete was gone.

*****

They'd heard him yell, and were tempted to run for help, run next door, run across the road. They did. But neighbour after neighbour turned them down, shook their heads, and told them to call the police.

Finally, Anna, Jasmine, Bella and Kyle converged back in the spot they'd heard Pete's cries and tried to make a decision.

"We can't go in, we just can't," Bella fretted, nibbling on both her lip and fingernail. "Why don't the neighbours want to help? Our friends are in trouble."

"*We* don't know that, and *they* don't know that," Kyle told her, winding and unwinding his candy bag cord around his finger. "We don't know what's going on."

"And that's the problem," Anna said. "We heard Pete yell multiple times. Yell Robbie's name, *not* 'help', *or* 'guys', *or* 'help someone'. He didn't yell anything but Robbie's name. He could have been yelling Robbie's name to find him, so Robbie could hear him. *That's all.* How long have they been gone?" She tugged on Kyle's arm.

He pulled back the sleeve of his Superman costume, feeling like a fraud since he couldn't even save his friends, and pushed the button to light up his watch. His eyes widened in surprise. It had only been a minute since the last time he'd checked when they were talking to their friends. So Robbie and Pete had been gone seven minutes in total. "That…can't…be…" he muttered, perplexed by the time. He tapped the watch's face and flicked the light on again. Still seven minutes. Something was definitely going on and it all had to do with 666 Derbon Street.

"What do we do?" Jasmine held on to Bella for grim death. "We have to go in."

"No, we don't, we don't," Bella's voice came out unsteady and high-pitched. "We don't. We can't go in, we can't. We won't come out."

"Don't be silly," Anna chastised and straightened her ball dress. "We have to, come on. Let's go."

Inch by inch they shuffled as a group across the threshold, leaving the old rusted gates open for their return.

"I think we should link arms," Jasmine whispered in the dead night air. "That way, we'll stick together and not get lost."

"Good idea," Bella whispered back, and since she was still clinging to Jasmine, inched closer to Anna and Kyle.

Kyle slid his left arm through Anna's right, while the girls were on the other side.

"Right," Anna murmured determinedly. "Here we go."

As a foursome, they slowly moved forward. One foot in front of the other, their gaze darting all over the place, their heads turning left and right for any sign of their friends. But all they saw was blackness. All they heard was silence. So they kept on, one foot in front of the other, arms linked with one another's, and they powered on in the pitch black.

"I'm scared," Bella murmured, her heart pounding in quadruple time. Her eyes were as wide as she could make them. "And it's creepy."

"It is," Jasmine agreed, her arms linked with Bella's and Anna's. "How far in is the house?"

Anna glanced up at the sky, but saw not a star twinkling, even though it was a clear night, and she knew the stars were out because she'd looked up at them periodically while they were trick or treating. "I don't know. Whenever I've seen the house you can definitely see it from the street, and the path seemed straight, but we've been walking for ages."

"And the path seems curvy," Kyle muttered. "We've been walking left to right and right to left."

"Yeah, I noticed that too," Anna replied. "We *should* be at the house."

There was no breeze, so no tree swayed. No moon, so no light to show the way. It was as if they'd walked into a black hole filled with nothing.

"Can we go back?" Bella glanced over her shoulder. "I can't even see the street anymore. I can't see any kids, no lights, no nothing." She looked at her friends. "I'm scared. I want to go home and let the police come and look for Robbie and Pete."

"We can't leave them," Kyle whispered loudly. "They're our friends. How bad would we look if we didn't do anything?"

"It would look even worse if *we* go missing while looking for our missing friends," Anna snapped. Her frustration with her two classmates was boiling over. "Of all the stupid, low down, idiotic things he could have done, Robbie had to come onto this property and be stupid." Her eyes narrowed and she saw the front porch. "We're nearly there, come on."

They quickly moved forward and hit the first step of the porch.

"We're at the house," Jasmine whispered, looking all over for any sign of her friends.

"And we haven't found them." Kyle peered at the house and barely made out the outline of the door. "We didn't come across them on the path, so they weren't coming back."

"So where are they?" Bella barely managed to speak, for the words were caught in her throat and choking her.

"Don't know," Anna murmured, more to herself. "But we need to knock on the door to see if they're inside." Staring at the door, her eyes adjusted to the very dim lighting and saw no other lights. At least, none on the inside, and there was only the pumpkin on the outside. "But it doesn't look like anyone's home."

"So where are they?" Bella repeated. "If we didn't run into them, and they aren't here, where are they?"

"Only one way to find out." Anna planted her right foot on the bottom step and rose to plant her left foot beside it. Her arms were pulled back because Kyle and Bella hadn't stepped up with her. "Guys," she whispered. "Come on, we have to knock on the door, come on." She tugged their arms to make them move, and reluctantly, they all stepped up beside her, and kept stepping up until they were standing on the porch and facing the door.

"I can't see anything," Kyle whispered. "Is no one home?"

"I don't think so," Anna replied. "But we have to find Robbie and Pete. So I'll knock, okay." She glanced at the others and saw them nod in the faint light of the pumpkin. Breathing in deeply, she stepped forward, raised her right hand, curled it into a fist, and knocked on the door.

The sound resonated throughout the house, empty, almost to its shell.

"Trick or treat," cackled from below them. "Do you want a trick or treat?"

All four of them looked down to see the light glowing brightly from the pumpkin with the evil face carved into it.

"Trick or treat…do you want a trick or treat…?"

"That looks a lot scarier than the other pumpkins we've seen," Kyle murmured as they gathered around it. "What *is it* with all of these pumpkins and the owners carving evil features on them? Ugh!"

"We want to know where our friends are," Anna told it. Her eyes took in the details and she swore she saw it move. Bending down, brow furrowed, she sensed it was watching them just as they were watching it. "Where are our friends?"

"Trick or treat," the pumpkin cackled. "Do you want a trick or treat? A boy named Pete, or lots of candy to eat?" The cackling laugh rose.

"What…?" Jasmine frowned. "What did it just say?" She glanced at her friends. "Did it just mention Pete?"

"Trick or treat, do you want a trick or treat, find out what happened to Pete, have lots of candy to eat, run scared till you hurt your feet." The pumpkin laughed, jiggling slightly at the fun and games it was having.

"I don't get it," Bella whispered. "Does it know where Pete and Robbie are or not? And who's making the voice? I'm scared, so can we go?"

"We aren't going without the boys." Anna straightened and nudged the pumpkin with her foot. "We need to find Robbie and Pete."

"Trick or treat." The pumpkin didn't appreciate being kicked and turned nasty, its voice retreating from the high cackle to the low growl. "Want to find Robbie and Pete, but they've both gone to sleep, candy they will never eat, and you will never see…" the pumpkin menaced, "them again!"

Scared, but curious, Anna bent over and peered at the pumpkin. "Neat trick, Mr Whoever You Are. How about coming outside to face us and tell us where our friends are, because I'm getting mighty ticked off!"

"Ticked off, ticked off," the pumpkin growled.

Anna kicked it, hoping to stop the mechanism making it talk. But kicking it just ticked it off even more.

The candlelight changed from yellow to blood-curdling red, the eyes narrowed into a slit, and the growl burst forth like an angry tiger on the hunt for prey. "Ticked off!" it growled and spewed forth the sleeping gas that knocked out every adult or child that dared to set foot on the porch on Halloween night.

"Ew, what's that?" Jasmine and Bella waved at the air in front of their noses and Kyle pinched his closed.

"Don't know," Anna said, stepping back. "But it stinks and is making me feel…" She became faint, wonky on her feet, light-headed. "Ugh!" She and the others slumped to the floor.

The porch tipped open and all four bodies slid down a metal slide into the basement of the house to land in a pile on the floor.

CHAPTER FIVE

"Ugh," Anna moaned. Her head, splitting from the pain of bashing against something, wobbled on her neck, and her eyes slowly blinked open as she tried to move.

"Mmm…" Jasmine breathed in and tried to shift positions, but couldn't. "Ugh. Did we…?" She thought she was at home tucked up in bed.

"Ugh…my head…" Bella lifted her head and tried to touch it, but found her arms wouldn't co-operate.

"Pete…Robbie…" Kyle slowly murmured. His brows furrowed and his vision blurry, he squeezed his eyes shut to clear them. He found himself at an odd angle in a straight backed chair, with his arms tied behind the back so he couldn't move them, and his feet tied to the front legs. He opened his eyes to see fuzzy versions of his friends, and blinked rapidly to clear his vision. When it did, he saw his two friends right in front of him in the exact same predicament he was. Tied to chairs in the basement of lot 666 Derbon Street. "Pete…Robbie?"

Their wide, scared eyes and shaking heads were

warning them to say nothing as their mouths were covered in gags preventing them from speaking. They nodded at the girls.

Kyle turned to his left and saw Anna, Bella and Jasmine tied up the same way, but like him, were without gags. And from the look of it, the girls were starting to realise the situation they were in.

"What the…?" Anna muttered and realised what was happening. Her head moved left and right, up and down, her eyes taking in the basement and all it encompassed. She saw her friends tied to chairs with panicked expressions, and saw Robbie and Pete sitting against the wall at a right angle to the rest of them, who were all lined up in a row. "What's happening? What happened?"

"Shhh…" Kyle warned in a whisper. "Keep it down." He glanced past her to Jasmine and Bella. "Keep your voices down." Looking around the basement, he tried to find something to untie them, or, at least, to help.

"Why do we need to keep our voices down?" Bella whispered loudly. "We need to scream so somebody can come and help us." She looked at all of her friends and saw Robbie and Pete furiously shaking their heads. "Why can't we yell for help? We need to get help."

"We need to be as quiet as possible," Anna warned softly, picking up on the hints from the boys. She moved her right arm up and down, trying to loosen her bonds, but they weren't shifting. "Whatever's going on, the person who did this could still be in the house waiting for us to wake up. So if we yell they'll know we're awake." She looked down at her feet and saw each one tied to a chair leg. "If we stay as quiet as possible, they may leave us alone longer, giving us time to escape."

"So what do we do?" Jasmine whispered, looking from friend to friend. Her right arm had gone numb and her left one had pins and needles rippling through it. "I can't use my arms. They're numb. How do we get out of whatever we're tied with?"

"Don't know." Anna was studying each shelf, each corner and wall in the dimly lit basement. Besides the usual tools, work benches and dirt flooring, there wasn't much else except for the glowing candelabra of ten candles. "Can anyone see anything sharp?"

Everyone peered into the dimness, but came come up with nothing.

"Okay, Pete, Robbie," Anna whispered. "Do you have any old nails poking out of the wall, or chair, that you can cut your ties with? And can you get your gags off? Push your chin against your shoulder and move the gag."

Pete nodded and rubbed his face against his left shoulder, hoping to push the gag down. Robbie took notice of how he was doing it and started working on his own.

After what seemed like an eternity, Pete finally got his gag down. "Argh…" he sighed. "That's better. Why didn't you guys go for help?"

"We did, but no one wanted to help us," Kyle told him. "We ran to all of the neighbours and none of them wanted to help, so the only thing to do was call the cops, or come and get you ourselves." He twisted his wrists around trying to loosen the rope. "So we came ourselves."

"And now you're trapped like us. Fat lot of good that will do. Who's going to save us now?" Pete whispered.

Robbie finally got his gag off. "I want to go home. It's not fun anymore."

"None of us is going home since they didn't bother getting help," Pete complained. "We could have been saved already."

Anna twisted her arms back and forth and finally worked one loose. "Try loosening the rope," she whispered. "Try getting yourself free."

The kids worked feverishly to loosen the ties that bound them, but made no headway. They were strapped in tight.

"How are we going to get out? I don't want to die here," Bella whispered, the chill seeping through her costume. She shivered and longed to rub her arms, but they were almost numb.

"We're not going to die," Anna said with as much determination as she felt. "We're going to get out of here and tell our parents and the police. That's what we're going to do." She tugged her arms against her bonds, but a cramp sped through her right upper arm. "Argh!" Her jaw clamped together so she didn't make any further noises, but when the cramp worsened, she whimpered. "I need to get out of here." Her whisper was barely audible through her tears. "We need to get out of here. Is anyone free?"

The others had been furiously struggling to free their arms and legs, but were also experiencing cramps.

"I found a nail," Kyle burst out, his fingers brushing against the sharp point sticking out of the wood of the chair back. He rubbed the rope around his wrists back and forth across the tip while the others watched on and rested a moment to see if Kyle made it free.

"I think it's coming," he whispered excitedly, straining against the rope, trying to pull it apart and cut it at the same time.

"Is it working?" Bella strained to see from the other end of the room, but all eyes were on Kyle and so no one noticed the old man silently enter the room and stand watching them; listening to what they were saying, watching what they were doing.

Always the same, he thought. *They always try and get away. To get out of the bonds that bind them. I see the other two have managed to slip off their gags.* He watched Robbie and Pete curiously, knowing they hadn't even bothered trying to remove their gags before their friends had arrived, had sat petrified, looking from one another to around the room. They hadn't tried to get their hands free, or their legs, had just sat there. *Of course, it could be the effects of the sleeping gas, they could still be running on half empty, but they look eager now.*

The old man's gaze wandered back to Kyle at the far end. *He won't get far; the ropes aren't meant to be broken by human hand. Human hand cannot break the ties that bind for these ties have a power far greater than human in them.* He watched on as Kyle finally broke free from the ropes.

"I've done it!" Kyle cried and swung his arms around in front of him. "I've done it. I cut through the rope. I..." He stopped and stared at the rope as a yellow light lit them aglow and magical beams turned the threads into vines that grew and rebound themselves to each other weaving in and out to strengthen themselves. "What the hell...?" Kyle murmured as his wrists were rewrapped. The rope took on a life of its own and swung his arms back behind him to bind them together once more, trapping him to the chair. He stared at the others, just as dumbfounded as them by what had just occurred.

"What just happened?" Bella asked, unable to see clearly past Jasmine and Anna. "Did he get free, or what?"

"He did." The old man shuffled forward and all six kids swung their heads in his direction. "But those ropes cannot be broken by human hand unless the hand is worthy."

"Who are you?" Anna gasped and eyed the man up and down. "What have you done to us? What do you mean they can't be broken by human hand? What are you going to do with us? What do you want...? Ugh..." She ran out of steam and gasped for air, tired after everything that had taken place.

"It's not me," the old man said. "It's him. He likes to play games, and what better night to play those games on than All Hallow's Eve when kiddies decide to dress up and play trick or treat when they're so fat and juicy and ripe for the eating." He stared at each child in turn. "You cannot escape. You cannot undo your ties. You cannot get out of this house."

"W-w-why can't we?" Jasmine stuttered. "I want to go home. I want my mum and dad." She burst into heaving sobs.

"You will not be going home," the old man said. "Unless you win the game."

"Game? What game?" Robbie asked. "I like games." He hoped by being positive, things might be easier.

"The game of *Trick or Treat*," the man told him. "And only if you answer each question correctly will you be able to go home." He clasped his hands together in front of him. "I fear no one will get it… again… No one ever does. No one ever wins, and so no one ever goes home. Turns out, kids just aren't smart enough. Never have been." His cold blue eyes pierced into theirs. "You will never leave unless you get the answers right. You will never leave because you're not smart enough. You're just dumb and fat and love candy too much."

"Hey!" Bella protested. "I'm not dumb *or* fat, thank you very much."

"Neither am I," Jasmine added. "I wouldn't've been able to fit into this costume if I was." She glanced down at her Elsa dress and found it dirty and rumpled. "My mother's going to be so mad that you made my dress dirty. Because *I* certainly didn't."

"I'm not fat either," Kyle argued, studying the man. He was average height, but hunched over, grey hair almost thinned away, wrinkled skin, and old-fashioned clothing that looked as if it was from the last century. "Who are you, anyway?"

"Who I am is of no importance," the man said. "I am just the gatekeeper, the bringer of food, if you will." He waved a withered hand at them. "And that is all you are. Food."

"For what?" Robbie demanded, having absolutely no idea what the man was talking about. "*How* are we food? *Why* are we food?"

"Quiet!" the man bellowed, sick and tired of the job he had to do year after year. "The rules of the game are easy. Answer all of the questions right and go free. Answer any wrong, and you will be food. Do you understand?"

"No!" Anna scoffed. "We have absolutely no idea who you are, what you're doing, why you're doing it to us, and all you tell us is, it's a game and we can't leave unless we win it. What happens if we lose?" She cocked her head and her ears pricked up. She'd heard something above them.

"I told you," the man said impatiently, almost petulantly, his foot stomping a little into the ground. "If you win, you go free. If you lose, you will be eaten. Master's going to dine well tonight. Six fat little blobs of boys and girls. He will be ever so pleased."

CHAPTER SIX

He turned to leave, but Anna stopped him.

"Who's the master? Where is he? I want to talk to him. Tell him I want to talk to him. I heard him upstairs." She belted the words out.

The man stopped and cast a glance over his shoulder at her. "You heard him? How do you know it was him? It could have been someone else, another child perhaps, or an adult who couldn't stay away. How do you know it was him?" *We'll have to keep an eye on this one,* he thought. *She's mighty inquisitive and could be a problem.*

"I heard someone, *or* something, upstairs," Anna replied defiantly. If she was going down, she was going down fighting. "Was it the master?"

"Never you mind who it was." The man turned and shuffled on. "Never you mind."

They watched him leave with Anna making note of where he exited the room. Once the door was shut, she said, "We need to get out of here, and if the only way to do that is answer those questions, then we'll answer those questions." She struggled against her bonds. "Or, more specifically, *I'll* answer those questions."

"Why you?" Robbie frowned, somewhat insulted. "Why can't *we* answer them?"

"Because *you're* stupid!" Anna exclaimed. "*You* were stupid enough to come here on Halloween. Stupid enough to get yourself kidnapped, and if you answer the questions, you'll be stupid enough to get us all eaten. I'm the head of the debate and maths clubs, read a lot, watch a lot, get top grades. If anyone's going to know the answers, it'll be *me*. Who's in agreement?" She looked from face to face. From Robbie's upset one, to Pete's thoughtful one. Kyle nodded in agreement and the girls did too. "Right, any questions that need answering, I'll answer."

"And here we go with the All Hallow's Eve quiz night." The pumpkin head from the front porch came sliding into the room, having grown long weed like legs with feet, and similar arms with hands. It wore a top hat and held a black cane. Coloured lights flashed off and on, and canned laughter and applause floated down from the ceiling. He addressed the crowd. "Hello, all you groovy guys and gals out there in Ghoul Land watching at home or on social media, we're here for the next round of *Trick or Treat*. I'm your host, Jack O' Lantern, but you can call me Mr O. As in Mr Oh No." More canned laughter floated through the air and Jack lapped it up. "Okay, and here we go." He whipped out a set of cards and the atmosphere grew sombre. "In what year did the tradition of Halloween start?" He did a spin kick and karate chop. "I repeat, in what year did the tradition of Halloween start?" He lifted up his top hat and removed a huge fob watch. "Time's a tickin'."

Jasmine, Bella, Kyle, Robbie and Pete all turned their heads to Anna, who racked her brain for the answer. She'd studied Halloween in history class so she *should* know the answer.

"Ah, the word itself dates back to 1745," she murmured and licked her lips. "But since you weren't specific as to which country it started in…"

"Speak up, I can't hear you," Jack said, and pranced closer.

"1745 is when the word Halloween was first used," she repeated, determined to get all of the answers right. "It started long before that, but there's no specific date on it than can be found and you didn't state in what country."

Jack pranced back and forth, laughed, and glanced at the answer. "And that is absolutely…" His face fell. "Right! Wait, what?" He flipped the card over to see if the answer was on the other side. But it wasn't. He flipped it back. "Right! O.M.GEE, the girl got it right. Luck of the draw and all that." His frown turned upside down. "But she won't get this one." He sashayed to his left and two-stepped to his right. "Let's see boys and girls at home, if she can get this one. In what year did the tradition of trick or treating first start?" He held up the fob watch which was bigger than his head. "Time's a tickin'."

Anna breathed in slowly, closed her eyes, and flashed back to history class. "Sometime in the 9th century, and the term trick or treat wasn't used until 1927 that we know of."

"*And time's gone…* Wait, what?" Jack stopped short and looked at his card. The evil eyes glowed red and the growl came out, but was gone in an instant. "And she's right, all you groovy ghouls and gals at home. Two down, three to go." He did a little dance as music came through the loudspeakers.

"Go Anna," Bella and Jasmine cheered, hoping they'd soon be freed.

"Okay, question *numero tre*, that's number three to all you groovy cats at home." Jack grinned into an imaginary camera. "When did vampires get involved in Halloween? Tickety tock." He danced back and forth while waiting for an answer.

"They technically didn't, but people chose to dress as them," Anna replied.

Jack frowned again, looked down at the card and flung it over his shoulder. "And what did Dracula have to do with Halloween?"

"Nothing," Anna said. "Vlad the Impaler is the supposed inspiration for Dracula. As Dracula never actually existed, Dracula himself, the non-existent version, had nothing to do with Halloween."

A buzzer rang out and applause filled the room.

Jack was not happy. "We've got a smart one here goblins and germs, oh so smart." He danced over to Anna and stuck his pumpkin in her face. "You think you're so smart," he growled, making her gulp and pull her head back. "But answer question number five. When did pumpkins become a part of Halloween?

Ha!" he screeched into her face. "Tell me that!" His bellowing made her blonde Barbie wig blow off.

When the bellowing stopped, she took a breath, shook her head and replied, "Sometime in the 19th century after the Irish immigrated to America. They realised pumpkins were better to use than the turnips they'd been using, because they were bigger."

"And she has it wrong." Jack thrust his hand into her face before realising what she'd said. "Wait... what...?" He flipped through the cards and still came up with the same answer. "She's right," he muttered. "She's right. No one's ever got them right before." Puzzled, Jack stumbled back, his legs folded in on themselves, as did his arms, and next second, Jack went poof and disappeared in a flash of smoke.

"Whoa!" Robbie cried. "Did you see that? So cool!"

The lights turned off, no applause or canned laughter came, and the basement was as dim as it had been before.

"What...just...happened?" Kyle asked, stumped by the chain of events.

"We won." Anna's brow furrowed and she tried to pull her arms free. "We won, but we're not free yet. Hey," she yelled out. "Hey, we won. I answered all the questions correctly. Let us go. You promised we'd be let free if we got them right. Hey, come back! Hey." She bounced her chair up and down hoping to loosen the legs or rope, but nothing worked.

"Why haven't they let us go?" Jasmine wiped her face on her shoulder. She'd been close to tears the whole time and now felt them roll in big fat lumps down her cheeks. She didn't want to break down in front of her friends, but knew she couldn't hold it in much longer.

"I don't know." Anna craned her neck hoping to see someone, such as the old man, or find another way out. When she couldn't, she stopped and sighed. "I have no idea what's going on, but that old man lied to us."

*****

"I didn't lie," the old man murmured. "You just misinterpreted what I said." He'd been upstairs watching the TV showing exactly what was going on in the basement, had been surprised when the girl had answered all five questions correctly, but knew that meant round two would be harder, and he daren't look at his master who was breathing heavily beside him.

"She is wise." The master's voice was gravelly and low. "We will need tougher questions that will stump her." He cast a dark look at Jack. "Make them harder."

"How hard?" Jack scratched his orange head. "We've never gone into round two before."

"Make them very hard. So hard she won't be able to answer them. But, as always, they must be about Halloween."

"All righty then." Jack disappeared in a puff of smoke and reappeared in the basement. "And here we are back with *Trick or Treat*. I'm your host, Jack O' Lantern." Canned applause filled the basement.

"You lied to us!" Anna declared. "You said we'd be set free if we answered correctly, I did, you didn't. You lied."

"Lies, schmies," Jack quipped and did a little boogie, gyrating from the hips. "And here we go with round two." He clicked his fingers and a wheel just like the one from *Wheel of Fortune* popped into the room except it was upright and facing them. "On the wheel there are ten questions."

"Ten!" Anna exclaimed. "We've already answered five."

"And you're only answering three now." Jack swung his hips side to side and did a spin. "I will spin the wheel and whatever the three questions are, you will have to answer."

"Oi!" Anna rolled her eyes. "Get on with it."

"Temper, temper." Jack's growl flared and he spun the wheel. Music filled the room and he danced around the wheel while waiting for it to stop. When it did, he asked the question. "If you end Halloween night with one thousand pieces of candy, exchange forty-five with someone else, swap one hundred and fifty-two with another person, give two hundred pieces away, and eat five hundred pieces, how many pieces do you have?" Jack thrust the fob watch in her face. "You have ten seconds."

"Three hundred," Anna answered. Not only was she head of the debate team, but head of the maths team as well.

"And that is in..." Jack put his hand to his ear and looked up at the ceiling, as if listening to someone in a non-existent production booth. "Wait…you sure…ah huh…right…okay… Correct!" His arms waved in a touchdown motion. "Three hundred is correct. And now onto the next question." He spun the wheel and danced again.

"Go Anna, you've got this," the others cheered her on.

Robbie's head bobbed along to the music. As much as he was scared and wanted to go home, he was also kind of enjoying himself.

The wheel rolled to a stop and Jack read the question. "If Dracula, a werewolf, a zombie, and Frankenstein all walked into a bar, how many of them would actually be alive? Your time starts, now." He jigged in place while the clock ticked down.

Anna raised her brow. "Two."

"And that is incorrectooooooo…wait…" Jack stopped. "Why do you say that?"

"Because Dracula, although he didn't technically exist, and the zombie, are technically dead, *humans* turn into werewolves, so *he's* technically alive, and Frankenstein was the man, *not* the monster, and you said nothing about the monster," she said smugly. "So *two* are actually alive."

Jack's face fell, literally. The carving in the pumpkin sagged to the bottom, as if it had melted, but after a few seconds it bounced back into its usual evil feature. "You are correct," he growled. His arm shot out and spun the wheel as hard as he could. It spun and spun and took a good while to come to a halt. Jack stared at Anna the whole time and didn't even bother to turn to read the question. He didn't need to; his carved face slid around the pumpkin to look out the back of his head. "What is Salem known for?"

"Witch trials," Anna said. "Or Stephen King's book on vampires, all depends on which one you mean. Which one *do* you mean?"

The carved face spun around to leer at her. "It was a trick question," it screeched and all of it, and Jack, disappeared in a puff of smoke.

"What is it *with* that dude?" Anna muttered. "*Seriously!*" She tried to work her arms free, but they were still bound. "And they're still lying."

"Why aren't we free yet?" Jasmine whimpered. "I want to go home."

"So do I," Bella, Pete and Kyle chimed in.

"I'm kinda enjoying myself," Robbie said. "This is fun. The best Halloween we've had so far."

Everyone looked at him in shocked horror. "Are you freakin' nuts?" Pete asked. "We could be eaten alive and not make it home to our parents, and you're *enjoying* yourself?"

Robbie half shrugged. "Well…yeah… I mean, it's better than crying, which Jasmine's been doing all night." They all turned to look at her and she ducked her head. "So we can enjoy it, or freak out about it," Robbie went on. "I choose to enjoy it."

"You are sick, dude, truly sick," Kyle muttered, shaking his head in disbelief. "How can you be enjoying this? I'm surprised you haven't cried over losing your candy."

"What!" Robbie perked up. "I'd forgotten all about it. Can anyone see it?" He arched his neck and looked all around, as did the others, but no one saw any of their bags of candy. "Naw, dude! They took it. Bugger." If he could have stomped his foot, he would have. "I lost all my candy. So. Not. Fair! Give me back my candy," he yelled at the ceiling.

CHAPTER SEVEN

"Oh, this is not good." The old man watched them on the TV. "No one's ever managed to get past round one, and now they've gone past round two. What do we do now?"

The master casually popped a Reese's cup into his mouth and dropped the wrapper on the floor beside his chair. He was done with the fun and games and wanted his yearly feed already, as chocolates weren't filling up the abyss that was his stomach.

"What now?" Jack asked. "I'm out of ideas. She's smart, that one. That's why she insisted on doing all the talking."

"Then we need to make her *stop* talking," the master growled. "Time for the final round." He disappeared in a puff of smoke and landed on all fours in front of his meal. The kids' screams filled the dead air of the basement and they pushed back in their chairs to escape the dripping fangs, glowing red eyes, and horns of the devil beast.

Robbie stopped screaming. "Hey wait, you look just like the dogs out of *Ghostbusters*. When that four-eyed dude, and what's her name, turn into the pet dogs of that evil chick." The beast advanced on Robbie, and while he quaked in his shoes and his bladder relieved itself, he made the choice to be brave. "Hey, where's our candy? I want my candy back."

"I ate it," the master growled, fluid dripping from its fangs onto the floor in front of Robbie. A slight wisp of smoke slithered upward and a hole was eaten away.

Anna saw it and ideas started forming in her mind. If its saliva was acidic, it could eat through the ropes tying them to their chairs and potentially be used against him.

"You eat chocolate?" Robbie scornfully stared into the face of the half beast-half mutt before him. "I thought you only ate fat kids. That's what the old dude said. *So I want my chocolate back. The whole bag!*"

"You want your chocolate?" the master queried and backed up. "Do you *really* want it back?"

"Yes! All of it," Robbie declared.

"Okay then." The master jerked, huffed, retracted its head, and regurgitated all of Robbie's candy stash he'd eaten during the night.

"Ew!" The kids turned their heads as the steaming pile of acidic candy was dumped in front of Robbie.

"There it is," the master said. "You're welcome to it."

And for the second time that night, Robbie hurled in front of himself.

The others tried to keep theirs in as the stench grew. With no air in the basement, the smell was becoming worse by the second.

The coloured show lights, canned laughter, and applause came back on, and the master reared on his hind legs, a top hat and cane appeared in his claws out of nowhere, and he did a little dance. "Da-da-da-da-dada, da-da-da-da-dada." He swung his cane and tipped his top hat, and when the music stopped he was back on all fours in front of Anna.

"Tell me, little girl, how smart are you?" He leant in close and sniffed her.

She pulled her head back and screwed up her face. "Ew!"

"How smart are you?" the beast roared and paced back and forth in the room. "Smart enough to escape the clutches of the master?"

"If I can," she muttered. So far, the questions had been easy, but that wasn't to say they'd stay that way.

"So…" The master sat on his haunches, crossed his forelegs and tapped his chin thoughtfully with a long nailed claw. "Let me see…I need to find the hardest question possible so that you get it wrong and I get to eat. Mmm…"

Anna glanced around the room. Now that the lights were on, she could see what else there was, made notes of where certain things were, and glanced at her friends. Bella and Jasmine looked as if they were going to be sick, but were also crying. Kyle and Pete kept their faces away from the steaming pile of vomit, and Robbie looked as if he'd passed out. *Well, that's not helpful,* Anna thought, trying to figure out what was going to happen next. Her gaze turned back to the master.

The master clicked its claws. "I've got it. It will be a three part quiz, each part harder than the last." He walked back and forth, his excitement growing. "There will be the Q and A section, followed by explanation, followed by the show and tell."

"What!" Anna frowned. "You said one question."

The beast leered in front of her. "I lied," it roared and backed away. Turning its back, it sat and stroked its chin in thought.

Anna noticed a wisp of white in front of her and looked down to see saliva had dripped onto the rope around her right foot. It was burning a hole through it and she thought back to what the old man had said, '...*cannot be broken by human hand unless the hand is worthy*'. But it wasn't a hand that had broken the tie, it was magical saliva and it was burning the rope right off her leg.

"I just need to think of a question." The master tapped his chin some more, and then cast a glance at Robbie. He clicked his claws and turned to Anna who swiftly sat up straight. He leaned in close. "How many Reese's Peanut Butter Cups have I eaten tonight?"

"How many...?" Anna furrowed her brow. "How would I know that? For all I know you have an addiction to them like Rob...bie..." She stopped and stared at Robbie then back at the master. "You've only eaten what was in our bags and since we traded our Reese's with Robbie, you could have only eaten them from *his* bag..." Her gaze moved to the vomit slowly burning into the floor and gulped. She thought back and vaguely remembered Robbie boasting he'd eaten fifteen to twenty pieces, hurled them into the gutter, and then ended up with more.

"Tick tock," the master growled.

Anna looked from Robbie to the beast and saw Jack sitting with his legs casually crossed on the bench behind him. She thought back to Robbie counting his Reese's a second time and trading candy for them right before they got to lot 666, and tried to remember what he'd said. "Sixty-six," burst out of her in excitement. "If you ate all of Robbie's candy then you ate sixty-six pieces of Reese's, and more than likely regurgitated them too." She cast a sickly glance at the pile of vomit. "Blech!"

"And how did you come to that conclusion?" The beast leaned forward in anticipation.

"He vomited his originals after trading them with us, he then gathered more and we did a second trade after going to the house next door. He had sixty-six."

"Mmm…" The beast growled from deep in its throat. Its red eyes widened, its teeth extended, and its forked tongue slid out to lick its mouth. "Now for the show and tell."

"No!" Anna commanded. "The old man told us if we got the five questions right, we'd be set free. We did, you didn't let us go, so that's not fair, and not ethical. You *lied*. We got them right and *you lied*. Let us go."

"Let you go?" the beast queried. "Let you go? As if I'm just going to let you go." He walked back and forth on his hind legs. "As if I'm just going to let you go. Why would I do that? If I did that every year, I'd never feed. I'd have starved away years ago, decades, centuries ago. Why would I let you go?"

"Because we did what we were told. We got the answers right." Anna knew that if she kept him talking long enough she might be able to distract him. She waited until he turned his back to her and then she turned her head to Kyle and Pete, nodded at the vomit and mouthed *'acid chemistry'*. They caught on and nodded.

"Yes, yes, you did." The beast spun around in an elegant pirouette and kept on spinning. "But, I am the master. I must feed, and so I lie."

"Do beasts like you not have a code of conduct?" Anna asked. Her gaze darted around for the things she needed. She couldn't exactly sit there and explain her plan to her friends, and Robbie was still passed out in his chair.

"Oh, well…" the master huffed. "*Of course* we do, but, being honest isn't in the code."

"Why not?"

"What do you mean, why not?" He stopped pirouetting to look at Anna.

"Why isn't honesty in your code of conduct?" she asked. "Should that not be in *everyone's* code?"

"No, because it doesn't work that way." The master cocked a hip and placed a curled up claw on it. "We're beasts, from other realms. We lie, we cheat, we kill. And then we feast on those kills. That's how we work."

"All of you?" Anna asked.

"All of us," the beast replied. "It's a hierarchy. We lie, we cheat, and steal our way to the top, and whoever kills the most generally wins because he's killed everyone else in his way, so there's no one to stand against him."

"So…you killed your way to the top? Are you on top?" Anna went on.

"*Of course* I am," he snarled. "I *wouldn't be here* if I wasn't."

"You'd be dead," Anna cut in.

The beast startled. "Well, yes, I would be. But since I'm not, I'm on top because I've killed everyone else in my way."

"What's it like on top?" Anna asked, noting the pool of vomit getting smaller and smaller. She needed to get away from the chair so she could set her plan into motion.

"Fabulous." The beast preened.

"Do you keep your style to yourself?" she went on. "I mean, your style of killing, otherwise, everyone would know how you do it and then be able to stop you."

"*Of course* I keep it to myself," he replied, turning his back to them and scoffing over his shoulder. "What do you take me for?"

CHAPTER EIGHT

Stupid, Anna thought, her gaze darting around the room. Jack had fallen asleep, but still burned brightly. "Do you play sport?"

"Sport!" The master pulled several bodybuilding moves. "*Killing* is my sport."

"What about things like *baseball,*" she stressed the word and stared at Kyle until she got his attention, then cast an eye at the pumpkin on the bench. "Or football. We're big on sports here."

"So I've noticed." The master turned around and sat on his haunches. "And yet you're all still fat."

"Well, technically we have an obesity issue," Anna corrected. "But we still love our sport."

"And I love you obese. You're so much more tasty and filling. But all that fat can get chewy sometimes and stick in my teeth, so I just use one of your ribs to pick it out. No harm, no foul." He crossed his forelegs. "But none of you is fat."

"Because we play sport," Anna told him, hoping he didn't see that her right leg was free. "We're all on a sports team at high school. Track and field, baseball, basketball, football."

"Ha," the beast huffed. "Please don't tell me you girls are cheerleaders." He held a claw to his forehead, pretended to feel faint, and put on a la-di-dah accent. "Oh, lordy dee, I do declare that all the girls are the same. Cheerleaders."

"Nothing wrong with that," Jasmine muttered. "It's very athletic and you get a good workout."

"Yes, yes," the master waved a claw, "but it's not actually a *sport* now, is it? Ugh!" He settled onto all fours and shook his head. "Cheerleading is *not* a sport. Sport is running, like running after your prey. And smashing, where you smash your claw across your enemy's face. Now *they* are sports."

"Is that what you do?" Anna asked. "How you kill?"

"*Of course.*" He rolled his eyes. "For a girl who's so smart and got herself and her friends this far, you're not very smart where it counts." He tapped his temple.

"And where does it count?" she asked.

"When it comes to what's needed to be done," he said.

The lights and music burst back on making Jack jump awake. The master danced on his hind legs getting his boogie on and Jack joined in, dancing for a few minutes more.

The master whipped out a card from behind his back and did a spin, landing on his hind legs. He read from the card. "And now we come to the final section of the show, *Shooowwwww and Tellllll*," his voice droned over the loud speakers. "This is the part of the show where you show me how you escape. For your lucky chance, I will untie you and your friends and you will show me what your last futile effort will be at freedom. You will have five minutes, and if by the time those five minutes are up and you have failed, I will eat you." A grin spread from horn to horn. "My absolute favourite part of the evening."

Jack pulled the fob watch out of his head and held it aloft. "Tick tock, tick tock, the mouse is running up the clock. Trick or treat is long over, and you're all about to be clam chowder."

The master gave him the side-eye. "That doesn't rhyme. Why would you try to rhyme with that?"

"It's the only thing I could think of," Jack said.

"But it doesn't rhyme, so why use it, and if you can't think of anything else, then don't say anything at all," the master fired back.

"Don't over and chowder rhyme?" Jack scratched his head.

"No, they don't." The master stomped a hind leg in exasperation. "I don't even like clam chowder. Have you ever tried it?"

"No, I haven't. Have you?" Jack asked.

"Yes, and it's god-awful." The master shook his head as he thought back to the taste. "It's slimy and the clams are…ugh…" He shuddered delicately, a claw going to his chest. "Awful."

"Can we get on with this?" Anna asked. "And why would you even eat clam chowder when you already admitted to eating monsters that get in your way? Did a clam get in your way?"

Jack sniggered, but was quickly shut down by another side-eye.

The master stared at Anna as though she were some brainless flea. "*No*, a clam *did not* get in my way. It's a long story, but needless to say, I was in Florida many a decade ago when *for some reason* I decided to try a bowlful. It was..." He rolled his eyes. "Ugh! Just horrible. Slimy and ugh... I've never touched human food again."

"You touched chocolate, and that's human food," Anna muttered.

"Yes," the master conceded with a knowing nod of his horned head. "But it's wonderfully, sinfully, delicious food."

"Okay." Anna rolled her eyes. "Sorry I said anything. Can we get on with this? I'm ready to go home and I know my friends are as well." She glanced left and right and saw hopeful nods. Even Robbie had come to and was perking up at the mention of home.

"All right, all right. Just remember the rules of the game. You show and tell," the master reminded her. "You have five minutes. Jack." He turned to the pumpkin who held up the clock. "And in three, two, one...go!" He clicked his claws and the ropes binding them to their chairs evaporated.

They all jumped up and huddled together while rubbing wrists and arms to get the blood flowing.

"I know exactly what to do," Anna whispered. "Jasmine, you and Bella get ready to run. Pete, you and I will do a little chemistry; just do exactly what I do. Kyle, get ready to play baseball, just like you did last year, and Robbie…" She saw his deteriorating health. "Since you look so sick, stand between the girls. When the sparks fly, we run the same way the old man did and either keep your arms linked, or hold hands so no one gets left behind. Got it?"

"Got it!" The five of them nodded, and they all broke the huddle.

"Naw, how cute," Jack said and watched them work. "They think they're going to make sparks fly. Tick tock, tick tock, time's a tickin'."

"Girls, take Robbie, Kyle, find yourself a bat, and Pete, come with me." She led him over to the bench where she'd noticed electrical cable rolled into bundles and she and Pete grabbed one each and unfurled them. The ends were cut and the wire was free. "Keep a hold of each end, you'll need them," she told him.

He nodded and followed her over to the remaining vomit the master had regurgitated and shoved one end of the cord in until it started smoking. Pete followed suit. When the end was vaporising, she headed for the power point nearest the door behind where they'd been sitting. "The other one's over there." She pointed along the wall to an outlet that was behind the chair Kyle had been sitting on. When Pete was in front of it, she nodded and shoved her cord into the outlet. Pete did the same and the outlets crackled and fizzed. She walked over to her friends and stood in front of them with the other end, and Pete stood next to her. "On the count of three, just like in chem lab last year." She watched him light up and nod.

"Stand next to Bella," she told Kyle, and he moved beside the girls and Robbie and prepared to take aim.

"Time's a tickin'," Jack reminded them. "One minute to go."

"And you have yet to show *or* tell," the master reminded her, intrigued as to what was happening.

"Last year in school we made sparks fly. Wanna see how?" Anna's left brow rose.

"*Of course.*" The master gave a nonchalant wave of his claw. "But I seriously doubt it's anything I haven't seen before."

"Oh, I wouldn't be so sure." She glanced at Pete. "Ready?"

He grinned, nodded and held up the wire. "Absolutely. Let's blow this joint."

"In three, two, one... Argh!" She and Pete yelled and charged at the master, thrusting the ends of the electrical cord into the master's mouth.

Surprised by the move, the master clamped down on the cords and jumped backwards. The acidic saliva in his mouth had the same effect the saliva on the other end in the outlet was having. Sparks flew and electrocution was imminent.

Kyle rushed forward and swung his improvised bat at a shocked Jack, and, being left-handed, he swung from left to right which meant Jack flew towards the master and got caught in the sizzling mess.

Anna and Pete jumped back. "Run," she screamed and saw her friends take off running.

The master thrashed his head around, connected with Jack's still-burning flame, and the cord crackled and sizzled. The cords flung every which way, and Anna and Pete ducked under one and jumped over the other as they ran in the direction they'd seen the old man take and found stairs leading up, pounding up them just as the master burst into flames, and those flames found their way through the ceiling, which connected to the next floor.

They flew through the door onto the ground floor and the master exploded, sending hungry flames through the bottom of the house to set it on fire. They saw the old man standing in the lounge room doorway surrounded by flames, pointing at the front door. They stopped for a millisecond and he mouthed *'thank you,'* before the fire enveloped him and took the floor out from under him. They saw him fall straight through before running for the door, the house exploding behind them, animalistic screams shattering the dead night air. Holding onto each other, they continued running down the path, not knowing how close they were, or how much farther they had to go.

A second explosion ripped through the air and the force flung them forwards. Screaming, arms flailing, they flew through the air and landed on their feet back on the sidewalk, costumes intact, candy bags intact, the night intact.

The burning house imploded and disappeared in a puff of smoke, leaving behind no trace of its existence.

The air was refreshed, the mood lighter, and all six looked at each other and breathed deeply.

"What's the time?" Anna asked.

Kyle checked his watch. "Seven twenty-eight. You asked me two minutes ago."

"No, I…" Anna frowned and noticed where they were. "Why are we here? Why have we stopped at lot 666? You know everyone avoids this place like the plague."

"We shouldn't be scared of a house," Robbie told them. "It's just a house." He waved a hand in frustration. "It's *just* a *house!* Why does it freak people out so much?"

"Because people have gone missing when they set foot on the property," Pete told him.

"Kids have disappeared at Halloween while trick or treating," Kyle added.

"Because they're stupid enough to go up to the front door and ring the bell," Bella chimed in. "Why take the chance on the stories *not* being true? We shouldn't go there. Period! Come on, let's go."

The girls started to move, but Robbie stopped them in their tracks.

"Well, I'm going in there."

Everyone stopped and reached out for him. "No…"

ALL HALLOWS POSSESSION

CHAPTER ONE

"Welcome to the *All Hallows Inn, in* All Hallows," Dirk Bently, the bus driver, mumbled into the microphone wrapped around his ear and bent in front of his mouth. "This is where you get off for the night." He pulled the bus to a stop, yanked the handbrake, and turned off the ignition. It had been a long ride from the city and he couldn't wait to have a hot meal and a beer.

"Children, this is what we're doing." Teacher Quentin Barrett clapped his hands and called out as he stood in the aisle. "You will file two by two off the bus and line up alongside it so we can collect our bags. We're only here for the night, but we need to be on our utmost best behaviours. Is that understood?" He levelled his gaze across the sixteen teenagers in the bus. Besides them and him, there were three other teachers.

"Yes, Mr Barrett," the kids chorused and eagerly got to their feet.

"Good. Now follow me." He led the way down the stairs and to the undercarriage of the bus, waiting for the driver to open the luggage compartment. Ten minutes later, they were standing in the lobby of the All Hallows Inn being booked in.

"There are four kids to a room for the children because the rooms have bunks beds, there are four doubles for the adults, and a single for the driver." The woman behind the front desk checked them in and handed over the keys. Once they were sorted, she sighed and looked at Quentin Barrett. "I'm Mrs Reeves, the manager, I hope you all enjoy your stay at *All Hallows Inn*. We have some special events on for Halloween, starting from five o'clock. Take these and have a read." She handed over a bunch of coloured brochures, almost shoving them into his hands. "We have trick or treating at five, a movie at seven, and ghostly tales at nine to finish off the night, with a few ghostly things here and there." The twinkle in her eye conveyed the message to the kids who all smiled in delight.

"Okay, kids, let's get you upstairs and to your rooms." Quentin ushered them over to the stairs and led the way up to the first floor. "Do you know who's sharing with whom?"

Some of the students hastily grabbed at their friends and chose roommates.

He eyed their choices over his spectacles and nodded. "Thought as much." The troublemakers; Cameron Murphy, Riley Landis, Damien Hennessy and Grady Ames had chosen to bunk together, leaving Nathan Bartlett, Morgan Chandler, Keenan Fielding and Caleb Walker to share a room. "Right, take those two." He pointed to the two rooms to his right. "Girls, you take the other two." He watched best friends Lena Ryker and Zara Winslow hurry into the room with Reagan Vaughn and Thea Elwood rushing after them. The girls were the clique of *Randolph High* and ironically, the so-called misfits all got to share. Olivia Guthrie, Gemma Hawthorne, Sydney Rourke and Hannah Macallister dragged their bags into the next room.

Barrett turned to the other teachers. "We all get the doubles to my left. I'll take the room at the end opposite the girls. Mr Cordell, why don't you take the last one opposite the boys?"

Jameson Cordell, the school's science teacher, nodded, accepted his key, and walked back along the hall.

"Ladies, the rooms in the middle are yours." Barrett nodded and stepped into his room.

Gina Grant, the art teacher, and Greta Halston, the history teacher, made their way into their rooms to find them most adequate.

Barrett leaned back into the hallway and called out, "You've got some time to freshen up, but I expect you in the hall in fifteen minutes." He found his room neatly laid out with old wood furniture covered in bright modern cloth. The four-poster bed oozed historic, while the covers screamed modern. "Mmm…" He set his bag on the bench at the end of the bed. "This will do nicely."

*****

"I *cannot* believe we're in this dreary old place," Gemma complained. She dumped her duffel on the bottom bunk along the left wall and sat down with a huff. "Who the hell wants to be here?" Scanning her bitten nails, she scratched some of the chipped black polish off. It suited her mood, the black. She'd lined her eyes with thick black kohl and her hair was black. So were her clothes. She wore a long-sleeved death metal group top, black ripped jeans, old Doc Marten boots, and an old black and white flannelette shirt was tied around her waist.

"Not me," Olivia replied. She threw her bag onto the top bunk and sat down next to Gemma. "But then, they argued that this would be beneficial for our education and would help us get a pass at the end of the year. Looks like our parents couldn't say no." Running a hand through her wavy black hair, she sighed. "I need to pass, otherwise I repeat this year next year and that will be *so* embarrassing." She wasn't the school layabout or dunce by any means, but her grades had been slipping due to her lazy eye and dyslexia.

"Did you see the cliquey witches all rush for a room together?" Sydney flung open the window. "Couldn't wait to get in there and show us who's the best in the group. Blech! They make me sick." Breathing deeply, she surveyed their surroundings of rooftops capped with mountain views and blue skies. "This place is pretty. Spring colours are coming in after a cold winter." She glanced over her shoulder at her schoolmates and shoved her unruly mop of brown curls out of her face. "Let's scare the witches tonight."

"How?" Hannah asked as she lounged on her stomach on the second bottom bunk. She wasn't an outsider or a misfit, just didn't fit into any group at school. Not that she really wanted to as she found a lot of the girls to be snobby and mean, especially to those less fortunate...such as all of them in that room. She'd been behind because her parents had moved a lot for work. They'd settled into the area a year earlier and found jobs, so Hannah and her brother could finish their schooling with some stability. She was being tutored by Sydney, the class nerd, for the small fee that her parents could pay each week.

"Like, oh, I don't know." Sydney's grin was mischievous. "Make some noises out the window, throw stones at their window, shove scary notes under their door at midnight." She sat down by Hannah and continued. "We could scare the bejeebus out of them. We could get some ideas tonight by picking up on the local stories." Shrugging, she glanced at Gemma and Liv. "What do you say? Feel like scaring the witches?"

Gemma looked at her, then her gaze flitted to the open window and the afternoon sky. "Why not? It might be fun. And the witches'll deserve everything they get. The boys probably already have something up their sleeves for later."

*****

Nathan had been searching his room, looking for any sign of Halloween. "Ah, bollocks! They haven't done anything."

"Why would you expect them to?" Keenan asked and finished laying out his tech gear on his bed. Being the resident tech head of the school came in handy, especially when the principal allowed him to use the school's technological devices for the trip. *Under strict supervision of the four teachers, of course.*

"Because it's Halloween," Nathan replied with a raised brow.

"God, what'd you bring the whole 'lectronics lab?" Caleb asked as he stood watching Keenan pack it all into the backpack he'd be carrying it around in.

"Seems like it." Keenan swung the bag onto his back and faced his classmates. They weren't friends outside of school, just in class. "I figured we might as well use it and see what works. Who knows, we might find something. It *is* Halloween, you know." He brushed a hand over his short afro and grinned. "We should scare the girls later."

Morgan heard him just as he came back from using the bathroom at the end of the hall. "Which ones? The cliquey witches or the deadbeat misfits?"

Keenan spun to face him. "The girls aren't misfits *or* deadbeats." Scowling, he added, "The cliquey witches."

"Er," Morgan teased. "Got a crush on a misfit have we? Which one?" He took in Keenan's geeky exterior. "I bet it's Sydney, she *is* the school nerd after all. You two should hook up. The geeky tech head and the nerdy misfit."

"They're *not* misfits," Keenan repeated with force. "Just the outsiders like all of us." He waved a finger at all of them. "We're not in cliques like the other lot. The girls *or* boys."

"Ugh…" Nathan groaned. "I can't stand those toerags next door. They're as bad as the girls. Poshy snobs, cliquey witches. They're hot messes, that's what they are. Pains in the neck and the bum and just want to make everyone else's life hell. I wish I didn't go to school with them," he grumbled and flopped onto one of the bottom bunks. "I cannot *stand* Cameron and Riley in particular. They're as bad as Lena and Zara. They should all just double date or something and get it over with."

"If they double dated it would be even worse," Caleb complained. "Double the snobbery, double the torture, double the—" His diatribe was interrupted by the girls screaming.

Everyone went running into the hall to see what had happened.

"Who screamed?" Barrett called as another loud shrill rang out. They rushed into the girls' room to find Lena, Zara, Reagan and Thea crowding on one of the top bunks.

"What *are you* screaming about?" Barrett demanded. "Come down this instant and *stop* screaming."

"No, we're not coming down, not until that th-th-thing is gone," Lena cried, her arm extended fully as she pointed to the opposite bottom bunk.

Everyone crowded into the room and stood

looking at the bed.

"What thing?" Nathan asked. He shrugged and looked at the others. "There's nothing there. What a pack of sissies."

"It's a spider; it's huge and black," Zara squealed, hanging onto Lena.

"And hairy," Reagan added. "It's under the bed."

Barrett and Cordell moved over to the bed and lifted the covers, bending over to peer under the bed. "Oh, for heaven's sake, there's noth—" Barrett was cut off as a big, hairy black spider slowly trundled out from under the bed.

CHAPTER TWO

Barrett and Cordell backed up and stared at it while the girls cried out again.

Keenan had removed a high-tech electronics device from his backpack at the first sight of the spider and stepped forward to scan the arachnid. At a good metre wide, it was more than enough to scare people.

"It's not a real one," Sydney told them and tucked a strand of fuzzy hair behind her ear. She stepped up next to Keenan and stared down at the spider. "Its eyes wouldn't glow red if it was; nor would it have hinges on its legs."

Everyone peered closer and Keenan thrust his device at it. "She's right. Electronic, running by remote control, I'd say."

"Or a timer," Sydney butted in, but refused to look at him since she had a massive crush. "Someone's idea of a Halloween joke."

"Ugh, I don't care," Lena complained. "Get it out of here. I won't be able to sleep now."

"You probably won't later, either," Gemma

murmured and watched Keenan pick up the spider and carry it into the hall. "None of us will get any sleep if this is what we're getting all night."

"Okay, everyone." Barrett clapped his hands. "Since that's over, let's head downstairs and get on with our trip. We have things to do before sunset, and trick or treating will be one of them."

They left the room and lined up two by two in the hall, with Keenan at the head of the line holding the spider, and walked downstairs, handing over the arachnid gadget to Mrs Reeves who at first looked surprised and then sheepish.

"It's all part of the Halloween fun," she explained. "You might want to watch out for more."

Nathan, Morgan, Keenan and Caleb exchanged excited grins, but the girls, still recovering from their shock, shivered delicately and clung to each other.

"The first thing I think we should do is a walk of the town," Greta Halston suggested. "Get a feel for what it was like, the history of it that is, and then stop at the museum last."

"Good idea, Ms Halston," Barrett said. "Please, lead the way."

With Ms Halston at the head of the group, they walked in two lines through the town, visited stores, the blacksmith's shop, the stables, had lunch in a tearoom, and bought souvenirs. They arrived at the edge of town in front of the history museum around three in the afternoon and filed inside.

A huge statue of the headless horseman, on a full-sized horse statue in a half rearing stance, greeted them in the lobby.

"Hello, and welcome to the *All Hallows Historical Museum*, I'm Mrs Reeves, and you must be the children from *Randolph High*."

They all turned to the voice to see an elderly woman with a mop of grey curls and glasses who barely came up to the chest of the horse statue.

"She's like *the fifth* Mrs Reeves we've met so far," Sydney whispered to Hannah. "That's weird."

"Hello, we're here for a tour of the museum," Barrett told her, not noticing her name was the same as four other women in town.

"Of course." Mrs Reeves placed a hand on the horse's chest. "We'll start right here, shall we? Our very own headless horseman. It's been seen many a Halloween by the townspeople. It's said, he was first seen some time in the 1690s, but details have been sketchy." She looked up at the statue of the headless man and then glanced at the skull in his hand. "People, through the centuries, have often wondered if that's *his* head, or the head of his enemy. No one knows. There's not a lot of written information from back then, and it's only been written about the last two centuries." Mrs Reeves looked back at the group. "It's said he was the founding father of *All Hallows* and did a deal with the devil." A small sly grin crossed her lips. "Let me tell you *that* story. Follow me."

She led them through the door she'd come through and over to the left wall of the rectangular room. Standing under a portrait, she waited for them to crowd around. "It is said that Jebadiah Jacobus

Hallows founded this town in 1682. He was a wealthy landowner with a wife and ten children, with money from oil and gold. He built the town and invited people from near and far to come and live. And they did." She peered over her glasses at them. "But it wasn't long before everything went wrong." Glancing up at the portrait of the stately looking man, she added, "We're not sure if this is *actually* him, as we have no other evidence, just an artist's rendering. Follow me." She walked along the wall to a huge ten by five foot painting. "This is the town of *All Hallows*. The way it was originally built." Pointing up to the left of the painting, she said, "That's where the Hallows family lived, on the homestead out of town. A huge two-storey sprawling home. It needed to be for ten children and two adults. There were also staff and cleaners, nannies, and cattlemen to help with the property and the animals they had. People came from far and wide to live in the town. He'd built houses, the bank, the corner store, the hotel bar, and many other places. But some people went on to build their own." Her finger moved to the right of the painting. "You can see the lake and river. It made the land prosperous, crops would grow, cattle could drink, but it also caused problems." Moving on, she turned to the right and stood in front of a list of people's names on the back wall. "In the summer of 1712 the drought hit. There'd never been one like it and it dried out the river, the lake, and the land. No one had water to drink or wash in, or to give to the cattle, and the cattle died off in their hundreds because there was no grass to eat, either. It drove Hallows crazy, according to the legend, and he blamed everyone but himself. Blamed the townspeople for using it all and not saving any. Blamed his cattlemen for letting the cattle drink it all, blamed his wife for having ten children that all needed food and water for their wives and families. It drove him so crazy…" Mrs Reeves sighed and licked her lips, looking from the group to the painting. "…that he killed everyone who lived in town, including his wife and children, and their families."

The girls gasped and the boys had the decency to look uncomfortable.

"Oh, no, that's horrible," Ms Grant murmured, her brow furrowing. "What happened next?"

"Well," Mrs Reeves went on, knowing she had their attention. "That's when he made a deal with the devil. Come." She waved them on to the next framed work on the wall. "This is the town two years later. As you can see, it was completely restored. New buildings, new homestead. The lake and river are in abundance, and there's greenery. This painting was done by one of the new townspeople who moved in. It was always questioned what had happened two years earlier. Hallows had apparently told a few people that the whole town had died off from the drought and had to be burned, including his wife and children because there had been no water. There were no crops, hence, no food. People starved, animals died, and all of their bodies were burned beside the Hallows homestead so no one asked questions. He rebuilt the town, after burning it down, claimed the drought made it easy work for a forest fire. But…" She breathed in and frowned. "A new arrival in 1714 painted this and a couple of others. You can see the homestead here on the left…" She pointed to it. "He rebuilt it exactly the same. And this gnarled mess here," her finger moved to below the house, "that's a tree that grew where he supposedly burned the bodies. It's still there, has lasted all these centuries, even after he hanged himself from it." She watched them all gape at her. "Yes, that's the next chapter of the story." Leading them around to their right, they came to a painting of a body hanging from the tree.

"Oh," the kids murmured, fascinated, but disgusted, by the horror.

"One evening, one of Hallows' farmhands found him hanging from the tree. Terrified, he ran into town and found the doctor. A large posse soon formed, and rode out to the homestead. They found Jebadiah Jacobus Hallows sitting on his horse, a rope around his neck, and him dead. They're not sure how, or why, the horse stayed there, or how he managed to die while sitting on the horse, but the horse refused to move while his master was on his back. They say animals are smart and loyal to their owners. I think the horse knew his master was dead and chose to stay with him until someone found him. One of the townspeople, the artist who sketched that last painting, did this one." Her head shook slowly. "No one knows why he did it. Many of the townspeople said he'd been as mad as a hatter when they moved in, and had grown even madder over the next two years. The year was 1716 and he hanged himself."

"But what's that got to do with the deal with the devil?" Cameron asked.

"Well…" Mrs Reeves stared him straight in the eye. "How would you explain the fact he killed everyone in town, buried them beside his own home, and then two years later, the town had prospered again? He'd lost a lot of money in the drought, had enough to live on, but definitely not enough to rebuild an entire town."

"Doesn't mean it was the devil," Riley muttered, thinking more and more it was nothing but a stupid story to scare tourists.

"Maybe not," Mrs Reeves replied. "But he didn't have his horse before all of that happened, only after. After he went mad he killed the entire town and burned it down, and after that, he rebuilt it. That horse itself was so much of a devil, that when the doctor and the sheriff tried to get Hallows down, he bucked, and hit the rope that was tied to the tree. The rope pulled and off Hallows' head flew. The rope fell free and Hallows' hand reached out to grab his own head. Once he had it, the horse bolted and didn't stop. The homestead burst into flames and burned down for a second time, and the artist who was drawing the painting," she pointed up to it, "swore on a stack of bibles that the tree he'd been hanging from started writhing and bending and twisting as if it were in pain, excruciating pain, its branches reaching out to Hallows, waiting for him to come back to claim it."

Her voice had risen, but now she calmed down and guided them to a long display cabinet in the middle of the room. "When the homestead stopped burning and the townspeople were able to go inside, they found a secret room in the basement that had survived. There were satanic circles and diagrams, bibles with satanic drawings on the pages; drawings of the devil all in red. You can see them here."

The children and teachers gathered around silently and gazed at the books and bowls of trinkets, reading the plaques that accompanied them.

"The doctor declared him deceased, and once they found his suicide letter where he clearly states what he'd done, including making a deal with the devil, the doctor declared him deceased *and* criminally insane. Since the body was gone and Hallows was dead, there was no need to do anything else. They razed most of the house, and filled in the room with dirt, but you can still see some rubble marking the corners of the house and some of the ground floor rooms. The tree is definitely still there. It's never burned down, rotted, or been eaten by termites. In fact," she chuckled lightly, "it's often said to be grown from the blood and bone of the people under it. Birds refuse to sit in it, it's never grown leaves, has always been twisted and gnarled, and nothing grows around it."

"Well…it's basically a cemetery," Keenan murmured. "Why would it?"

"True," Mrs Reeves agreed. "And that's the tour and the history of *All Hallows*."

"The town clearly survived," Gemma piped up. "*Thrived* by the looks of it."

"It did." Mrs Reeves walked into the lobby and checked the clock on the wall. "We've done well since October 31, 1716."

"Halloween?" Sydney frowned. "Today? Today's the anniversary of his death?"

Mrs Reeves turned to her, a twinkle in her eye as the sound of thundering hoofbeats grew audible.

CHAPTER THREE

The hooves thundered to a stop outside of the museum and a horse's whinny floated through the air.

"Oh, no, he's here," Lena cried, and clung to Zara. "The Hallows man is here. He's here. We're going to die."

"Oh, for God's sake, get a grip," Gemma snapped at her and strode over to the door. She flung it open and gasped. There in front of her was the headless horseman.

The black steed snorted at her, sweat dripping down its neck from being ridden hard. The body, or man, or whatever it was riding him, was headless. At least, its head wasn't between its shoulders, but in its hand. The horse reared and whinnied again before bolting off down the main street in a cloud of dust.

"What the hell…?" Gemma muttered, scared, shocked, surprised and unable to move.

"It's him, he's here to get us," Lena sobbed. "I don't want to die. I want to go home." She burst into tears, not even caring that her classmates were watching.

Zara hugged her, scared out of her wits herself,

but unable to speak.

"And right on time." Mrs Reeves smiled. "Gets the tourists every time."

Mr Barrett glanced sharply at her. "*What do you mean* right on time and gets the tourists?"

She stared him down. "It's five o'clock, time for trick or treating. Our horseman is our local blacksmith. He volunteers to play the role every year to add to the tale. It gets the blood pumping, wouldn't you say?"

"Certainly did that," Hannah murmured, and clutched her chest. Her heart was still racing and she wanted it to stop. "I don't think I want to trick or treat after that. Definitely not walk around town doing it."

"No," Ms Grant agreed, on edge after the performance. "I say we go back to the hotel and have dinner. We did bring some things for you kids, sweets and such; you don't need to go trick or treating."

"The hotel will have something for the children, if they're not game," Mrs Reeves told them. "They make lovely desserts in all kinds of spooky images. They may be all you need."

"Okay, kids, we'll head back to the hotel then." Barrett sent them on their way with the other teachers before turning to Mrs Reeves. "Thank you for the…" Struggling to find the right words, he finally said, "Entertaining performance."

"Oh, *thank you*," she replied. "But it's only the beginning."

They arrived at the hotel in better spirits and the boys insisted on going trick or treating.

"Just because the girls are scared doesn't mean we

are," Grady complained. "It's already five-thirty, trick or treating started half an hour ago and there's a movie on at seven. That means we've got an hour at least to do something." He nudged Damien who nudged Riley.

"Yeah," they agreed. "Let's do it."

"Well…" Barrett turned to confer with the other teachers. "Jameson, you and I could take the boys if the girls don't want to go. Gina, you and Greta could stay with them."

"Yes, I think that would be best," Gina murmured. "That was quite a story she told."

"Yes," Jameson agreed and fixed his cardigan cuffs nervously. "The real life horseman definitely added to its authenticity."

"Right. Ladies, stay here with the girls and have dinner. We'll take the boys and be back in," he checked his watch, "just under an hour."

"Good. Girls, we're staying in, let's go and have dinner." Gina herded them into the dining room with Greta, while Quentin and Jameson procured pumpkin buckets from the manager for the candy. In five minutes, they were off.

Even though they didn't have costumes, it didn't matter. The residents still handed out sweets to them as they did to the children of the town.

"This stuff's pretty generic," Cameron complained as he looked into this bucket. "Just wrapped up stuff like chocolates and hard chews."

"Be grateful you're even getting that," Nathan told him. "You don't even say thank you to anyone.

Clearly your parents didn't teach you any manners."

Cameron spun on the spot to face him. "And what did *yours* teach *you*? How to dress like a hobo and leech off others?" He sneered in Nathan's face and smirked at his friends.

"*Enough*, Cameron," Barrett warned. "Continue and I'll give your candy to someone else." He kept the boys moving onto the next home.

"Trick or treat," the boys chimed.

"Oh, there you are." Mrs Reeves from the museum opened her screen door. "I wondered when you'd get here. Here you go." She handed the boys a good sized bag of candy each that fitted in the palm of their hand. "Don't forget to eat dinner first, and make sure you have the desserts. Bye, boys." She waved and closed the door.

Cameron weighed up the bag he'd just received. "Not bad; a good weight. Should have some decent stuff in it."

"God, you are such a greedy guts," Morgan complained. He'd never liked Cameron, and thought he was the school dick, while Cameron thought of himself as the king of the crowd. He wasn't. Rolling his eyes, Morgan led the way back to the street and started for the next house.

"This will be it, boys. We need to get back to the hotel," Barrett called out. It was the last house on the street anyway and soon they were done.

*****

"I am *loving* these ghost meringues." Lena picked up her white swirly dessert and bit into it. A smooth lime crème oozed into her mouth. "Mmm…"

"The pumpkin doughnut balls are delish, too." Zara licked her fingers to get every speck of sugar off. "It's like one of those Jaffa chocolate balls. Chocolate on the inside, orange on the outside."

"This spider cupcake's awesome." Gemma shoved hers in Lena's face, making her squeal and shrink back.

"Get that away from me." Lena flapped her hands in front of her face, closed her eyes, and turned her head away. "Get it away from me."

"Gemma, stop teasing her," Ms Grant reprimanded. She and Ms Halston were down one end of the table with the girls either side. "It's heading for seven and the movie starts soon. Quentin said he'd be back by six-thirty."

"Must have become caught up in trick or treating," Greta replied and finished off her coffee. She noticed Mrs Reeves as well as several wait staff stop what they were doing and wander towards the door with blank expressions on their faces. "What on earth? Where are they going? Are you girls finished?" She saw them nod. "I'm just going to check outside and then we'll get ready for the movie." She rose from her chair and happened to look out the window into the fading lights. A frown crossed her brows. "What the hell? Where are they going?" Hurrying out to the front porch, she found Barrett, Cordell and the boys. "What's happening?"

"We don't know," Cordell murmured. "It just

started a few minutes ago. Everyone just started walking towards the end of town."

"What's going on?" Gina stopped beside them with the girls. "Where's everyone going?"

"We don't know," Barrett repeated and continued watching.

Sydney and Gemma moved forward, both excited by what they were seeing.

A possible possession!

"They've headed for the Hallows homestead," Keenan murmured and hastily pulled his bag from his back. He dug through it and brought out the gadget he'd used on the mechanical spider. It wasn't as if he had any *real* ghost hunting equipment.

They watched as the townsfolk walked out of town and up to the homestead on the hill. Watched as their torches were lit and waved around.

"What time did Mrs Reeves say they found Hallows hanging from the tree?" Nathan asked.

"Which Mrs Reeves?" Gemma asked with an arched brow.

Nathan sniggered. "Yeah, there do seem to be a few of them in this town."

"Just a few," Gemma replied. "You mean Museum Reeves?"

"Yeah, that one," he muttered.

"Evening." Keenan raised his binoculars to his eyes. "Like just about now." He focussed the lenses and watched. "Holy crap! They're near the tree and there's a guy on a horse with ropes around his neck."

Barrett yanked the binoculars from Keenan's hand

and raised them to his own eyes. "Jesus!" he muttered. "There is. What are they doing, re-enacting it?"

"Well, it did happen on Halloween," Sydney reminded him and heard a horse whinny. "Oh, no, it didn't?"

Barrett watched in horror. "It did. The horse is headed this way."

"What!" Ms Grant and Ms Halston gasped. "The children."

The thunder of hooves sounded in the distance, but rapidly grew louder, and harder, faster than any horse could possibly go.

Keenan held up his instrument in the hope of getting a reading. And he got one all right. That horse bolted into town as if the devil was after him, but came to a shuddering halt in front of the teens, its eyes blazing red as the head of Jebadiah Jacobus Hallows hung from the rider's hand.

Everyone stood frozen as the horse reared, snorted smoke from its nostrils, and the rider held up the head, shaking it as some kind of ominous warning. Then they took off, flying down the main street, dust at their heels, smoke wafting through the air.

"What the hell…?" Damien murmured, staring in horror at the scene that had just unfolded. "Did we just…? Did he just…? What *was* that?"

"Real," Keenan said in an authoritative tone. "Not a machine, no electrodes about it." He lowered his gadget. "That thing was as real as you and me."

"How can it be real? It had red eyes!" Cameron argued.

"Smoke and mirrors." Keenan packed away his machine and binoculars and slung his backpack onto his shoulder. "Could have been red lights around the horse's eyes. Special glass lenses on a hood. Anything." He shrugged. "It was scary, but it's Halloween and they probably relive that every year."

"Oh, there you all are." Mrs Reeves popped out the door. "The movie's just about to start; are you going to watch it?" She looked bewildered as they all stared at her.

"How did you get here so quickly?" Ms Halston asked. "I saw you walk out to the homestead."

"Oh, silly, I've been here the whole time." Mrs Reeves smiled brightly. "I can still serve you gentlemen and the boys if you want dinner. You can eat it while you watch the movie. Come, come." She waved them inside as the town went about its business.

"What movie?" Gemma asked, disturbed by the whole ordeal.

"*Sleepy Hollow,*" Mrs Reeves replied, and walked ahead of them.

CHAPTER FOUR

The teens stopped in their tracks and looked at each other.

"She *cannot* be serious?" Nathan said.

"Come along, children. Boys, you need to eat." Barrett waited for them to walk ahead of him and followed up the rear. While he, Cordell, and the boys ate, the others settled in to watch the movie.

"Oh, this one," Gemma murmured, seeing Johnny Depp's name on the screen. "Seen it. I'd rather watch the TV show. At least Tom Mison is hotter."

They sat through the next two hours and then gathered in the lounge room for the ghostly tales section of the night.

"Do you think that was real, before?" Hannah murmured to Sydney. They were sitting in a large easy chair by the fireplace.

"I don't."

They turned to see Keenan sitting at the table behind them playing with the school's gadgets.

"But it must be." Sydney kept her voice low and leaned towards him.

"Why?" He leaned in so he was closer to her as he had a huge crush. "It clearly wasn't electronic, but it wasn't a ghost, either."

"That's not what I meant," Sydney kept on. "I mean *real*, as in, someone on a horse. Maybe the blacksmith, like earlier, to entertain the tourists on Halloween. We're not the only tourists in town."

"No, we're not," he agreed and set the mini conductor on the table. "All of this is of no benefit for catching ghosts. The only thing it can do is detect electronics."

"What if this is like a Scooby Doo cartoon?" Sydney slid out of her chair and sat at the table. "We'll end up being those meddling kids if we solve a mystery." She shoved her hair behind her ears and noted hers was as curly as Keenan's.

"This isn't a mystery, either." He raised a brow in amusement. "It's clearly just a show for tourists on Halloween and nothing more."

"It was pretty scary," Hannah went on, despite feeling left out of the conversation. She knew Sydney had a crush on Keenan and vice versa.

"It was," Sydney agreed. "And weird. Especially when Mrs Reeves popped up out of nowhere and acted like nothing had happened." Her gaze darted from person to person and saw how tense the girls looked. The cliquey witches didn't look as if they were having too much of a good time. "Do you still want to scare the other girls tonight?" she asked Hannah.

Keenan grinned. "You too?" He saw her puzzled

expression and told her he'd suggested it to the boys before. "Nathan, Morgan and Caleb, that is." He glanced over his shoulder at the posh crowd. "Don't care for Cameron, Riley, Damien and Grady."

"We could scare them, too," Sydney whispered.

"After everything that's happened?" Hannah whispered back. "Why bother?"

"True." Sydney nodded in agreement. "Let's see what happens."

"Hey, I just remembered Manager Mrs Reeves said earlier that there might be more Halloween fun. I wonder if that show before was a part of it." Keenan watched Nathan, Morgan and Caleb join them at the table.

"Yeah, I remember that." Nathan stuck a piece of candy corn into his mouth. He'd been munching on his trick or treat stash since dinner. "Can't get any worse than what's already happened."

Keenan stared at the window and pointed. "You think."

The headless horseman stood on the porch outside, head hanging in his hand.

"Ah, it's him," Hannah squealed and dived for the other side of the room behind the teachers.

"Who's him?" Barrett asked and glanced towards the window. He saw the silhouette outside. "Children, get away from the window this instant."

They grabbed their stuff and backed away, not taking their eyes from him. The arm drew back and threw the head flying through the window, smashing glass in every direction.

The children cried out and other people came running.

"Oh, no, it's him," Mrs Reeves cried out and raced back the way she'd come.

"Get away from the window," another patron yelled and picked up a chair. He used it as though he was taming a lion, but the horseman just grabbed the chair and flung it over his shoulder as if it were as light as a feather. He held up his hand and his head levitated then flew at him. He caught it easily.

"Oh, this is ridiculous," Barrett snapped. "I'm going outside." He marched from the room, through the lobby, out the front door, and along the porch to stand outside the broken window.

The horseman was nowhere to be seen.

"Where did he go?" Barrett asked through the window. "Where did he go?"

"He just vanished," Jameson called nervously. "He…just…poof…vanished." His bewildered facial expression said it all.

"I really don't like it here," Gina murmured. She was beside Greta and keeping the children back. "Something weird is going on."

Staff members came in to clean the mess up and closed the window's shutters. The handyman nailed them shut until the window could be replaced.

"Something *really* weird is going on here," Gemma murmured to those around her. "And I have a feeling someone's playing silly buggers." It was an old saying she'd picked up from her parents.

"Whatever they're doing, it's working," Lena told

them. "I'm scared and want to go home." She huddled with Zara, Reagan and Thea for comfort.

"So do we," Cameron and Riley said in unison, whereas the others just traded glances.

Gemma turned her back on the cliques and faced her friends. "Something weird is going on. Now, I don't know whether it's all a part of the shtick they've got going on for Halloween, but it's freaking me out. What about you guys?"

They nodded and nervously looked at the window. As much as Gemma never admitted to being upset or scared, or anything else for that matter as the school's rebellious Goth, she never said or did much of anything. But this was different.

"If this is all for Halloween, then yeah, I get it," Nathan said. "Well done to the town of *All Hallows* for reliving a story hundreds of years in the making. But how far are they willing to take it?"

"What if they burn down the whole town?" Keenan asked, a thought having occurred to him during the conversation. "They've already recreated the death." He noticed the weird looks they were giving him and shrugged a shoulder. "They may try and recreate the town burning, or killing everyone. It *is* three hundred years since it happened, you know." He glanced from puzzled face to puzzled face. "Did you lot not figure that out?"

"No." Nathan frowned in thought. "What *is* going on in this place? *Are they* trying to recreate the whole thing? But then, the town was burned down *after* the drought, *after* he killed everyone, then he rebuilt it and then killed himself."

"They're going backwards," Caleb said. "The hanging, then it will be the town rebuilt. Would a window do?" He nodded towards it.

"No," Sydney butted in. "It's out of order. The drought, the murder spree, the burial, the burning, the rebuilding, the hanging, and *then* his house burned down again. That hasn't happened. This isn't the first to last or last to first, it's out of order."

"So, what, it's whatever the hell they wanna do to scare the crap out of us," Gemma told her. "I don't get it. *Regardless* of whatever order they do it in, I just don't get it."

"I want to go home," Liv murmured. "I'm with the others. I just want to go home." Her friends saw how scared she was.

"It's okay, Liv." Hannah put her arms around her. "We'll stick together. We're all in the same room. We'll look out for each other."

"Cold comfort if the town burns down," Liv muttered. She'd been silent most of the day, just taking everything in and enjoying herself until the museum tour, after that she was just trying to be brave. She'd been excited by this trip, but the weirder it became, the creepier it became, and the scareder *she* became.

"She's right," Caleb said. "It will be no good if the town's burned down while we're asleep."

"Who can sleep tonight?" Morgan asked. "This place is giving me the heebie-jeebies. I won't be sleeping." The others nodded in agreement.

"I wonder if the whole town's in on it." Sydney rubbed her neck, a habit when she was nervous.

"Would have to be," Nathan told her. "To pull off an elaborate scheme like what we've seen, they're *so* in on it. The whole freakin' town!"

The grandfather clock in the lobby softly chimed ten.

"Two hours left," Sydney muttered. "Wonder what they have in store for us?"

Barrett approached them. "Okay, kids, I think it's time to get you up to bed. The window's locked, they'll lock up the hotel in a minute, and I think it better if we just go upstairs and try and get a good night's sleep."

"You are kidding, right?" Ms Grant asked scornfully. "There's *no way* we'll be able to sleep." She glanced at Ms Halston who agreed. "We've already agreed to share my room because neither of us wants to be alone with some weirdo running around. God knows what he'd do, especially to a single woman." She wrapped her cardigan tighter around her.

Barrett sighed. "Well, I'll guess we'll just have to do it the best way we know how. Lock our doors, keep our phones on, and stay dressed if we have to run out in the middle of the night." He addressed the students. "Stay dressed and keep your bags packed just in case we need to dash out in the middle of the night."

"It nearly *is* the middle of the night," Ms Halston pointed out. "It's just past ten and I've had enough."

A ringing bell sounded from somewhere outside,

grew louder, whizzed past the hotel, and then faded.

"That was heading towards the Hallows homestead," Keenan said and dashed out of the room to follow the crowd of staff and other guests out to the porch where they stood watching as the homestead went up in flames, or, at least, the ground where it had once stood.

"Now *that's* weird," Sydney said. "There's no house there, so why set the ground on fire?" She watched the flames leap high into the black sky.

"As some sort of significance?" Nathan replied, puzzled even more by everything.

"It has to be all part of the game." Keenan shook his head and turned to his friends. "It *has* to be a game. This *can't* be real. It's all a game for Halloween to get tourists to keep coming back year after year for the experience."

Gemma glanced around at all of the faces and got the nagging feeling that someone was missing. She saw five Mrs Reeves, the other tourists staying at the hotel, other people they had met during the day, but there was someone… "The bus driver!" She snapped her fingers. "Where's he in all of this? I haven't seen him since we got here."

"What? Are you saying he's the one doing all of this?" Keenan guffawed. "Yeah, right. Like that dope could come up with everything we've seen."

Gemma shrugged. "Whatever. It's a possibility and his disappearance is noted." She crossed her arms defiantly and turned her back on him.

Barrett saw the fire was nearly out and ushered

everyone inside. "Okay, kids, looks like they've got it under control. Let's get you up to bed. If you want to sleep two to a bed and bunk up like Ms Grant and Ms Halston, feel free and lock your doors." They reached their rooms and went in, but heard a yell from the boys' room a second later.

CHAPTER FIVE

Everyone rushed into the room that Cameron, Riley, Damien and Grady were sharing and stopped short.

On the wood floor, right in the middle of the room between the bunk beds, someone had painted a satanic circle in what looked to be blood.

"Paint!" Keenan exclaimed. "You can smell it. If it was blood it would smell metallic."

Barrett sighed. "Can this night get *any* worse?" He reached down and dabbed the paint with his finger. "Still wet. We'll need newspaper or something so you don't get it all over you. Jameson, can you—"

"I'll run down." Jameson was out the door in seconds.

Barrett straightened and stretched his neck which was starting to ache. A migraine was also growing at the base of his skull. "As I said before, if you all want to sleep two to a bunk and share the one room, go ahead. The rest of you," he looked at the teachers and students, "go and carefully check your rooms."

They hurried off and were thoroughly searching their rooms when Jameson came back with multiple newspapers and helped the boys cover the diagram so they didn't get paint on the rest of the floor, or traipse it through the hotel.

"So far, that's the girls who get the spider and the boys who get the diagram." Gemma bit her lip and curled a strand of hair around her finger. Flopping onto her bed, she looked around the room. "We've got nothing. Were those guys targeted on purpose and not us?"

"Maybe the *rooms* were targeted," Sydney suggested and sat on the bunk opposite her. "Maybe it has nothing to do with us at all; they just picked a room."

"And Mrs Reeves *did say* to look out for stuff, so maybe the diagram was, *is*, a part of that. We saw the same one in the diaries and books in the museum," Liv told them. "I studied each book and it's the same as in his bible."

"Good for you, Liv," Hannah said. "At least one of us was interested. I just wanted to get out of there it was so creepy."

"Yeah, but it's not like the diagrams mean anything to *us*," Gemma went on. "They have nothing to do with us and everything to do with Jebadiah Hallows."

"Maybe that's where everything comes from." Sydney looked at her friends. "From the room under the house, the one they found after the fire. If he was worshipping the devil and made a deal with him, then it would be whatever's in that room."

"Buried under ten tonnes of dirt," Hannah reminded her. "They filled it in."

"Okay." Sydney nodded. "Then it's in whatever *came out* of that room. Like those diaries and papers in the museum. Everything on the wall was technically an artist's rendering, so wasn't Jebadiah's. So all they have of his are the books and papers in that cabinet."

"Unless there's something we're missing," Keenan said from the doorway.

The girls looked up to see Nathan, Morgan and Caleb were with him.

"What do you mean?" Sydney asked, and scooted over to make room. The other girls did the same.

"What I mean is…" Keenan sat on the bed next to her eliciting secretive glances between their friends. "We were talking, and either this is a prank, or this place is actually haunted."

Gemma scoffed. "I don't believe in ghosts and don't believe that horseman *is* one. I think the town is playing silly buggers and we've been caught up in it. I just don't know why they think that everything they're doing is fun. It's not. It's scaring people, especially the others, who I don't care about, and it's freaking the rest of *us* out. It's not funny."

"No, it isn't," Nathan agreed and scratched his head which itched from his having not washed his hair in a month. "But I can't come up with any other reason for why it's happening and I don't believe in ghosts either."

"We were talking before," Morgan jumped in. "About why the others have had it happen to them. We've had nothing."

"Neither have we," Hannah declared. "Neither have the teachers."

"The night's still young." Keenan looked at his watch. "Just about to chime eleven."

They paused and waited for the faint chime from the lobby clock to ring out. But it didn't.

Keenan frowned and tilted his head. "That's strange—"

"It's chimed every other hour," Sydney muttered. "I wonder what stopped it."

Keenan stared at her and marvelled at the way her brain worked in sync with his.

"We should go and see what happened," Sydney suggested.

"You can," Liv told her. "I'm not interested. I just want to get ready for bed and try and have an uneventful night. Hannah, come to the bathroom?"

"Sure." Hannah grabbed her toiletries and followed her out the door.

"Don't really care about a clock either," Caleb said. "I'm heading back to our room." He stood and stretched his back muscles. "Ugh, I think I ate too much candy. I feel sick."

"So do I." Morgan stood as well. "See you guys when you get back." He followed Caleb out the door and three doors down the hall to their room.

"Do we sneak downstairs or what?" Nathan asked. "Or just boldly walk down and the teachers won't figure it out either way."

"Quietly leave the room and quietly rush down the hall," Keenan said and headed for the door. He stuck his head out to see if anyone was around, and when he saw no one, frantically waved to the others and took off down the hall. They followed and fled down the stairs. Arriving at the lobby, they walked over to the grandfather clock and saw immediately why it hadn't chimed.

Mrs Reeves walked into the lobby. "Oh, I thought you children were going to bed. I was just coming to see why the clock didn't chime when it was supposed to. Oh…" She stopped next to them and saw the door wide open and the pendulum disc missing. "Oh, well, it should have still chimed, even without the pendulum." She peered up at the face and noticed the clock had stopped at 6:48. "That's strange," she murmured. "I could swear it's been going off all night on the hour."

"It has." Keenan stared at the face and noted the time. "What happened at 6:48?"

Mrs Reeves tilted her head, but couldn't look at him. "What do you mean?"

"*What I mean is*, that clock chimed at ten, it chimed at nine, and eight, and seven before that. It chimed at midday when we arrived, and since the last chime was," he checked his watch, "one hour and eleven minutes ago, why are the hands on the face set to 6:48 when it's already been working all day." He studied her face for any kind of expression, but she had her poker face on.

Mrs Reeves took a slow, deep breath before answering. "Well, 6:48 is when Jebadiah Hallows was found and released from the rope. It was when his head fell and the horse bolted." Embarrassed, she glanced away. "The clock was gifted by Jebadiah when he rebuilt the town. It's sat here ever since." She hurried away and into the small office off the lobby.

"Well, well, well," Gemma murmured. "Another connection to the headless horseman." She pointed to the clock. "Anyone know if that was intact at ten?"

"It was," Keenan replied. "Every time we've walked past the clock I've looked at it. That pendulum disc was decorated, though I'm not sure what it was. If I'd had my phone with me I would've taken a photo." One of the rules of the trip was the children left their phones at home and had to take cameras instead.

"Liv!" Sydney exclaimed. "She's been taking pics all day."

"Let's go see what she's got." Nathan led the way back upstairs and to the girls' room, managing to avoid the teachers.

"Liv, you got your camera?" Gemma asked. "Did you take a pic of the grandfather clock downstairs? You'll never guess what; Jebadiah Hallows gave it to the hotel when he rebuilt it."

Liv grabbed her bag, dug out her camera, and flicked through the photos until she came to the one of the clock. "I took it at noon when it chimed." She handed over the camera and kept getting ready for bed.

They crowded around to look at the tiny screen, but couldn't get much detail.

"Does this thing zoom?" Gemma asked and

found the button. She clicked it a few times and made the pendulum bigger.

"Oh, what does that look like? Like the circle on the boys' floor." Sydney peered at it. "But I can't tell unless we see it up close."

"Or on a bigger screen." Keenan dashed out of the room and was back moments later holding his laptop while it booted up. "Thought this might come in handy. Give me the SD card." Gemma pulled it from the camera and handed it over. Moments later, he was uploading the pictures onto the computer, and once done, handed the card back. "Now, let's enlarge this shall we." He clicked on the clock photos and zoomed in, moving it so it was just the pendulum disc in the shot. "Liv, is this what you saw?" He showed her and she nodded. Pulling up a photo of the diaries in the museum, he found the one with the same diagram. "They match."

"So does the one on the boys' floor," Liv said. "I took a photo of that too."

Keenan found it and enlarged the image. All three diagrams were the same.

"That has to mean something," Sydney murmured. "That circle keeps popping up."

"It's not the only place, either," Liv said. "The sundial under the statue in the middle of town; same diagram." She watched their eyes widen and Keenan hunt for the photo. "It's also in the symbol above the church door at the end of town. What's the bet, the homestead, or the tree, is in direct line to both. *Right* down main street. And…" She took the laptop from

Keenan and looked for a photo of the town drawing in the museum. "It also forms the shape of the town." She turned the computer around and they saw all five pictures on the screen, silently screaming at them to do something about the town. "Weird, huh?"

"*Weird* is now an understatement." Sydney breathed. "Wow!"

"*Wow*, is an understatement," Gemma replied. "Hallows was up to something when he rebuilt this town, and whatever it is, it's satanic and otherworldly in nature. It's depicted by everything he did."

"And possibly still does," Nathan added. "This is *seriously* weird shit."

"Children, time for bed," Barrett called and clapped his hands for attention. He strolled the hall, glancing in every room. "Time for bed. Make sure your windows are locked. Share rooms if you have to. Make sure your bags are packed and ready to go in a hurry. You don't want to leave anything behind if you do have to run. Boys…" He stopped at the girls' room and saw them all looking at the laptop. "Time for bed. Girls, lock up." He waited for the boys to leave the room. "Keenan, make sure that laptop is locked away. Is it yours or the school's?"

"Mine sir, and I'll pack it away before bed," Keenan replied and walked into his room.

They shut and locked the door and made sure their things were packed before turning in, but Keenan kept his laptop out. He wanted to search for more diagrams throughout the town and tried to pull up Google to do a search. It didn't work. "Drat, no Wi-Fi," he mumbled and checked the connection. "The town must have it."

"Or the hotel, anyway," Nathan mumbled and climbed into bed fully clothed, but without shoes. "We'll be going home tomorrow; let's not bother with it until then." He settled back and watched the others get into bed. He watched Keenan as he scrolled through the pictures, his face illuminated by the light once they turned off the lamps above each bed. He watched until he fell asleep, only to be woken by an almighty crash of splintering glass.

CHAPTER SIX

"What the hell!"

All four boys flicked on their lights and looked around.

"There." Keenan pointed to the dead crow covered in what looked to be blood, lying a few feet from the window it had just smashed through.

"Boys, what happened?" Barrett pounded on the door and rattled the handle. "Let me in. Is everyone all right?"

Morgan jumped out of bed to flick the main light on and unlock the door. "We're fine, but the bird's not." He pointed to the animal under the window.

The teachers hurried in and surveyed the damage. "This night gets weirder and weirder," Barrett said. "I'm going downstairs for a dustpan and broom, and to have a stern word with the manager." He hurried from the room and downstairs to the front desk, impatiently ringing the bell.

Mrs Reeves appeared from the back office. "Yes, Mr Barrett."

"I need a dustpan, broom, and a bin. It seems your bird life has also gone crazy, and a crow killed itself by flying into one of the windows. As if this town wasn't weird enough." He tapped his foot impatiently. "Now we're being attacked by the Corvus family."

"Oh, no, I'm so sorry," Mrs Reeves murmured and her hand flew to her mouth in shock. "I'll get you what you need straight away." She hurried back into the office and seconds later produced what he'd asked for. It was as if she'd already had them waiting.

Surprised, Barrett accepted them and went back upstairs to the boys' room. Everyone else was in there chattering excitedly. "Okay, kids, get back to your own rooms and lock your doors. I'll take care of this." He swept up the broken glass and bird into the bin, then closed the window shutters to keep out the cold night air, and pulled the curtains tightly over them.

The kids had been milling around and Liv had taken photos, but as she quietly slipped into the hall, she saw a dark shadowy figure sneak down the hall away from their room. After quickly snapping a photo, she hurried back to her room, but saw nothing awry or out of place…at least from the quick glance over she gave it.

"What's wrong?" Sydney stopped beside her and looked around.

Liv pulled up the picture on her camera. "Someone was sneaking away from our room, but it doesn't look like they've touched anything."

Sydney walked around the room and surveyed it, hands on hips. "Cool. I was just saying to the boys they've finally had something happen and now we have too."

"We have what, too?" Gemma asked as she walked in with Hannah behind her.

"A visitor." Liv showed them the photo. "The boys get the bird; we get a human."

"Cool," Gemma murmured. "About time. Not that you can see who it is." She walked over to the window and flung back the curtains. "Nothing." She rifled through the desk beneath it. "Nothing. You?"

"Not yet." Sydney checked under her bed and pulled the covers back down, but something stopped her and made her look again. Peering into the darkness, she asked for a light. The girls looked around for one, but it was Liv who pulled a torch from her bag and handed it over.

"Well…looky here." Sydney noticed the upended floorboard. Not too much, just an inch or two that poked up. She dug her nails in and lifted the plank, and then crawled under the bed, where she aimed the torch into the hole. "Aha!" Gingerly putting her hand in, she pulled out an old leatherbound book, had a quick search for anything else, and shoved the plank back in place so rats and spiders couldn't get in. After wriggling out, she sat on the floor and leaned against the bed. She opened the book. "Now, doesn't this look familiar?" Holding the book out, they saw Jebadiah Hallows' name on the first page. "How did we get this?"

Liv clicked her camera and took pictures of every page Sydney turned to.

"It was left for us," Gemma declared, but was cut short.

"Girls, back to bed," Ms Grant called into the room. "Just like before. Stay dressed and keep your bags packed. And lock your door."

"Yes, Miss," they replied and Hannah locked the door behind her.

Sydney flicked through the book. "I can't make anything out. It's not in English, but here are those satanic circles." Her finger moved over several drawings. "And they're the same as all the others."

"The whole town's full of them," Liv murmured. "The town *is* one."

"Is that what's making it cursed?" Hannah asked and brushed some dust off Sydney. "Because he built the second town in the shape of one of those things?" She pointed to the diagram. "The whole town is cursed?"

"Let me look." Liv held her hand out for the book and flipped through the pages. "There are two main lines crossing in the middle. It looks like a cross, or plus sign, but its horizontal line is shorter. The vertical is the main line." She pulled up the town's painting and studied the layout. "The vertical line is the church, the sundial, and the house. The house was destroyed, but is technically still there in ruins. When it burned down the lines were still connected, so the circle is still intact. *And*, if there is a curse, so is that."

"Perfectly good reasoning," Gemma surmised. "*If* that's what it is. What about the horseman? What's he got to do with it? Does he represent the cattlemen, the drovers, Hallows? Who?"

"Mrs Reeves from the museum first mentioned something about they don't know if it's Jebadiah's head or the head of his enemy. But from the story she went on to tell, it was Jebadiah's body sitting on that horse with the noose around its neck."

"What if it wasn't?" Sydney asked. "What if *all* of this is a lie and there *never was* a Jebadiah Hallows. He *never* killed the people of the town, *didn't* burn it down, rebuild it, or do a deal with the devil? What if it's *all* a lie and *all* of this is just purely an act for Halloween?"

"Another perfectly good thought," Gemma said. "But, at the end of the day, or night, what are we meant to do about all of this?"

Sydney shrugged. "Don't know. But I'm tired, so let's go to bed." She cleaned herself off and put the diary into her backpack beside her bed. Slipping out of her shoes, she slid under the covers and turned out her light.

*****

"This is getting creepier by the minute," Nathan said and sat watching Keenan who was back on his laptop. "Found anything?"

"No, it's all the same," Keenan murmured. "The diagrams are all the same whether it's in the diary, the town map, or on the pendulum disc from the clock. They are all the same symbol."

"Maybe that means something." Caleb yawned and tried keeping his eyes open. "Maybe that's a clue."

"Maybe." Keenan flicked between the pictures. "I get the feeling something's staring me right in the face and I'm not seeing it."

"Maybe it's because you're too tired." Morgan curled up under his blankets. "Get some sleep." But even as he said it he heard the soft whistle of the wind coming through their broken window, and since he was on the top bunk, it was going to be hard to follow his own advice.

"I'm with Morgan." Caleb curled up in the other top bunk. "Get some sleep."

"What's the point when stuff keeps happening," Nathan muttered. He heard the wind and pulled the blankets over his head, leaving just his nose uncovered so he could breathe.

Keenan sat cross-legged on his bed and leaned back against the wall behind him, his covers over his legs to keep him warm. "Is all of this shit for real, or what, just some elaborate hoax by the townspeople to scare the bejeebus out of people every year? What if it *wasn't* real? What if it was? What if there's *really* a headless horseman, supposedly Jebadiah Hallows, running around town every Halloween? That horse and man we saw just before seven was definitely real. My gear said it was. So it was probably the same person that played him this afternoon at five when we were in the museum. Wait!" He snapped his fingers. "At five, it was time for trick or treating. At seven, it was time for the movie. At nine was when story time was happening. That's those times, two hours apart."

"And at eleven?" Nathan yawned and breathed deeply to stay awake. "The clock didn't chime because the pendulum was missing and someone probably jammed the mechanism to stop it."

"But we had all that other stuff happen as well. The electronic spider, the satanic diagram on the boys' floor, the bird in our window. The girls and the teachers haven't had anything yet, that we know of." Keenan's gaze scanned more pictures. "But the horseman has appeared three times and he wasn't around at eleven."

"So what...he missed a chance to scare us." Nathan frowned and lifted his head to look at his friend. "*So* unlike him."

"Don't laugh." Keenan glanced up from the laptop. "That could be the case, or he's planning something bigger for 1 a.m." He checked the laptop clock. "It's after twelve now and I definitely didn't hear the clock chime downstairs. Did you?"

"No." Nathan shook his head and scrunched back down under the covers. "How long you gonna stay up?"

"Don't know. Until I figure out what's going on."

*****

In the room next door, there was giggling afoot!

"Do we want to scare the girls?" Cameron asked his roommates. "Put a note under their door or something."

"Crawl out on the roof and make noises through

the window," Riley suggested. "Scare the knickers off them."

"Gross, Riley," Cameron berated him and thought some more. "We could tap on the window, or throw stones or something at it."

"But what if they fling the window open?" Damien asked. "We'd fall off the roof and be in bigger trouble than we already would be."

"And where would we get the stones?" Grady pulled the covers around his neck. "We can't go out and find some, it's after midnight."

"I collected them all afternoon," Cameron boasted. "Made note of those satanic circles too, and since no one noticed I brought cans of red paint with me, no one's figured out it was me who spray painted the diagram on our own floor."

Damien chuckled. "I *cannot* believe you did that. And people call *me* evil." He'd gone around in a hockey mask the year before for Halloween and scared the hell out of people by sneaking up behind them. Of course, his name also didn't help when it came to horror movie villains.

"Yeah." Cameron preened at the attention. "I did. Figured, *why not*, it *is* Halloween after all, something had better happen, and if it doesn't, then I'll add to the excitement a little. Little did I know we'd have a real headless horseman, the girls would get a fake spider under their bed, and the boys would get a dead bird smash through their window. It's been eventful."

"You know the deadbeat misfits are beside them,"

Grady said. "If you crawl out on the roof, throw stones at their window as well."

"So, what will it be?" Cameron shifted to the edge of his bed. "*Notes* under the door, *noises* at the door, or crawling out onto the porch roof and making noises, or throwing stones at the window?"

"Stones," the boys replied and watched Cameron pull a small bag of stones he'd collected all day out of his backpack.

He flung open the curtain, opened the window, and came face to face with the horseman.

CHAPTER SEVEN

"H-h-h-horse, C-C-Cameron," Riley stuttered, seeing the dark figure out on the roof.

Cameron was staring into the face of Jebadiah Hallows hanging from the hand of the headless horseman. The steed was prancing on the metal roof of the porch below which brought him, and the head, level with the boys' bedroom window.

As scared as he was, Cameron did the first thing that popped into his mind. He reached out, grabbed the head, and threw it with every ounce of energy he had.

The horseman, not expecting such an act, directed the horse to jump off the roof while he waved his hand in the air. The head levitated, just as he and the horse did, and hovered in front of the boys' window.

"Hey, what's going on out there?" Nathan and Keenan stuck their heads out of their window and gasped.

Cameron, not wanting to be outdone, or to be seen as weak in front of his fellow classmates, started throwing the only thing he had at the horseman; the stones he'd collected all day to throw at the girls' window. He thrust his hand into the bag and started pelting the horseman who threw his arm up to protect himself and then galloped away.

"Yeah." Cameron high-fived himself. "I scared the horseman off." Turning his head to boast to Nathan and Keenan, he saw they had disappeared back into their room. Shrugging, he closed the window and turned to see his friends cowering in their beds. "Bunch of pussies!"

"What do you say to that?" Nathan asked Keenan. "What's the time now?"

Keenen checked his laptop. "It's 1 a.m."

"Does that mean we need to expect something to happen at three and five?"

A tap came from the window, and surprised, Nathan opened it to see Sydney and Gemma outside. "What are you doing here?"

"We saw what happened," Sydney whispered. "We want to check out the driver's room. Want to come?"

"Which room's his?" Keenan set down the laptop and moved over to the window.

"The one at the far end of the hall, but on the other side," Gemma murmured. "We'd have to either break in from the hall, or see if we can look in the window."

"Okay." Nathan quickly grabbed his torch and quietly climbed outside. "Lead the way."

They followed as the girls led them past the other students' rooms and around the side of the building. There wasn't much light from that side, so all were glad they had torches.

Finding the room, they shone their lights in. The curtains were only open a sliver, so from what they could see, there wasn't much *to* see. The bed was made and looked as if it hadn't been slept in. The driver's bag sat neatly at the end of it.

All four traded glances, and Nathan pointed to the window then put his finger over his lips. He tried to lift it to see if it was unlocked, and found it slid open easily. Surprised, they climbed in one by one, careful to not make a sound, and closed the curtains tightly so their lights wouldn't be seen. They quickly searched the room and the driver's bag, but found nothing of any significance except the bus keys.

"I think we should keep these," Nathan whispered and pocketed them.

Puzzled, Sydney frowned at him. "Why?" she whispered back. "He'll know someone's been in his bag."

"Let's just say I'm beginning to agree with Gemma," he replied, surprising both girls. "I think he's up to something and we may need a getaway."

"There's nothing else here, so we should go." Gemma turned for the door to see if it was locked and jumped back in horror. The horseman was standing right in front of her.

"It's a costume hanging on the door," Sydney murmured in her ear and went to take a closer look. She rifled through the pockets, but found nothing. "Weird."

"I'll say," Keenan muttered. "We need to get out of here. If the driver *is* the horseman then I don't want to be here when he gets back." Peeking out of the curtains to see if the coast was clear, he slid them aside and climbed out onto the roof.

Nathan and Gemma followed, but while waiting, Sydney's torch flicked across something white poking out between the mattress and the bed frame. She lifted the mattress and pulled it. It was an A4 piece of paper folded in three.

"Come on, Sydney," Gemma urged, and Sydney followed her out of the room. They pulled the curtains across and Nathan slid the window pane down.

As quiet as church mice, they made their way along until the end of the hotel when they turned left. They were in the homestretch, but hoofbeats stopped them. Grabbing each other's arms, they turned off their torches and quietly flattened themselves against the porch roof, trying to make themselves as small as possible. With eager eyes, they looked out for who it could be and saw the person *they didn't want* to see. The headless horseman casually trotted his jet-black steed past the hotel and kept on going. They waited until they could no longer hear a sound and hurried along the roof to the girls' room which was first. Gemma and Sydney crawled in, followed by the boys who shut and locked the window before drawing the curtain.

"Hey, what are the boys doing here?" Hannah sleepily called. "Are you hooking up with Keenan, Sydney? We all know you have crushes on each other."

Gemma and Nathan sniggered while Sydney and

Keenan blushed.

"Go back to sleep," Sydney chastised and unfolded the paper she'd taken. Reading it under torchlight, they saw it had something to do with the Hallows family tree. Under Jebadiah and his wife were ten names, with ten spouses and multiple children's names under that. All had a red cross through them except for the wife and eldest child of the eldest son. "What does that mean?" she whispered.

The boys shrugged. "It's just a piece of history we already know. Jebadiah killed off his family with the rest of the town. Burned all of the people in a mass grave beside his own house and that weird tree grew from it," Keenan said. "That's just his family tree."

"Yeah, but why are two names not crossed off?" Sydney pointed to them.

Another shrug. "I don't know, but I'm going to bed," Keenan whispered. "If the timing's right, the horseman will appear at three and five, and the night's not over yet. Bad stuff could still happen. So be alert and ready to go. We'll sneak down the hall to our own room. I left it unlocked."

"That was a stupid thing to do," Gemma muttered and unlocked their door. She looked before opening it all the way. "Quick, hope the boys didn't get eaten." She watched them move silently down the hall to their own room and enter before closing and locking the door.

"Three and five," Sydney muttered. "But we just saw him trotting past like someone out for a casual ride. Does that not count?"

Gemma shrugged. "Dunno, but what do we do if he reappears?"

"Be prepared." Sydney sat on her bed with her back against the wall and her notebook and pen in hand. Something was urging her to think straight and put a plan in motion, but *what sort* of plan, she didn't know. Scribbling some things down, she tried to figure out what it all meant, and being the resident nerd who knew too much, she knew she should put that to use and have something sorted in case of another encounter.

*****

Once the boys arrived back at their room, Keenan went straight back to work to come up with a plan. He knew that something, *anything*, had to be done to break the curse and that meant breaking the line down the middle of town. He checked the photos on the laptop and zoomed in. There it was; the symbol was above the door of the church, and it faced directly down the road to the old homestead with the sundial in the middle. "We need that ornament," he muttered. "A chisel, axe, hammers, something to pry it off and destroy it."

"And where do we get those?" Nathan asked, as he slipped into bed.

"Tool shed." Keenan shrugged and clicked on a photo of the sundial. "It's probably concreted on; we'll need acid or something. And we have to destroy the sundial, get the rest of the books from the museum, and get to the homestead. Somehow destroy the tree and destroy all of these symbols."

"And how do we do that?" Nathan had a feeling this was making Keenan a little loopy and hoped that nothing happened between now and the cold light of day when they could go home.

"I don't know." Keenan sighed and rubbed his eyes. "But I just have a *really* bad feeling that it will still happen. It's after two now. He still has visits for three and five to go."

"That's *if* he comes." Nathan pulled his covers up around his head. "Night."

"Mmm, night," Keenan mumbled and started making a list.

Out in the hallway, the headless horseman silently walked past their rooms, stopping a moment to make note of the faint light under the boys' door. He moved on, coming to the stairs, and as he stepped down, he slid his left gloved hand down the banister. He made it to the bottom and waited, listening to the silence. He knew what he had to do. He had to make an impact, had to make it worthwhile. Had to make it so dramatic that the whole town would end up out in the street to witness what was about to unfold. It would be something so momentous the town would be talking about it for *another* three hundred years.

He walked over to the grandfather clock and stood in front of it for a moment, watching the hands go in swift motions around the face. His hand went to his pocket and removed the pendulum disc he'd taken hours ago. He replaced it, and removed the small screw he'd stuck in the mechanics so it didn't chime. Closing the door, he went about his business.

In the kitchen, he found what he needed. Cloth, long wooden spoons, and fuel. Having wrapped the cloth around the spoons, he hosed them down with lighter fluid and set them ablaze. As he walked back down the hall, he flicked a burning torch into each room he passed, causing the cheap polyester curtains and carpeting to go up in flames. When he was satisfied, he moved back to the lobby and walked out the front door.

The alarm blared into the night waking everyone, and Mr Barrett smelled smoke in his room. Switching on the bedside light, he knew the sound was the fire alarm and quickly threw back the covers, and slipped into his shoes. He grabbed his overnight bag and phone, and met everyone in the hall. "Into your shoes and get your bags; this is what I warned you about. Quickly now."

The kids ran back into their rooms in a blind panic, slid into their shoes and grabbed backpacks and overnight bags to line up two by two in the hall.

Other tourists were fumbling around in dressing gowns asking what was happening.

"Fire," Barrett boomed. "Get out as fast as you can." He led the children and other teachers along the hall and down the stairs to see much of the bottom floor on fire. "We'll have to get out through a back way," he yelled, seeing the front door covered in flames. "Does anyone know where the back door is?"

"I do; follow me." Mrs Reeves held up the keys and marched down the back hall as a horse let out a terrifying whinny at the front of the building just as the grandfather clock chimed three.

CHAPTER EIGHT

Stunned, half of the kids stared through the fire at the horseman right outside the door on the porch. They stared at the blood-red eyes on the horse, and smoke rising from both horse and rider.

Liv snapped out of it and turned her attention to the clock. Sliding her backpack over both shoulders, she ran over to the clock, opened the door, and yanked the pendulum disc out. "May need this for later," she muttered and ran after the others.

"We need hammers, chisels, axes, anything that can destroy the sundial and get those metal circles," Keenan was gasping through the stifling smoke.

"Acid!" he and Sydney exclaimed at the same time and both detoured into the kitchen as there was a bottleneck of people trying to get out of the back door. Quickly rummaging in cupboards, they found what they were after and re-joined the group. The girls were crying and Barrett was yelling.

"Where do we go now? We need to get out of town for safety reasons. It could all go up and we'll need the bus. Oh, for heaven's sake, where's the driver?"

"Don't need him." Nathan held up the keys. "You drive."

"And where exactly did you get those from, Bartlett?" Barrett asked, hearing a whinny down the street. "Never mind, on the bus." He took the keys and opened the door. "Quickly, quickly, take your bags. Put them on the floor."

"Sir, there are things we need to do, things we need to get," Keenan babbled. "If we're going to stop the horseman forever, we need to break the curse."

"There *is no curse*, Fielding." Barrett bellowed. "There's no such thing. Just a stupid tale that someone made up." The whinny came closer, above them, and they looked up to see the horseman on the hotel's second storey roof. The blood drained from Barrett's face. "Okay, we need to break the curse. What do we do?"

"Get in and let's go," Keenan told him and boarded the bus with Barrett behind him. He took a seat while the teacher started the ignition and drove out of the parking lot behind the hotel. "Where to?"

"The museum first. We'll drop a couple of kids off there." Keenan turned to his fellow classmates. "Liv, you get the diaries and books from the museum. Take a couple of the others with you. We'll need the boys to work on the sundial while we get to the church."

"You're breaking the chain," Sydney gasped. "Excellent!"

Keenan grinned at her exuberance. "We're gonna try. Do whatever's necessary, but we need the diaries and bible, and that metal disc from the sundial. Get it. We'll take the church."

"And just how are you going to get it?" Barrett managed to find his way down the street to the museum, seeing fire engines in the street behind him at the hotel.

"We have tools." Keenan directed the group. "Damien, Grady, go with Liv and Hannah and get what we need. Wait until we get back for you."

"I don't think that they should be doing this on their own," Jameson Cordell argued. "Quentin—"

"Just go with them, Cordell," Barrett instructed. "Do what's necessary. I have a feeling this town's not going to care come morning." He pulled to a stop in front of the museum and opened the door. "Go. We'll be back to get you."

Liv, Hannah, Damien and Grady jumped off the bus with Cordell reluctantly following. He was grumbling as Barrett pulled away.

Doing a u-turn, Barrett headed back up the main street. "Where's this sundial you keep mentioning?"

"Past the hotel. You may need to go on the wrong side of the road," Keenan said, seeing the fire trucks outside of the hotel, and they veered over to the other side to pass.

*****

"Boys, ever wanted to kick down a door or smash in a window?" Liv asked.

Damien and Grady grinned and picked up the first thing they saw; pot plants and rocks.

"Now, just a minute," Cordell demanded, but was too late as shattering glass rang out into the night.

*****

Barrett pulled to a stop at the sundial and opened the bus door.

"Sydney, you and Gemma get that disc. You got the acid?" Keenan asked her.

"Got it." Sydney dashed past him. "And the tools."

Gemma followed, as did Cameron and Riley and the rest of the girls.

"We can't leave them here on their own," Gina cried and stood behind Barrett, watching the kids run over to the sundial.

"Both of you stay with them, and help them destroy that damn sundial," Barrett told her. "Go." He watched the ladies leave the bus and run over to the small garden roundabout that held a statue of Jebadiah Hallows and the sundial that the kids were already working on.

"We need to get this ring off and destroy the pedestal," Sydney explained. "Start bashing." They went to work, smashing the concrete base while she poured acid around the metal disc to dislodge it.

Barrett hit the accelerator. "Now where?"

"The church. Park so the door faces it in case we need to make a quick getaway." Keenan handed tools that he'd found in the kitchen to Nathan, Morgan and Caleb. "We need to get the disc. It's above the door."

Barrett swerved right to pull up outside the

church's gate. "Let's go." They ran up the walkway to the building, the security lights came on, and they saw the disc right above the door.

"We have to get it." Nathan came up with a way. "Guys, give me a boost." They held out their hands and he stepped into them, and was hefted up until his face was right in front of the metal object. "Chisel, hammer." He held out his hands and got a bottle instead. "What's this?" He stared down at Keenan.

"Acid, to break whatever's keeping it glued to the wall," he said. "Just don't get it in your eyes."

Frowning, Nathan carefully sprayed it around the outside of the disc and watched it bubble away.

"Here's the tools." Keenan handed up the chisel and hammer. "It should come off."

"That doesn't smell like acid, Fielding," Barrett said. "It smells more like—"

"Coke, vinegar and bicarb." Keenan grinned. "It'll rot your gut if you drink it, but awesome for cleaning and getting metal discs off walls and sundials."

"Got it." Nathan pried the metal disc from the wall and was lowered to the ground. "Good thing that wasn't real acid. I wouldn't be able to touch it."

"Would I do that to you?" Keenan grinned again. "Come on, let's go."

They turned to hurry down the path and found the horseman between the church fence and their bus.

"Damn it, what do we do?" Caleb muttered.

"He can't come on hallowed ground," Keenan told them. "It's the church."

"Unless he was born of the evil that built it,"

Nathan said and looked down at the disc in his hand. "Get ready to run." He broke into a run down the path, and once he made it to the gate, launched himself into the air like a long jumper and swung his right arm past his body. He angled the disc just so and it sliced through both rider and horse.

The horse reared, steam bursting forth from its nostrils.

Nathan landed in a crouch and jumped up to slash again and again, and unable to contain the horse, the rider held on while it bolted down the street. "Come on," Nathan yelled and waved for the others to move. They bolted down the path and onto the bus.

Barrett gunned the engine and turned into the main street.

The church burst into flames behind them.

"And so that's done," Keenan murmured, watching out the back window. They pulled up beside the sundial and opened the door. "You got it?" he yelled.

"Got it." Sydney triumphantly held it up and they ran for the bus and up the stairs. "Got yours?"

Nathan held it up "Yep. He attacked us, but I sliced him with the disc and he ran off."

"And it looks like he's going to try again." Keenan stared out the back window. "He's outside the church. Floor it, Mr B."

Barrett floored it down the main street, past the hotel, and screeched to a halt outside the museum where the others were waiting.

"Got them?" Keenan asked as they boarded.

"Got them," Liv replied and took a seat next to

Hannah.

"Good. Head for the homestead, Mr B, he's coming." Keenan saw the horseman charge down the main street, homes and businesses exploding as he passed. He swung his head and knocked the head off the Jebadiah Hallows statue in the roundabout which then burst into flames and made people scatter, not knowing which way to run. As they drove out of town and away from the lights, he saw the horseman pass the museum which also burst into flames. "Floor it hard, Mr B. Park between the tree and the ruins. Nathan, you, me, Sydney and Gemma need the diaries and the bibles. We have to head for the house and try and get above where he had his devil's room. We need something to stab them. Anyone keep the tools?" Everyone shook their heads no.

"I've still got acid," Sydney said, holding up the bottle and a packet of matches. "And fire!"

"And I've got the salt," Keenan added. "We'll need a piece of that tree as it's all a part of it. Liv, you and Caleb go and get a piece, a thick end of a branch or something, but it needs to be cut fresh. And take a disc, it cut the horseman, so it might cut the tree."

"Got my own." Liv held up the clock's pendulum. "It's the other part."

"Awesome. Okay, we're here. Mr B, leave the lights on." Keenan jumped out, and by the light of his torch and the fires in town, ran over to the old ruins. Nathan, Sydney and Gemma joined him, spreading the bibles on the ground, sprinkling salt around them and laying the two discs onto the exact drawing in each book.

Liv and Caleb ran for the tree, while the teachers kept the rest of the students back and the bus idling.

"What do we get?" Liv flashed the torch around looking for branches.

"Ah, Liv." Caleb was looking up at the old, gnarled tree.

"What?" She shone her light up to see it twisting and writhing, faces emerging and disappearing in its trunk. Its branches, like sharp points waving and snaking towards them. "Whoops?" Liv's legs were grabbed and she tumbled, slashing at it with her disc as she squirmed on the ground trying to get out of its grasp.

The tree wailed and let go, dropping the end of the branch that turned into a hard black substance. "Perfect." She snatched it up and ran, but saw Caleb grabbed around the waist. Like a kung fu fighter, she jumped into the air and slashed at it, making it let go of Caleb, and wail into the night before bursting into flames. "Gotta go." They ran over writhing ground, writhing with bodies of the long dead, past the bus, and over to their friends.

"Here." She handed the branch and disc over and watched Sydney place the disc on a page of the third book, the bible from the museum, and lay the branch on top. She sprinkled salt and acid.

A horse whinnied, hoofbeats sounded, and they looked up to see the horseman flying through the air on his steed towards them.

Sydney flicked three matches and threw one on

each book, picked up the branch, and raised it into the air. The grass around them magically burst into flames, creating a wall between them and the rider.

"Syd," Gemma and Liv cried, seeing the horseman was nearly upon them.

Just as the horse leaped off the ground and over the wall of fire towards them, Sydney stabbed the branch into the centre of the disc on the bible. It exploded in bright white light, and as the horse's front hooves touched the ground, the ground collapsed beneath all of them…

"Ugh," Nathan groaned and opened his eyes. Dust danced all around them and he shifted his head to look for the others. He spied them through the light of the full moon and glanced over to his left where he saw Jebadiah Jacobus Hallows nod, mouth *'thank you'*, and disappear.

*****

The children were helped from the rubble in the cold light of sunrise. The police and emergency services had come to their aid after the fires in town extinguished themselves, except for the statue and the church, and the buildings had magically appeared undamaged. But they'd noticed the old homestead on fire and gone to investigate, finding the teachers trying to get down into the hole.

One by one they helped the students up from their tomb and wrapped them in blankets, giving them hot soup or tea to get them warmed. All were uninjured bar a few scratches and scrapes and were looked over by their teachers and the local doctors.

The teens watched as the body of the horseman was brought to the surface and finally unmasked.

"That's Dirk Bently, our driver," Nathan told the sheriff. "We thought he was up to something." They watched the body be taken away.

"Bently…" The sheriff stroked his chin in thought. "I remember…he came looking for information on his ancestors. He's a Hallows."

"What!" the whole class exclaimed.

"Mmm…" the sheriff went on. "The eldest son of the eldest son. His mama had taken him to visit her relatives when old man Hallows went on his killing spree. When she found out, she moved in with her family and remarried years later. Generation after generation led to Bently."

"That's what that paper meant," Sydney burst out. "All the family was crossed out but him and his mother. The rest of them were dead, but *they* weren't."

"And what paper would that be?" the sheriff asked.

Realising she'd made a mistake; Sydney reluctantly pulled the paper from her backpack. "I found this," she said meekly.

The sheriff read it and then refolded it. "I'll just be keeping this as part of the case."

A shot rang out from the hole.

"Ah, you shouldn't've heard that," the sheriff muttered. "We had to put the horse down. It broke all four legs in the fall. We'll bury him when we fill in the hole."

"Oh, that's awful," Gemma cried. She was an animal lover and hated seeing any animal in pain.

"Can't be helped, I'm afraid." The sheriff tipped his hat. "How about you folks having a nice hot meal before you go? You deserve it."

"I agree." Barrett ushered the children towards the bus, and along with the other teachers, got them on board.

Gemma, Sydney, Nathan and Keenan came up the rear, and as they neared the bus they heard a whinny in the distance. Turning, they stared open-mouthed at the rider on his jet-black steed, but this time, Jebadiah Hallows' head was firmly where it was supposed to be.

He gave a salute and rode off into the distance before vanishing into thin air.

THEY RISE ON A BLOOD MOON

CHAPTER ONE

"I *cannot* believe we're going to a dumpy old campground," Flynn Jefferson complained to his best friends Sebastian Montague and Jarrett Powell.

Flynn's family had broken up the year before with his mum leaving them for a used car salesman, and his dad hitching up with a school teacher. *His* school teacher. He glanced over at his friends and rolled his eyes. His dad, Marcus, had started dating Martina York four months earlier after meeting at a parent-teacher night, and this was the first time they'd gone away together.

"And the problem is," he whispered and leaned over to his friends. "We have to put up with *her daughter* and her friends."

Casey York turned around in her seat to stare Flynn in the eye. "Just like *we* have to put up with *you* and *yours*." She raised an arched brow and narrowed her eyes. "Do you *really* think I like my mother dating your father any more than you do?"

Casey hated going to school at the same place her mother worked. Even though she loved history, which her mother taught, as it was always awkward and meant a lot of teasing and bullying.

Flynn sneered. "Yeah, right. Just stay out of our way *and* our tent."

"Why would I need to go into *your* tent?" Casey peered at all three of the boys in the backseat of the van. Typical filthy teenage boys. "*We'll* have our own. We don't need yours."

"Good, so stay out of it," Flynn repeated and cast another glance at his friends. "We don't need no girls lurking around our tent."

"That's not even grammatically correct." Casey rolled her eyes and sat back facing the front. "Jerk," she muttered under her breath and heard her best friends, Bethany Tripp and Sherri Sadler, giggle softly. The only way she'd agreed to come on the trip was if her best friends came too, so it wasn't so uncomfortable. Her mother and new boyfriend agreed, so both she and Flynn had their friends along. Ugh! She just *could not* get over the fact her mother was dating another student's father. *Especially* Flynn Jefferson's father. While she didn't mind Marcus and thought he was polite enough, his son didn't even *come close* to having manners. She heard a loud burp behind her, which proved her point, and hit the window's down button. "You are *such a pig*, Flynn Jefferson."

"Flynn, I heard that," Marcus called and looked in the rear-view. "You have better manners than that."

"Yes, Dad," Flynn droned. "Sorry, my bad." Another eye roll and glance at his friends scored him another scolding.

"I saw that, Flynn! No bad manners. I was serious about that."

"Yes, Dad." Flynn slid down in his seat, hit the window's down button and sat staring out of it while the crisp, cool, late autumn air hit him in the face and ruffled his dark curly locks.

It was October, and almost Halloween, and he'd planned on going trick or treating with the boys. Now he couldn't, because his father had planned this trip with his new girlfriend. Rolling his eyes hard, he shook his head to stop the tears that threatened. It had happened all too fast. His mother was barely gone a year, the marriage barely over, and he hadn't heard anything from her whatsoever, and it sucked. On top of that, his dad had been dating his teacher for the last four months. *And* she had a daughter who was in his class. It was all too much. He was only fifteen and it was all too much to deal with. Not to mention she was his history teacher and all of the kids in their class teased him mercilessly about his dad getting it on with Ms York, and how she was going to be his new mum. He didn't want a new mum, he had one and wanted her back, but the used car salesman was much more important than he was. Clearly. No card, no letter, no call, no visit. He hadn't heard from his mother in nearly a year. And because of the teasing and bullying, he'd been in trouble by beating up the kid who'd teased him. The kid just kept going on and on about Ms York being his new mother until finally, he'd gone over to him and hefted his closed fist into his face. The kid's head had hit the locker and the lock had dug into the back of his skull, making both sides of his face bleed. He'd been in so much trouble for that he'd been suspended, even though the principal had understood why. He'd suspended the boy for bullying and Flynn for physical violence, which is why his dad and Ms York were taking them on a five day break from school, hoping to get some sense of adventure and fun back into Flynn's life again. Not happy with the situation, he kicked the back of the seat in front of him.

Casey felt the kick and jerked her head around to the left. She was sitting in front of Flynn and knew what a jerk he could be. He glared silently back at her scowl, and after a few moments, she turned her head back to the front.

Sighing, she rolled her eyes and clutched the door handle, her knuckles turning white. Clearly, Flynn Jefferson had forgotten what a bully he'd been to her three years ago when word had spread through the school about her father being killed in a car accident. He'd been a palaeontologist and travelled the world searching for dinosaur bones, giving lectures in museums and schools about bones and clues and how you could tell what they ate and how they pooped. It made her so proud of her father. The way he'd tell her bedtime stories and make her laugh. Make her mother laugh. He'd take them to foreign lands to dig for bones and always made it fun. She'd go back to school after the holidays with stories and photos and bits of bone and fossils her father had allowed her to keep. And her mother had only worked part-time as a teacher, but since her father's death, Martina had to work full-time just to pay the bills and keep the household running. Casey didn't mind. She knew her mother liked her job and had no issue working full-time. But Casey also had space and didn't see her mother that much during the day because of the bullying that had gone on three years ago. They drove to school and left school and still went grocery shopping once a week to spend mother-daughter time together. But now that her mother was dating a fellow student's father, there was less time.

Ugh, she thought, *out of all the parents, all the people in town, it had to be Flynn Jefferson's father for God's sake.* She stared at her mother and Marcus and saw her mother's head bob up and down in time to the music on the radio. She was laughing and turning her head to Marcus, reaching out her arm, her hand lightly touching his arm before it slid its way down to his hand which eagerly encased hers in it.

Casey's head had tilted while watching the whole sordid scenario, a scowl on her pretty face.

Hard breathing from behind her made her turn her head and she saw Flynn staring over the seat at their parents' hands. He noticed her staring at him, scowled, and slunk back into his seat.

Sighing, her gaze moved to her friends to see what they were doing before turning for the window. She'd been looking forward to trick or treating this year, but because of Flynn punching some kid in the face, their parents had decided it would be better to get away from civilisation. So not only was Flynn being punished, so was she. With another sigh, she tuned out everyone in the car, slid her dark sunglasses on, and sank down in her seat.

As they travelled along the road, densely populated with towering pine and fern trees, the air grew crisper and cleaner.

"Smell the air, kids," Marcus told them. "Isn't it fresh!" He manoeuvred around the bend and the trees gave way to the view of the lake. Its dazzling brilliance used the reflection of the sky to make it brighter and shinier. Its circumference was filled with towering trees that only added to the eerie quiet that blanketed the scene below them.

Marcus carefully negotiated his way down the side of the mountain until the road flattened out and became level with the lake. "We'll be in town shortly, and you can get out and stretch your legs while I get petrol. The campgrounds are on the other side of the lake."

Within minutes, the town came into view; a typically beautiful picturesque postcard town that had long settled into the side of the mountain for protection. Each house was the same, each road named after a different tree, and the colours blended into the surrounding greenery.

"Everything's green," Seb muttered, peering over Flynn's shoulder one moment, Jarrett's the next, as he was stuck in the middle of the back seat.

"It's because they wanted to be environmentally friendly and make sure everything they built blended in with their surroundings," Bethany told them over her shoulder. "Do you learn *nothing* in school?" She rolled her eyes and turned back to stare out the windows. "It's so beautiful."

It's so beautiful, Seb silently mocked her behind her back, making the boys grin.

"Okay, here we are." Marcus drove into the service station and pulled up beside a bowser. "I'll get the petrol. You kids don't go far."

Four doors opened and six kids and two adults alighted.

"I'm going to the rest room," Martina told him. "Girls…do you need the bathroom?"

The boys sniggered, making the girls blush.

"Do you *boys* need the bathroom?" Martina raised an authoritative brow at them, making *them* blush.

"No miss," they muttered, glancing away and scuffing the tips of their shoes into the chipped concrete under their feet. "We're just um…going…"

Flynn frantically looked around and saw the local tourist centre right next door. "We'll be in there." He pointed and he, Seb, and Jarrett hurried away.

Martina shut her door and glanced at Marcus who shook his head. "We'll go and freshen up. Come along, girls." She led the way into the station and found the restroom.

Marcus continued to pump petrol and watch the world go by, wondering why it was so quiet except for the small cavalcade of cars leaving town.

Meanwhile, the boys were perusing the shelves in the tourist centre to see if there was anything they'd consider taking home. They found nothing of worth to waste their money on.

"An' what're you young'uns doin' in this neck o' the woods?"

The boys spun around, but saw no one.

"Who said that?" Flynn asked.

"I did."

"Argh!" The boys jumped and spun back around to see a grizzled old man with white wispy hair and a long white wispy beard.

"Normally, folk would leave town this time a year." The old man stroked his beard and his pale blue eyes glanced over them. "So, what're you doin' here?"

"My dad thought it was a good idea for us to get away for Halloween," Flynn mumbled.

"Mmm." The old man continued stroking and looked from the boys to the road outside to see more cars leaving. "Most people get outta town 'round Halloween, especially when it's a blood moon. Although…" He frowned and trailed off. "That's only an old wives' tale, but no one takes a chance in case it's not on a blood moon but Halloween instead. Although…it has been both, but everyone returns to town an' finds everythin' normal an' how they left it…" He shuffled around the boys and behind the counter.

"What *are* you talking about?" Flynn finally asked, sharing frowns with his friends.

Seb twirled a finger next to his temple and rolled his eyes.

"What am I talkin' 'bout?" the old man muttered, more to himself than the boys, as he pottered around behind the counter. "The zombie plague, of course."

CHAPTER TWO

The boys traded glances. "What?"

The bell rang out above the door and Martina walked in with the girls who wandered off to one side of the store. Marcus followed a moment later.

"There you are boys, ready to go?" Martina noticed the old man and smiled. "Hello. What a lovely town you have. It's so quiet and peaceful."

"Aye, that's 'cause everyone leaves this time of year," the old man repeated. "They like to get outta the way for Halloween."

The boys were still waiting for the old man to elaborate on what he'd said a few moments ago, but the parents were in the way.

"And why's that?" Martina walked past the counter to look at the paintings on the wall. "Why does everyone leave? They're lovely paintings. Local artist?"

"Aye," the old man mumbled. "Young lad with an eye for it. He's the only one who stays at Halloween, 'sides me."

"And why is that?" Flynn jumped in before their

original conversation could be hijacked by Martina once again. "You told us before, about the blood moon and Halloween."

"Aye." The old man peered at the boys. "Can't rightfully 'member. Somethin' to do with a blood moon on Halloween. The dead rise from their graves." His voice lowered. "Walk through the town scarin' the bejesus outta everyone. Scared the whole town so the whole town runs. Don't want no dead bitin' 'em. Don't want no dead attackin' 'em. Don't want no dead livin' in their homes." His voice had risen and lowered with every sentence and he scratched his head in thought. "Young'un would know. The young artist boy." Waving a finger at the painting, he added, "He knows the history of the lake an' what happens. He's not scared of 'em an' what they represent. No, no, no." His head shook in time with his finger. "Get out of town now, or lock yourselves away. Go back to where you come from, don't get eaten, don't get bitten, don't get sick, avoid 'em, avoid the plague, get out of their way." He shuffled into the back room and slammed the door.

"Okaayy," Flynn mumbled, his brows rising in shock. "Weirdo."

"Flynn, that's not a nice thing to call someone," Marcus chastised his son.

"Well…he is." Flynn shrugged. "Before you came in he was talking about a zombie plague on Halloween and that everyone usually gets the hell out of Dodge. My words, not his. So tell me he's not weird."

"He was talking about zombies?" Casey came to a stop nearby. "I don't want to be bitten. I don't want to die. Mum, can we go home?" She turned to her mother who'd taken down a painting from the wall. "Can we go home, please?"

"Don't be silly." Martina set the painting on the counter. "There is no such thing as zombies, regardless of all the plagues in the world, or some countries and religions believing the dead come back, it just isn't true." She pulled her purse out of her bag and removed six twenty dollar notes before putting it back. "Repeat after me," she told her daughter, *"There are no zombies."* She tweaked her daughter's chin before knocking on the door. "Sir, I'd like to buy a painting."

A few seconds later, the door flung open and the grizzled old man came out. "What's that?"

"I'd like to buy that painting." She pointed to it and walked back around the counter. "Do you know the artist's name?"

"No, no, just a young'un I do business with," he mumbled and rang up the sale on the register. "That's $120."

Martina handed the money over and waited for the receipt. Once she had it, she picked up the painting and turned to leave, but saw all six children standing wide-eyed and somewhat terrified. "Oh, for goodness sake, there's *no such thing as zombies.* I just told you that before. Plenty of plagues and diseases, but *no* zombies."

"Not that you know," the old man muttered,

scratching his head. "You don't live 'ere, you don't deal with the dead risin' on Halloween, or a blood moon, or whenever. When I was a baby they took my mammy an' pappy, nearly took me right outta mammy's arms. Had it not been for the neighbour, I'd be a dead'un just like them. Don't sleep out in the woods, don't go for a walk, don't be out come Halloween night. Lock yourselves up, lock the windows, the doors, don't even make a run for your car 'cause they'll get you." His mumblings became low. "They'll get you." He hovered on the spot, shifting one way and then the other while everyone just stared at him. "Where are you folks stayin' anyways?"

"The *Eagle Ridge Campgrounds*," Marcus replied, an uneasy feeling in his gut.

"Don't camp, don't use tents, they'll walk right over you. Get inside, stay inside, don't go out," the old man warned and waved his fist at them. "They'll get you."

The bell above the door tinkled and they all jumped.

"Ah, hello, I did not mean to scare anyone," the young man said and noted the expressions on everyone's faces. "Has Harold been telling the tale of the zombie plague on Halloween again? You all look a little scared." He pointed to the painting in Martina's hand. "Thank you for buying one of my paintings."

"Oh, you're the artist!" she exclaimed and turned it around for him to see which one she'd picked. "You're very good; you capture the light and shade beautifully. How long have you been painting?"

He beamed a wide white-toothed smile at her compliment and choice of picture. "Ah, yes, that is my best one. I love that spot. I chose it for the magical elements of the setting sun hitting the water and tree tops. But to answer your question, since I was a little boy. My father and grandfather taught me; they were artisans too." He had slowly walked over to them while talking, and saw the children still looked scared. "Do not worry about Harold's story. As long as you stay inside and lock all the doors and windows, nothing will happen to you." Grinning, he wandered around the counter. "My cut please, Harold."

Waiting for Harold to get his share of the profits from the till, he explained that for every painting, Harold took forty dollars while he took the rest. "That is our business contract." He pocketed the money and patted Harold on the back. "I will walk our guests out. Come." Indicating for the family to follow him, he led them back to their car. "Where are you staying? Do you have directions?"

"At the camping grounds on the other side of the lake," Marcus told him and pulled open the back of the van for Martina to slide her painting in.

"Ah, yes, I know the one. I run it for the owners and am headed back that way," the young man said. His milk coffee coloured skin and jet-black hair glowed in the afternoon sun. So did his sparkling brown eyes.

The girls stood mesmerised and Martina noticed.

"Well, that's very nice of you, thank you. Girls, into the car, please. Boys, you too." She watched them shuffle past her and then directed her attention back to the artist. "Perhaps you can show me the spots you paint from. I'm a history teacher and love art as well. Studied both in college."

"Oh, you dabble in painting." The young man bestowed his dazzling smile on her and stepped closer.

Martina bristled a little at the word *dabble*. "I minored in it at college. Studied all the techniques and the most famous artists in the world. Came top of my class, and my brushwork was the best my teacher had ever seen in a college student." She wanted him to know she was no lightweight amateur when it came to art.

"How excellent." The young man nodded. "We can talk about depth and composition, but for now, I must get you to your cabin. Night fast approaches, regardless of daylight savings, this time of the year. Do you have enough food and water?" He waited for her to get into the van and shut the door.

"We have enough. Brought supplies," Marcus, slightly aggravated, said from the other side of the car before getting in. "Where are you parked?"

"Just over there." The young man pointed to the beat up old ute off to the side of the station and then rested his hand on his chest. "I am Chatan, by the way. Local artist, camp manager, and storyteller. Next to old Harold, that is." He tilted his head and smiled. "Please, follow me back to the camp and I will get you checked in." His steps were light and athletic, almost a dance, as he ran for his car. Within moments, he was backing out of the car park and leading them out onto the main road around to the campsite which was relatively empty. It had been a ten minute drive, but was over quickly.

After pulling up beside the main office, Marcus alighted to sign in and pay the bill, and then Chatan was showing them the way to the main cabin just down a small road from the office. It boasted unprecedented views of the mountains, forest and lake, and had the rustic old-style log appeal with a porch on the front.

"Oh, how lovely," Martina said as she slid out of the van. "So authentic looking."

"This is how they were made," Chatan told her. "Please, make sure you pull the car into the garage on the side and lock it up tight. We get animals trying to worm their way into cars and trailers. Lock the garage door, and make sure all of your windows and storm shutters are locked tight as well because we don't want anything happening to you, or animals getting in."

The boys glanced at each other and frowned. *Now why would he be saying that?*

The girls just stood staring dreamily at the tour guide, and Martina saw that look and thanked Chatan. "Kids, get your bags from the trailer, and help with the containers of food. Let's get inside."

They unloaded the trailer and car within twenty minutes and locked it up in the garage. Chatan had disappeared, so Martina and Marcus sat on the porch sipping the wine they'd brought while the kids unpacked and settled into their rooms.

"I really wish Harold hadn't told that story," Martina fretted. "I think he freaked them out. Especially the girls."

"Oh, I think the girls were too busy mooning over Chatan to worry about an old ghost story." Marcus chuckled. "A little enamoured, I think they are."

"Well, they *are* at that age when boys and young men will interest them, just as the boys are at the age where girls will interest *them*."

"Ugh." Marcus groaned and threw back his head. "Don't remind me. I just have no idea how to talk to Flynn about girls. His mum's not around, and while my sister helps out, I don't know whether I *should* do this or not, but I've considered asking the sex ed teacher at school to make sure he gets told about the birds and the bees."

"Marcus!" Martina exclaimed. "You can't leave stuff like that up to us poor teachers. We have enough on our plates as is. It's *your* responsibility to teach him about sex, not ours." She glanced at his face. "And don't even *think* of asking me to talk to him. I have to make sure Casey's educated about *boys*." Shaking her head, a light laugh left her. "Or in this case, young men that are too old for her."

"I thought it was cute." Marcus sipped his wine. "Is it her first crush?"

Martina thought about it. "I don't think so; definitely won't be her last."

From the shadows beside the cabin, two eager eyes watched while two eager ears listened.

CHAPTER THREE

"I can't believe we're stuck here in the middle of nowhere with our history teacher and her daughter," Flynn grumbled to his friends. He'd scored the single bed while Seb and Jarrett had the bunks. Both beds were flat against the walls on either side of the window, and matching wardrobes were either side of the door. He finished shoving his clothes into the cupboard and shut the door. "I just wanted to spend Halloween trick or treating, and *now*, because of Snobby Bobby, I'm stuck here with my dad and *Ms York*."

"I don't mind her." Seb pulled his soccer boots from their bag. "At least she's one of the better teachers at school. Makes things fun to learn and gets us involved in it. So if your dad was gonna date anyone…"

"Yeah, but why not another student's parent? Why a teacher?" Flynn moaned and threw himself face down on the bed.

"Technically she *is* another student's parent," Jarrett reminded him. "She just also happens to be our teacher." He grabbed Seb's soccer ball from his bag and bounced it a few times before trying to bounce it on his head.

"Better be careful with that, don't want to break the window," Flynn muttered and raised his head to stare out at the darkening sky before letting it drop back down. "Guess we'd better lock up, too."

Jarrett managed to bounce the ball five times in a row on his head before it skewed towards the bunk, bounced off the railing, flew across to the opposite wall above Flynn's bed, bounced back across to hit the bottom bunk bed, and eventually roll under Flynn's bed.

"Dude! Awesome trajectory." Seb grinned.

"Bugger!" Jarrett exclaimed and scrambled to his knees.

"At least it didn't hit the window." Flynn opened one eye and peered at his friends. "Better get it."

"I can't see it." Jarrett flipped the bedding onto Flynn's bed, covering him, and looked underneath the bed. "I think I see it, but it's too dark. Gotta torch?"

Seb dug one out of his soccer bag and handed it over. It was a small, but powerful, Maglite he used for late night soccer training.

Jarrett flicked it on and directed the beam under the bed. "Whoa!" He leaned back in surprise and then looked again. "You've *got* to check this out."

"What?" Flynn didn't move. "A pile of dust mites?"

"Oh…this ain't dust mites," Jarrett told them from under the bed.

Seb fell to his hands and knees beside his friend

and peered under the bed. "Besides getting my ball back what else could be…oh…" His brows rose. "Oh, Flynn…you've *got* to see this."

"Argh, what!" Flynn rolled over until he was hanging halfway over the bed and able to see what was underneath it. "What am I looking at?"

"*That!*" Jarrett pointed to the floor.

"What?" Flynn finally noticed and moved his body until his head was right side up. "What the…?" The rest of him slid off the bed until he was on his hands and knees next to his friends. "Whoa. Can we move the bed, or lift up the mattress for a better look?" He placed both hands between the mattress and frame and lifted it up and against the wall. "Whoa, it's huge."

"What is it?" Jarrett stood beside him and aimed the torch down.

Painted in red was a symbol they didn't recognise.

"Those are Native American symbols," Martina said from the doorway. "Symbols to represent safety and protection, but mainly protection from the look of it. Whoever painted it knew what they were doing." She took a few steps into the room and frowned as she stared at it. "Two arrows facing each other with a circle in the middle of them, separate arrows facing right, above and below them. Looks to be surrounded by two moons, maybe, or a full circle. The paint looks old, worn, so it's been there a while," she murmured and wondered why it would be there at all. "Why don't you boys fix the bed, lock your window, and wash up. Marcus and I are about to get tea ready." Looking up at the boys and their inquisitive expressions, she smiled. "Don't worry, it's a good symbol." Exiting the room, she left them puzzled.

Jarret dropped to his knees to look under the bunks. "It's here, too."

"The same one?" Seb asked and retrieved his ball before Flynn reset the bed and fixed the blankets and sheets.

"Looks like." Jarrett climbed to his feet and dusted off his hands. "It's under both beds. Weird."

"Mmm…" Flynn turned for the window and saw it was almost dark. "Better lock up before the zombies get us," he muttered and pulled the glass pane down and locked it, then closed and locked the wooden shutters on the inside. "Hey, look." He stepped back and all three boys stood staring at the symbol on the shutters.

"It's the same symbol," Seb muttered. "It's the same…why?" He looked at his friends, still puzzled. "Why? Why on the shutters over the window? Why on the floorboards under the bed? Why?"

"And where else is it?" Flynn asked. He grabbed the torch from Jarrett and headed out of the room, but took a few steps back and stared at the door. He aimed the torch at it and moved his head from left to right, shifting this way and that. "I can swear the symbol has been etched into our door, but it's painted over." His fingers traced the outline. "Yep, it's been carved in."

"Why?" Seb asked again. "Why put that symbol everywhere?"

"Don't know, but let's see if it's anywhere else." Flynn sneaked down the hallway to his right, past the girls' room, and into his father's and Martina's room. "Ugh," he muttered under his breath. "They're sharing a room after four months. Seb, you check the window shutter, Jarrett, check the door. I'll check the bed." He quickly kneeled down and waved the light under the bed. "It's here."

"And here." Seb pulled the curtain back.

"And carved in the door," Jarrett added.

They quickly left the room and stopped at the bathroom they had to share with the girls, finding the same symbol on the door under the paint and on the window shutter.

"Jesus, it's in every room," Flynn murmured and shook his head.

"Are you just gonna stand there all night long? We gotta use the bathroom."

He turned to see Casey behind him and flung the torchlight into her eyes, making her throw her arm up to cover them. "Have you found that symbol on your door and floor?"

"What symbol?" she asked. "Put that damn torch down, you're blinding me."

He lowered it and pointed to the bathroom window shutter. "That one."

"Oh, yeah." Casey blinked at it while her vision came back. "It's a mix of Native American symbols for protection and safety. We have it on our shutter as well."

"And carved into your door?" Flynn advanced on

Casey, making her back up into the hallway. He stopped at her door and traced the outline with his finger. "It's carved into the doors as well. Is it on the floor under your beds?"

Casey looked over her shoulder at Bethany and Sherri who shrugged.

"Well, look," Flynn urged. "Quickly."

The two girls scurried to the beds and looked underneath. "There's one here," Sherri said from under Casey's single bed.

"And here." Bethany got to her feet and brushed off her hands. "What does it mean?" They huddled around Casey who was staring at Flynn intently.

"As I just said, it's a mix of symbols for protection and safety, comes with a spell that can only be performed by someone of that descent. It's complicated. You need herbs and berries, etc. and the red is usually from an animal that you sacrifice for its blood."

"How do you know so much?" Flynn pointed the torch into Casey's bright green eyes, but she pushed it away.

"My mother majored in history and my father was a palaeontologist. He also studied other cultures and their beliefs." She stared defiantly into Flynn's eyes. "Remember my dad; you bullied me over his death three years ago." She watched him frown and then his eyes widen at the memories. "Guess you got your comeuppance last week when you got bullied over your mum. You punching that kid is what I wanted to do to you three years ago. Instead, Flynn

Jefferson, I cried myself to sleep every night over the loss of my father and the bullying I received from you. Sucks to be you, huh!" Taking in his curly brown hair, dark ocean blue eyes, and rather good looking features, she scoffed, and pushed past him into the bathroom with the girls following. They shut the door in the boys' faces.

"I *cannot* believe you just did that," Sherri whispered. "You stood up to him and gave him the old one-two with that quick wit of yours."

Casey shakily washed her hands and gave a half smile. "I was so nervous, though. I've never brought it up before. *Especially* to Flynn Jefferson."

"First time for everything," Bethany whispered and quickly went to the toilet which was in its own room off the bathroom.

"Yeah," Casey murmured and thought back to being twelve years of age when she'd lost her father and gone back to school. The teachers had been sympathetic as had most of the girls in her class, but the boys were horrid. Especially Flynn who'd teased her mercilessly for a week before the teachers finally put a stop to it by talking to the classes about death and how it just wasn't funny to tease someone who'd lost a parent. Flynn never apologised, but had stopped tormenting her.

Out in the hallway, Flynn had been stunned into silence.

"You okay?" Seb asked. He took his torch from his friend, turned it off to save the batteries, and shoved it in his pocket.

"Um…" Flynn's memory had gone flying back to three years ago and how he'd relentlessly tormented Casey. "Shit!" After everything his mum had done, and the feelings of pain and loss he'd experienced and then the bullying he'd endured from Snobby Bobby, he finally realised how it must have hurt Casey all those years ago. Even though his mother was still alive, the fact she'd left him for another man and not looked back hurt him deeply and may as well have been a death because he never saw her. Never heard from her. Nothing. She may as well have been dead.

"You okay?" Seb repeated and watched the emotions fly over his friend's face. "You don't look good. You gonna be sick? Can I have your share of tea? I'm starving."

Flynn snapped out of his memories and frowned. "*No*, you *can't* have my food, you guts. You eat like a garbage disposal and never get fat. What *is it* with you?" He looked his friend up and down and saw the tall skinny Jamaican kid he'd known since fifth grade when Seb's family had moved to Australia for a better life.

Seb shrugged. "Can't help it. I'm always hungry."

"It's because you're always growing," Jarrett told him, disgusted that Seb could eat anything and not gain weight, while he did nothing *but* gain it.

The girls came out of the bathroom and cast cool glares over the boys before moving off.

"Casey." Flynn stopped her, but she didn't turn around. "I…" He heaved a deep sigh from his gut and struggled to pull out the words. "I'm…ah…sorry…"

Surprised, Casey turned around. "What?"

Flynn took another deep breath and wiped his hands on his jeans. "I'm…ah…sorry. You…ah… didn't deserve all of that three years ago. We were mean. Those of us that teased you, I mean. Especially me." Glancing away in embarrassment, he went on. "You were right. I did get it over my mum and didn't like it. And I know it's not as bad as what you got, but I kinda know what it must've been like, and for me, I'm sorry…"

Stunned, Casey opened her mouth to speak, but not a word came out.

Bethany and Sherri just glanced from their best friend to Flynn, to Seb and Jarrett, and the boys did the same. They were all unsure of what to say or do. Until…

Bang…bang…bang…

CHAPTER FOUR

Six heads spun in the direction of the front door.

"Did your parents lock the door and close the shutter?" Seb asked, his heart pounding in double time.

Bang…bang…bang…

"Don't know," Casey and Flynn replied in unison.

Bang…bang…bang…

They saw Marcus move from the kitchen towards the door.

"Dad, no!" Flynn sprang into gear, and with an outstretched arm, he raced for his father.

Marcus stopped. "Flynn? What is it?" He saw the other kids hurry after his son.

"Don't answer the door," Flynn gasped. "Did you lock it and close the shutter?" He spun around and checked all the windows and doors in the main room, noticing the shutters were closed and all had the symbol painted on them. "It's on them, too."

"The symbol's on every door and window," Martina called from the open kitchen. "Someone's deadly serious about protecting the people in this cabin."

They had all looked at her as she'd spoken, but turned their heads back to the door as the bangs continued.

"Hello…it is Chatan. Can you let me in, please?"

"Oh…" The kids all sighed in relief and Marcus went to open the door.

Chatan stood grinning and carrying a huge box. "Hello, it is just me. I have some supplies for you."

Marcus unlocked the screen door and let him in, closing it behind him.

"It is just a box of batteries, matches, candles, etc. Since it is still autumn, the lights might go out and I do not think I have restocked the cabinet yet." He set the box down by the kitchen bench. "My, that does smell good." The pots of spaghetti and meatballs in Bolognese sauce made his mouth water.

"There's more than enough if you want to stay," Martina told him as she put a pile of plates on the counter.

"Ah, no, thank you. I must get back to the office and lock up for the night. Thank you, anyway." His grin beamed across the room and the girls all sighed.

Marcus, hearing that, and seeing the boys all screw their noses up at the girls, thanked him. "I hope we won't need them while we're here. But it's good to know we have them in case."

"Of course. Sorry I did not bring them around earlier. We do not actually get campers this time of the year and so I forgot the supplies." He nodded and gave a slight bow. "Good evening."

"Wait." Flynn stopped him as he headed for the

door. "What's that around your neck?" He eagerly peered at the gold pendant he'd seen when Chatan had bowed.

"It is a pendant in the symbols for protection and safety." Chatan pulled the necklace out from under his shirt and showed the kids as they gathered around him. "It is passed down from generation to generation; my grandfather and all before him."

"That's the symbol on the floor under the beds, and carved into the doors, and painted on the shutters," Bethany said.

"Yes." Chatan smiled. "All cabins and tent sites have it somewhere as protection."

"Against what?" Flynn demanded. "What's out there? Zombies?"

Chatan's smile grew larger. "Against wild animals, evil spirits, you name it, it protects you from it. I must go now. Goodnight." He tucked the necklace away and strode out the door. "I will lock all of your outdoor shutters for you. Make sure you lock your door and do not need to come out for anything. Good night." He closed the screen door and quickly locked the shutters over it. They heard him do the same for all of the front windows.

Marcus locked the screen and front door, then the inside shutter. "All of this seems a bit excessive, doesn't it? Outside shutters, inside shutters, protection symbols everywhere. I'm finding it just a *bit* ridiculous."

"But if it stops the zombies getting in—" Jarrett started.

"There's no such thing," Martina cut him off. "Now, come and sit, tea's ready."

*****

The next day, Martina announced a trip into town. "I think it would be relaxing. We can walk down each side, lunch in a café or nice family restaurant, and see what the town's about."

"Dead, is what it is," Seb muttered to Flynn and Jarrett. "All the people have left."

"And we're not a family, so why lunch in a family restaurant?" Flynn replied, eyeing off his father and his teacher. He still didn't care for the whole trip, didn't care for Martina as his father's date, but at least his hostility towards Casey had vanished. It's not that he hated her, or even resented her; she was just the daughter of his father's new girlfriend. It was the fact he resented his father having a new girlfriend when his mother was barely gone a year. And he certainly didn't want to be a family. He had one, him, his dad, and his mum. Even though his mum was long gone, he still had her, and Martina would never replace her.

"But everyone was leaving," Casey reminded her mother. "Will anything even be open?" She rinsed off her plate and put it in the dishwasher.

"I don't know; we'll find out when we get there," Martina said and tidied up. "I really don't know why everyone would leave. It's beautiful this time of year." Putting the leftover food back into the fridge or hampers, she added, "Even if the shops aren't open, we'll still be getting fresh air and exercise." Wiping down the counter, she shook the crumbs into the sink and rinsed it all out. "Who's up for it? We did bring Halloween goodies for you kids, but we may be able to find something else in town."

"I think it's a good idea," Marcus said. "And we can drive around town, and maybe go up to the lookout, which I see is up the mountain and should have some spectacular views. Kids, finish getting ready and get your stuff."

All six hurried off and Marcus went to get the van ready. "Oh, hello, Chatan." He spied the young man coming towards him. "We're just heading off to town." He unlocked the garage and opened the door, waiting for the young caretaker.

"That is good, the town is very pretty this time of year," Chatan replied, a huge smile on his face. "Most stores are still open. Will that be all you are doing?" He watched as the teens came out the door and Martina locked up after them.

"We'll probably be going to the lookout this afternoon." Marcus clipped the garage doors back and opened the driver's door. "I can't wait to see the view." He drove out of the garage and stopped for the kids to climb in, alighting to close the garage doors. "Is everything all right? Was there something you wanted?"

Chatan had been making small talk with Martina. "No, no, just wanted to see if you had a good night and what your plans were for today. If you are going to the lookout, make sure to take your cameras. The view is stunning. Do you know the way?" He hovered around the car doors and waited for Martina to settle herself in before shutting it for her.

"Yes, we do. We have maps of the town and surrounding areas from the tourist brochures," Martina said out her window. "And we had a very pleasant sleep. The air here is so fresh. It's just a pity we couldn't leave our windows open." She and Marcus had discussed the symbols before bed, wondering why there were so many of them.

"In summer, you can." Chatan laid his hands on the window ledge. "But in winter and autumn it is best not to, as it is very chilly and we do not want anyone catching colds, or wild animals coming in for the warmth. They have made burrows in the cabins before and we want to discourage that as it is not their natural habitat. Plus, it keeps the tenants safe." He nodded. "Enjoy your day. Remember to be back by sunset and locked up safe inside. It gets quite cold around five."

"Yes, it does," Martina said, and thanked him. "A good day to you, too."

Marcus slowly drove off. "That was strange."

Martina hit the button to raise her window. "Yes," she murmured. "Why do I get the feeling there's more to all of this than just animals making burrows."

They left the campground and drove towards town.

"Don't know, but all of those symbols don't help." Marcus glanced in the rear-view. "You kids got your warm coats on?"

"Yes," chorused six times.

"Good. Don't want you catching a cold because you didn't keep warm enough." He glanced at Martina. "That sounded like bunkum."

"It did," she murmured. "You also don't catch colds from the cold, they're viruses"

Marcus rolled his eyes at her and continued on with what he was talking about. "That's what I thought, but I think there's a lot more that he's *not* saying."

"So do I." Martina peered out the window at their surroundings. "It's going to be a sunny day today. I hope it won't be too cold, especially up at the lookout. Did everyone bring their cameras?" She looked over her shoulder to see six confused faces and sighed. "Your phones, then."

"Yes!"

"Of course!"

"Wouldn't leave home without it."

"I'd be lost without mine."

"We *so* need to post to social media!"

"Ooohhh, we should do videos and post them," Bethany told Casey and Sherri. "That would be so cool. The kids at school will all be *so* jealous."

Flynn rolled his eyes. "Why would you think that *anyone* would want to see pictures and videos of you three? Besides, you don't have that many followers." He glanced at the smirks Seb and Jarrett were giving the girls.

"For *your* information, Flynn Jefferson, I have *double* the number of followers on Instagram that you do, *triple* the followers Seb has, and *quadruple* the amount Jarrett has. Why? Because the three of you are not as popular as you think you are. Even Sherri and Casey have more followers than you, and it's all because we're girls," Bethany told him over the back seat. "You may think you're popular at school, but you're not. And the girls all follow the girls, so there are always more people to follow. Why would we follow you icky boys when we can follow fashion-loving friends? Even celebrities are more entertaining than you, but then," she cocked her head, "you barely post anything. And all of your followers are boys on the sports teams who want to *be* you, or the deadbeats who think you're the best. You're not, ergo; I have more followers." Turning her attention to the girls, she added, "We *really* need to make videos and upload them. We're the only ones having another holiday right now after going back to school weeks ago, all because of Flynn." She gave him a side-eye glare.

"Oooh, I know. We can take photos in town and post them, and then take a video at the lookout. The view will be spectacular," Sherri said. She had almost as many followers as Bethany and just needed to post some awesome pictures to take the lead.

"How about we take your picture with a zombie?" Flynn snickered. "It's nearly Halloween." He saw Casey twist her head around to the right to look at him.

"You know there's no such thing, Flynn Jefferson. You're just trying to scare us after what that old man said yesterday."

"Not at all." Flynn smirked. "It's just that there's one right outside your window…"

CHAPTER FIVE

"Oh, for God's sake, Flynn Jefferson. There's no such thing and you know it." She spun around in her seat and looked out her window. "Argh!" Her high-pitched scream bounced around the car. "A zombie. A zombie. Kill it, kill it. It's after us."

The person standing at her door leered in the window, both hands flat against the glass. Bandages wrapped around his head and hands, his piercing blue eyes were pinpointed, and blood dribbled down his face from a cut on his forehead.

"What in the hell?" Marcus muttered as the kids screamed. "Who the hell is that?" He was about to get out of the car when two paramedics came rushing up to them.

"Sorry, he got away from us," they called, and the male gently guided the man away while the female stopped at the passenger window that Martina rolled down. "Sorry about that. We had a call out and he took off running. Hope he didn't scare you folks much." She looked from annoyed adults to petrified girls to laughing boys. "Guess it's just the girls. So sorry. We'll take care of him now." With a nod, she raced after her partner and patient.

"O.M.Gee." Sherri clutched her chest as her heart pounded out of it. "That. Was. Scary."

"You girls are such wusses!" Jarrett exclaimed. "Thinking that was a zombie. And man, are my eardrums shattered with all that screaming." He stuck a finger in his ear and shook it. "I can't hear anything."

"That's because your finger's in your ear, stupid," Bethany chastised. "You're such an idiot, Jarrett." With a huff, she shifted in her seat to face the front, crossed her arms, and sighed. "Boys! Who wants 'em?"

Martina heard her and hid a smile before pointing ahead of them. "Park there. It looks about the middle of town. We'll walk down one side and up the other. And the stores seem to be open. Maybe we'll find some more things for Halloween. I wonder if they do trick or treating. The kids could go after all," she suggested to Marcus and unlocked her seatbelt.

"Maybe," he managed before being cut off by his son and future stepdaughter. Now that his divorce was finalised, he was considering proposing to Martina that weekend.

"Ah, no way. Not after that nutjob back there tried eating us," Casey said.

"And the old dude says everyone clears out for Halloween," Flynn added. "So I'm surprised the shops are open now. Thought everyone would've been gone." He looked out the window and opened the rear door to step out. Stretching his back and legs, he turned around to look at the main street. "They may be open, but there's no one around. Look how quiet it is. How boring."

"At least there are no weirdos roaming the streets," Sherri said and wrapped her neon pink sheepskin coat tighter around her. It matched her pink jeans and boots.

"Except you lot," Jarret told her. "You're the weirdos." He elbowed Seb and snickered, but didn't get anything out of his friend who was too busy looking in the window of the store in front of them. "Seb?"

"Huh?" Seb spun around and saw everyone was ready. "Can we go in here first?" He pointed his thumb over his shoulder. "It looks like they have some cool Halloween stuff."

Marcus came to a stop beside Martina and slid an arm around her waist. "I guess we could start here. Just behave yourselves," he implored to his son and friends.

Martina slid her handbag over her shoulder, smiled knowingly at Marcus, and followed the teens into the store.

After buying a few things, they moved on down the street, the girls walking arm in arm three abreast, the boys following, and Marcus and Martina behind them so they could keep an eye on all six.

"At least they haven't had massive quarrels," Marcus said under his breath. "Just a few jibes in the car on the way up yesterday. Today hasn't been too bad, either." He kept his eyes on the girls who darted along the street to a clothing store.

"Yes." Martina watched the boys go into an electronics store. "They haven't killed each other yet." They waited for both sets of teens to come out of the stores before moving on.

"I can't believe I found gloves to match my jacket." Sherri excitedly slid her cold fingers into her brand-new sparkling pink sheepskin gloves. "And only five dollars. What a bargain!"

"Not that you *needed* another pair," Bethany told her. "You already have your grey ones with the pretty snowflake print that you've been wearing. If you don't want them, can I have them?"

"What, girl, you mad!" Sherri shook her head. "Just because I've hunted high and low for pink glitter gloves *does not* mean you'll be getting my grey ones."

Bethany looked past her friend to Casey and shrugged. "I tried."

Casey giggled and came to a stop outside of a store, a marking on the window catching her attention. It was the protection symbol that was all over their cabin.

"I've seen them on other shop windows and doors." Flynn stopped behind her. "They're small, almost unnoticeable. But once I saw the first, I kept seeing them. Clearly, the whole town wants to be protected."

"But since zombies don't exist, what is it they're being protected from?" Bethany asked.

"Are you going inside?" Martina wondered why

they'd stopped. "Otherwise, we'll head down the other side of the street and stop somewhere for lunch." She checked the time. "It's only eleven, but by the time we finish up it will be about one and time for lunch."

Casey looked from her mother to the store and didn't find sewing equipment and knitting needles to be to her liking. "No. I just noticed the symbol on the door and window. It's the same as the one in our cabin."

"Yes, I've seen them. The only thing I can put it down to is that the folk in the area are really into protection spells." Martina glanced up and down the street. "It's really quiet today. I wonder what it's like on a normal day." After scanning the street, she turned back to the teens. "Oh, well, let's move on then."

As they crossed the street to the other side, Casey wondered why her mother was so nonchalant about the symbols. She knew her mother was just as informed as she was about such things, but for some reason, the symbols didn't seem to bother her mother. Yet they bothered her. Why were they on all the shop doors and windows? Why were they all over their cabin? And why did the dreamy Chatan have one around his neck? Was he the one painting them all over town? Sighing, she realised she wasn't about to get any answers and decided to put it out of her mind.

"Girls," Martina called. "This shop looks good. Why don't we go in here?"

They all looked up at the sign above the door. *Eagle Ridge Secondhand. Where we just might have the knick to your knack.*

"Ugh, good grief." Casey rolled her eyes and reluctantly followed her mother into the store. "Mum, can we not?"

"Hush, Casey. You know I love secondhand bric-a-brac stores. We've found all sorts of goodies from them."

"Ew, it's so dirty in here," Sherri complained as she looked around and wrinkled her nose at the smell. "I'll get my pretty new gloves dirty."

"Then take them off and put them in your pocket," Marcus told her, surprised by how big the store was on the inside. "You can wash your hands later."

Reluctant to get her gloves dirty, but not wanting to make her hands cold, Sherri decided to keep her hands to herself and not touch anything.

As they wandered down different aisles of the store, Casey found herself walking towards the back of the shop and into a smaller room. Dark and dingy, the lone bulb hanging from the ceiling barely gave off enough light to see by, but something had made her walk into that room. After digging out her phone from her bag, she flipped on the phone's light and waved her hand slowly from left to right. The phone illuminated the space enough for her to see the room was full of baskets, busted boxes, and buckets of rubbish. Old kettles and other electricals, dirt-riddled magazines with torn corners, old blankets that smelled as if they'd been dunked in sheep dip, and piles and piles of stuff surrounded her. She screwed up her nose and wondered why she was in there.

The owner shuffled past and saw her. "Don't know why you're in there, girly. Just rubbish meant for chucking away."

Casey glanced over her shoulder and saw the man shake his head in bewilderment. Flynn was standing beyond him, watching intently. The man walked off and Casey turned back to the piles in front of her. "Why am I here?" she whispered. "Why am I here?" And just like that, something shiny attracted her attention. She waved her phone at it, hoping it would catch the light, and when it did, she reached through the pile of rubbish and grasped what had been winking in the light. Pulling her arm out, she saw it was a small square old wood box with no opening. "Why would I pick this up?" Her brows furrowed and she turned the box this way and that under the light, noticing the round indent on one side. She found no lock, no latch, and no way to open it.

She turned it back to the side with the indent and noticed a small metal stud in the middle; as if something clicked into it, or around it. She pushed the stud, but nothing happened.

Flynn watched her examine the box and silently approached. "What did you find?"

She gasped and dropped the box, nearly dropped her phone, and nearly punched him in the arm. "Don't sneak up on people."

He picked up the box and turned it over. "Sorry, I

saw you looking at it. Why did you come in here? Why...*how* did you find it?"

Casey shrugged. "Don't know. I just saw something shining in the phone light." She watched Flynn shake it, raise it to his eyes, and trace his nails over all six sides before grabbing her hand to bring the light closer to the box.

She gasped at the contact, and the electricity it sent through her, reminding her of the crush she'd once had on him. And it didn't help that the blue and brown plaid soft flannelette shirt with the rolled up sleeves, and sapphire blue puffer vest he was wearing brought out the blue in his eyes even more. His roughed up blue jeans and scruffy old boots added to the look, as did the curly lock of hair that flopped over his forehead.

The crush had been long before her father had died and the bullying she'd suffered at his hands.

"Sorry, didn't mean to grab you so hard." He was apologetic and released her hand. "But look here." He held the box under the light and his finger traced a very faint marking in the indent. "What does that look like?"

Casey peered closer and made out the very faded red marking. "Oh, my God, it's the symbol." Her gaze moved up to Flynn's. "It's the same symbol we keep seeing everywhere. It must've had a metal version attached at some point. But where is it now?" She aimed her phone at the pile of rubbish she'd dug through, and started pulling everything out of the box. After a few minutes, all she had was an empty box and a dirty hand. "It's not here. I can't see it. It must've been lost…"

"Or Chatan has it," Flynn murmured and squinted when she pointed the light in his eyes. "He has the symbol on his necklace, and did you notice the weird carvings on the bottom?" He turned it upside down and pointed to them. "Bet he knows what this says. They're the only two identifying marks on the box and he knows all about that symbol. You should buy it." Flynn handed it back. "If it's got to do with everything else going on, buy it."

"But we don't know that it does." Casey looked at it, turning her hand this way and that. "We don't know that it has to do with anything."

"And yet you found it anyway," Flynn said, and left the room.

Puzzled, Casey followed him and approached the store owner. "Hi. I found this in that back room. How much?"

The owner glanced at the box and shrugged. "You can have it. It's just rubbish. Prob'ly woulda been chucked on the fire." He shuffled off and she thanked him.

Deciding to wait for the others by the door, she saw Chatan walking down the opposite side of the street, and wondered if she should run over and ask him about the box, but Flynn appeared at her side.

"Do it," he said, reading her mind and staring out the window. "Come on, let's go find out." He pushed the door open and dragged Casey by the elbow over the street and after Chatan. "Hey," Flynn yelled out.

"Chatan, can we talk to you a second?"

He watched him turn around with a huge smile on his face, but when he saw the box in Casey's hand, the smile faded.

"*Where* did you get that? *How* did you get that? *Why* do you have that? You need to get rid of it immediately." He clutched the pendant around his neck and silently murmured something.

"I just found it in the secondhand shop buried under piles of rubbish. Why?" Casey was bewildered by the sudden turn of attitude in the young man.

"Because you must get rid of it," Chatan replied, unsure of how much to reveal. "It is manifested from evil and will bring about the end of life as we know it unless it is used for good."

CHAPTER SIX

"What!" Casey and Flynn exclaimed.

"You're kidding, right?" Flynn shook his head at the dramatics and put his hands on his hips. He may have only been five foot ten to Chatan's six feet, but he could still pack a punch, as Snobby Bobby had found out.

"No." Chatan shook his head and stared at the box. "Did Old Joe say where he got it from?"

"The owner? No," Casey murmured. "He just said it was a pile of rubbish and he was going to burn it. Why?"

"Because *that* box was buried under the lake a hundred years ago by my forefathers. Back then, there was no water in it and it was just flat soil where my family lived. The rains came and covered the area, and turned it into a lake. My ancestors all thought it would remain buried."

"Clearly it didn't." Flynn grabbed the box from Casey's hand and shoved it in Chatan's face. "Do you know what the carvings on the bottom mean and if *that* round indent is meant for *that* pendant?" He pointed at the one around the young man's neck. "Are they a match?"

Chatan breathed heavily and stepped back. His eyes never leaving the box, his fingers played with the amulet around his neck that shone brightly in the autumn sun.

Casey noticed it, her gaze drawn to it, almost as if it was calling to her. The brightness acted as a beacon and she wondered why the pendant was brighter than it had been before. In the sun she could see the markings on the symbol, similar to those on the painted symbols all over town and their cabin.

Chatan noticed her gaze, saw her lips moving, and knew exactly what she was saying. He felt the warmth of the pendant under his fingers and against his skin. It was starting to burn, and the only time it did that was when it was near a tribal genetic link, such as the box, or a tribal genetic ancestor. *But could this young girl be...* he thought. *Could she be the one to break the curse and stop the rising from happening?* It happened only once every hundred years, and his father and grandfather had passed down the story of the burial of the box. They said, if the box was ever uncovered then only an ancestral link could stop the rising from happening again. Could this girl be the link?

"Um...Casey...is it?" Chatan asked, his smile beaming brighter than the gleam coming off the pendant. "What are you descended from? Your forebears?" He watched her slowly come out of her trance.

"Huh?" She stared dreamily at him. "Descended from?"

"Yes, your ancestors. What is your mother, for example?" Chatan needed to know as it was imperative to their survival.

"Mum was born here, and her family is European. Why?" Casey asked, her eyes staring into his lush brown ones.

"What's it got to do with anything, especially this box?" Flynn was irritated that Chatan hadn't answered his question.

"And your father? Where is he from?" Chatan saw the parents come out of the store across the road and wave. He waved back.

"My father?" Casey glanced across the road, and said, "That's Flynn's father. Mine's dead. Why?"

"Oh, so sorry to hear that," Chatan pushed on. "What descent was he?"

Casey shrugged. "Don't know. I know he was born here, but his parents weren't."

"Do you know where they are from?" the young man asked.

"Don't know. You'd have to ask Mum." Casey frowned and backed away, a knotty tense feeling in her stomach. "We need to go. Come on, Flynn." She grabbed the box, and after looking left and right, ran across the street with Flynn following.

Chatan followed a few moments later, not giving up so quickly.

"You okay?" Martina asked her daughter. "What were you guys talking about?"

"He wanted to know where you and Dad were born; your ancestry," Casey told her.

Martina raised her brows in surprise. "Why?"

"Dunno." Casey shrugged and glanced away in thought.

"Ah, hello again," Chatan said to everyone. "A nice day today."

"Why were you asking my daughter about our ancestry?" Martina asked him, coming straight to the point. "That's rather personal, isn't it?"

"Ah, yes, I am sorry if I upset Casey." Chatan bowed his head in apology. "I was talking about my ancestry and my forefathers, and saw your daughter's fascination with my pendant. It seemed only natural to ask her about hers. I am sorry if that was rude." He hoped to ease the tension, but to also find out if his thoughts were correct. "I was just wondering if your daughter was of Sioux descent."

Martina's eyes widened in shock. "How do…why would…I didn't…?" Pursing her lips, she scowled at the young man and rushed off down the street.

"Mum?"

"Martina?"

"Whoa!"

Marcus and Casey hurried after her and left the others standing there in shock.

"Well, you ticked her off, so thanks for that," Flynn told him snidely. "Now she'll be in a right mood for the rest of the day."

"Not that there's much of it left." Bethany checked her phone. "It's already three. It'll be teatime soon because we spent so much time in the secondhand shop we lost track of it. We'd better get going. Bye, Chatan." She gave him a wave of her fingers and took off down the road with Sherri.

Flynn scowled at Chatan and followed with Seb and Jarrett at a slower pace, leaving the young artist standing there wondering why Casey's ancestry was such a big secret and if she was the one his tribe had been waiting for.

"Mum…" Casey caught up to her mother and slid her arm through hers. "What's wrong? Why did you run away?"

Martina slowed her pace. "I didn't," she gasped. "It's just—"

"Martina?" Marcus came to a stop on her other side. "Is everything okay? Why would someone asking about Casey's ancestry upset you?" He cupped her elbow and watched the expressions fly over her face. "What is it?"

"It, ah…" Martina took a few deep breaths. "Just that…with ah…Casey's father gone…it doesn't seem right to talk about it." She tweaked her daughter's chin. "I'm sorry I made such a fuss. Your dad's family tree was complicated and things happened that we didn't want you to know."

"Was he right?" Flynn and the others came up behind them. He'd been thinking about what Chatan had said about Casey's ancestry and from Martina's reactions, Chatan had been right.

"About what?" Martina's gaze darted from her daughter to Flynn and back. "Casey's heritage is *our* business, Flynn. There's nothing *to* discuss. Now, since we spent so long in the secondhand shop, I suggest we finish off the street and have an early tea instead." Wanting to change the subject, she indicated to the two huge shopping bags in her hands. "I bought so much in there I hope we can find space in the van or trailer when we head home. With the painting I bought yesterday, I seem to be buying out the town. Shall we move on?" Putting a bright smile on her face, she encouraged Marcus to keep walking, leaving the teens standing there in bewilderment.

"What was *that* all about?" Flynn asked and took Casey by the arm.

Casey glanced sharply at him and removed her arm from his grasp. "How should *I* know? But what I *do know* is Mum's right. It's none of *your* business." She hurried after her mother and Marcus with the girls right behind her.

"Not only is this *place* weird, but now the *olds* are acting weird," Flynn grumbled. "Great!" He took off after them and they wrapped up their shopping around five, had a nice meal at the local family restaurant, and were back at the cabin just after six-thirty. And even though it was almost dark, Chatan had the campground lights on so it was as bright as day. He was also waiting for them on their porch.

As Marcus locked the car into the garage, Martina approached the door silently, ignoring Chatan who was standing beside it.

"I came to apologise," he said solemnly, watching each face for a reaction. "I did not mean to cause an issue. And if you have not told Casey of her heritage that is your business." He watched Martina's eyes flicker his way as she unlocked the door. "But if Casey is of Sioux descent, then it is imperative that I speak to her about something our ancestors did. Something only she can stop from happening."

"No…it isn't," Martina replied coolly and led Casey inside. The others followed, with Marcus bringing up the rear and closing the door in Chatan's face.

Chatan muttered, stood on the porch stairs, looked up into the night sky and sighed.

Casey put her things away and freshened up. Troubled by all that had been said, she realised her history had never been revealed, never talked about. And she figured that if Chatan could tell her she was Sioux descent, then why couldn't her mother? She pulled the framed photo of her family from her suitcase and stared at it. Her dad didn't look Native American, and neither did she, but if she *was* of that descent, why didn't she know about it? Her finger slid over her father's face, his grin as broad as can be. They were in Egypt, the sphinx and pyramids in the background, and she was sitting in front of her father at ten years of age. Her mother was leaning down on her husband's shoulders. They all looked incredibly happy.

If Chatan can tell I'm of Indian descent after just one day, first of all, how can he do that, and second, why is Mum making such a big deal out of it? She slumped on her bed. The other kids were watching

TV in the lounge room and she could hear Marcus and her mother in their bedroom next door talking about something. Wondering if they were talking about her, she considered whether it was time. Deciding it was, she went and knocked on their door. Silence followed, until Marcus finally opened the door and let her in. "I'll be in the lounge." He left and closed the door behind him.

Martina noticed the picture frame in Casey's hand. "You always take that with you?" She was sombre as she finished tidying up.

"How does Chatan know when I don't?" Casey asked her mother. "How does *he* know my heritage when *I* don't?"

Sighing, Martina finally turned to her daughter. "I guess it's time I told you."

CHAPTER SEVEN

"Come and sit." Martina indicated for her daughter to sit beside her on the bed, and when she obliged, Martina started the story.

"Your dad never knew about his ancestry when I met him. Wasn't really interested in it. But once we had you, and his work took him all over the world, he figured, why not. He was digging up other people's pasts, why not his. So..." She grasped her daughter's hand and kissed it. "We dug into his history."

"Why's it such a big secret? You freaked out when Chatan mentioned it." Casey slid closer to her mother.

"It's not that I..." Martina frowned and thought back. "It's not that I freaked out over your heritage, I freaked out because a complete stranger guessed it, knew it, sensed it somehow after barely talking to you. We didn't tell you for a reason, sweetie. There's too much death and despair and we figured we'd wait until you were old enough."

"I'm fifteen, Mum, just tell me."

Sighing, Martina steeled herself. "Your dad was

born here in Australia to American-born parents. They moved here, as you know, before your dad was born. But their heritage is, *was*, a little sketchy until we dug into it. Your dad's paternal side, as in your grandfather, is descended from Sioux Indian. Now, you wouldn't know it from looking at them, and they didn't know much about it. But it's in the male lineage. Your *father's* great-grandfather was full blood Sioux, *your* great-grandfather half, your grandfather one quarter, your dad one eighth."

"Wow," Casey murmured.

"Well…you can say that." Martina pushed her long dark hair out of her face. "But they were massacred by white men, so, it's not really a great story to tell."

"So that makes me what…one sixteenth Indian!" Casey said. "That's pretty cool."

"I guess it could be." Martina squeezed her daughter's hand. "The family chose to forget their past because of the bloodshed as they moved on with their futures, and moved around, met and married white European descended women. Although, eventually, the percentage will be inconsequential."

"So…how did Chatan know?" Casey's brow furrowed in thought. "How did *he* know, and why does that symbol keep popping up? I think I need to talk to him tomorrow and find out what he knows."

"I'm not sure he'd know anything," Martina told her. "He may be of Sioux descent, but that doesn't mean he knows *your* heritage."

"We're of the same lineage," Casey argued. "For

all I know, we're related."

Martina's brows slid into a frown. "I'm not sure I like the idea of that, although, it's entirely possible."

Casey shrugged. "What harm could it do? If anything, it'll make a great story for Halloween. Which *is* tomorrow."

*****

October 31st dawned bright and sunny. The sky was clear and fantastically blue, with no clouds, no breeze, just sunshine and blue skies, and at 9 a.m. there was a knock at the door.

Casey opened it to Chatan who smiled and gave a slight bow of his head. "Hello, come on in; we need to have a chat." She'd called the main office the night before and left the message for him to come over.

"Hello." Chatan nodded at everyone and cautiously stepped inside. He saw Martina's frown and crossed arms. "I did not mean to pry. I am sorry if I caused you sorrow or worry, but I think your daughter and I are linked."

"By our Indian heritage, you mean?" Casey offered him a seat in the lounge area. "Mum told me the basics last night. If we're both of Sioux descent, we could be related." She sat opposite him and saw Flynn frowning, arms crossed, wearing the blue puffer vest over a red and blue flannelette shirt and looking rather cute. She blinked and looked away. She'd told the girls her news after they'd gone to bed, but hadn't told the boys. Wasn't their business, and she doubted

Marcus had told them either.

"Yes, it is entirely possible." Chatan sat with his knees together and his hands flat on top of them. "I will start the story." Clearing his throat, he kept his concentration on Casey as her mother was standing behind her. "Many decades ago, my great-great-grandfather and his tribe travelled to this land. They found their way here and settled. My forefathers had many rituals and ideologies, traditions that they believed in, and it was all handed down to my grandfather, my father, and now me." He reached under his shirt and pulled the pendant out. It glittered like gold in the light of the room and all eyes were on it. "This is a double arrow, known as warding arrows, with two single arrows pointing right, surrounded by two moons. The arrows are a symbol of protection. This has been handed down from son to son, made from the gold of the earth that my forebears forged it from. It is sacred, the pendant and the symbol, and we use it on everything we need to protect. Unfortunately," he sighed and stared at the handmade amulet. "It also comes with an inexplicable horror that only the chosen one can prevail over." He looked dead straight into Casey's eyes. "When you showed me the box, you saw the pendant glowing, and you murmured something."

"Did I? I have no idea." Casey shrugged a shoulder. "I just remember being mesmerised by it." Her eyes hadn't left the pendant since he'd removed it from under his shirt. She was drawn to it.

"And I see that now, you are mesmerised also. It

has that power of the Sioux. It is forged from our blood as well. That is its power, and that will be its demise."

"What do you mean?" Martina asked, noting Casey's blank expression as she stared at the necklace.

Chatan looked up at her. "It was forged from the gold of our earth, and the blood of our soul. My forebear who made it cast a powerful spell over it for all who are descended from the lineage. I am, Casey clearly is, and it affects both of us in different ways. I have worn it since my father's death. He wore it after his father's death and so on. The problem is, that in our lineage, our forefathers created a curse they did not know about. A curse that goes with this pendant." He twirled it around, watching the small gold gleam it gave off. "When my forefather forged this pendant, he did it for protection and safety, to protect his people, his tribe from death and destruction, and it does, to an extent. However, it is also said, that the moment he mixed his blood with the gold, an evil force was joined with it. We do not know how, but it has brought evil to the world every one hundred years. And my people have suffered for it. That is why my great-great-grandfather travelled to this country, hoping for a fresh start for his people. But we did not get it, as the curse followed, and every one hundred years, it rears its ugly head. Literally."

"And what's the curse supposed to be?" Flynn demanded. He was annoyed at the rubbish going on and felt Casey was being taken advantage of.

Chatan gazed thoughtfully at him, sensing

resentment and anger. "It is when the dead rise from their graves."

"Zombies!" Seb rolled his eyes. "That's what the old man in the tourist centre said."

"Are you trying to tell us that everyone who ever died will rise from their graves, and what, walk around town and bite whoever's alive?" Marcus demanded. He'd only heard that from his son and his friends, not grown adult men.

Chatan stood and faced him. "I know it is hard to believe, but it *does* happen, and from what my forefathers told me, it could only be resolved when a descendant from the other side of the lineage would find the box that this pendant goes with. The man who forged it made the box to go with it. When the two sides of the family re-join, and both pieces are reunited, only then will it be stopped. I have the pendant; Casey found the box. That box was buried by my great-great-grandfather under what is now Eagle Ridge Lake." He pointed out the window and walked over to it. "My family settled here when there *was* no lake. The box was buried ten feet down, and once the water came, it was covered over for what we thought was eternity. But, here it is, in Casey's hand. She found it." He turned back to her. "That is a miracle in itself. I went to see Old Joe, the owner of the secondhand store, and asked him where he got it. He said, he dredged the lake as he always does looking for rubbish, and up it popped. He figured it was just an old piece of wood he could burn. But, instead, Casey found it yesterday."

"And when did *he* supposedly find the box?" Flynn asked, his hands on his hips stance showed his attitude towards the campground manager. He knew in his gut they were all being taken for a ride.

Chatan smiled. "The day you came."

Casey looked up at him. "You're kidding? He dredged it up the day we arrived?"

"Yes." Chatan nodded. "Come, I must show you what you need to do and where you need to do it." He headed for the door and opened the screen. "Please, I must show you, because only you can do this."

Casey stood up and followed. So did Martina. There was no way she was leaving her daughter alone with him. But she told the others to stay.

Chatan walked them down to the small jetty and motioned for them to get into the small boat. "Please, I must show you where you need to go. The exact spot the box was buried." He helped them into the boat, untied the rope, and started the engine. When it roared to life, he aimed for the centre of the lake, and once there, he turned it off. "Lore says, the other descendant must come to the middle where the box was buried and place this pendant into the indent of the box. The stud in the box needs to be locked into the hole between the two arrows here." He showed Casey on the amulet. "And it must be straight. Once the two pieces are joined, our forefathers will do the work. The box will open, and all will be righted. Evil will be removed, and good will prevail. Only *you* can do it, Casey. But you must remember. *This spot.*" He pointed to the big pine tree to their left. "That is one of the points. The other is the big rock to our right." He aimed a finger at the massive boulders to the right side of the lake. "They are fallen from the mountain where the lookout is. They fell centuries ago, but you can still see the pathway up the mountain."

Casey's gaze wandered from the boulders up the mountain to the top. "I see it."

"Good." Chatan nodded. "The other two points are the tallest mountain there in front of you, and the old totem pole back that way. My forefathers built it as a marker." Looking at her, he added, "*Our* fore-fathers."

Casey's smile was small as she was so over-whelmed. She had forefathers. "Why me?"

Chatan shrugged a shoulder and sighed. "I do not know. This may be *our* legacy, but the *history* is out of our hands. We must fix what they did wrong. I have the amulet; you have the box. Whoever finds the box must do it."

"Oi!" Martina let her head drop to her hands. "I'm beginning to regret bringing you here. This is just…too fantastical and completely ludicrous."

"I know," Chatan told her. "But once the blood moon rises, as it will tonight, you will see how true the story is."

"And *when* is my daughter meant to do this?" Martina ran her hands through her hair and lifted her head to look at him. "Which I still find is a load of bunkum."

Chatan smiled softly. "You will see. Once the

moon is on show, they will rise. Casey must do it at precisely midnight when the moon is at its highest."

"Do I have to do it by myself, or can someone help me?" Casey's stomach tied in knots to the point her whole body was shaking.

"There will be someone to help you." Chatan nodded. "They will prove themselves worthy of helping you, and when it is all over, you can go home knowing it will never happen again. Please, take a good look at the four markers so you remember tonight."

They spent a few minutes more absorbing the locations before motoring back to the dock where everyone met them.

Marcus helped Martina and Casey from the boat. "What was that all about?" he asked in Martina's ear.

"I'll tell you later," she murmured and followed her daughter up to the cabin.

"So please, keep your box within reach, and when the time is right, I will bring you the amulet," Chatan told Casey.

"You're not giving it to me now?" Casey asked, confused as to why she wasn't getting it now so she had both pieces.

"No." Chatan shook his head. "The timing has to be right. They cannot meet until midnight. I will give it to you just before you leave."

"And what if the zombies get you before then and I don't get the amulet?" Casey asked seriously.

Chatan chuckled. "Fear not, I have seen the future and know exactly how it will all go. Don't worry, you will be successful. I'll see you later, but don't be out all day, you need to be back before dark." He bounded down the porch steps. "Oh, I forgot to tell you, every spirit comes alive, so be prepared for some things you'll never see again." He walked backwards and waved. "I'll see you later."

"Bye." Casey waved and then realised how silly she must look and put her hand down. As she turned, she saw Flynn's scowl, the girls' dreamy expressions, and her mother's frown. "I know it's weird, but he said we'll see proof soon enough."

Martina sighed and shook her head. "I say it's ridiculous, but considering what your father did…" Reluctantly, she walked into the cabin and screamed.

CHAPTER EIGHT

Everyone ran inside to see Martina staring wide-eyed and pointing to the kitchen.

"What is it?" Marcus demanded and looked to where she was pointing. "What is it? I can't see anything."

"A head," she muttered, her hands over her mouth. "It popped up and then disappeared."

"What do you mean…a head?" Marcus queried.

"Oh no, are the zombies out already?" Bethany squealed and jumped behind the boys. "Kill it, kill it!"

"Oh, for God's sake," Flynn muttered and strode into the kitchen area. He looked around and found the culprit. "Not a zombie, just a possum."

The possum looked up wide-eyed at Flynn, food in its paw, tail bushy and curled. It did the only thing it could think of. It jumped onto the cupboard and dive bombed over it, to land flat on the floor, and stop short at all of the people yelling or screaming.

Chatan came running through the door. "What is it? I heard screams."

"Possum." Casey pointed to it. "Do they have rabies?"

"Ah, the little critter just wanted food." Chatan slowly stepped towards it, but it bolted down the hallway and into the master bedroom.

"Oh, no, get it out of there," Martina cried. "I need to get my bag."

"I will get it for you," Chatan told her. "And then I will get the possum out. You go about your day. I will deal with this." He silently walked down the hall and into the bedroom where he surveyed the situation. After closing the door, he retrieved Martina's bag from the bed and slid out the door. "Here." He handed it to her. "The door will keep him in until I can get in there with some food."

"Um…thank you," Martina murmured and took her bag. "We just need a few minutes to get our things." Glancing at Marcus, she motioned for him to go into the kitchen where he hefted the food cooler off the counter.

"Boys, grab the hampers and help load the van," Marcus told his son and his friends.

They helped, and within ten minutes they were gone, leaving Chatan to remove the possum.

With a sigh of relief, they settled into the car for the trip to the lookout.

"We didn't get here yesterday," Marcus reminded the teens. "And since it's nearly lunchtime, we're having it at the lookout."

"Plus, we have some special treats," Martina added over her shoulder at them. She noticed Casey's frown and faraway expression as she looked out the window. "Case, you okay, sweetie?"

Casey turned her head to give her mother a half smile before looking back out the window. She was trying to digest everything Chatan had told them, but still didn't believe in zombies or the undead. So, what the hell was she going to do come midnight? And how was she going to get the amulet from him to put in the box? And how was she going to get to the middle of the lake?

Sighing, she rubbed her neck and the back of her head, feeling a migraine coming on. She only got them when she was stressed, such as exam time or when her father had died, or when her mother had told her she was dating Marcus Jefferson. *That migraine had lasted a week.*

Dad, she thought. *What would you know about all of this? Mum dating again, me being descended from Sioux Indians. The dead rising on Halloween's blood moon? You'd probably love that one. The undead. That was your job, to unbury the dead, tell their story, bring them back to life. Yeah, you'd love that and it looks like I'm following in your footsteps.*

Wiping away a lone tear, she stared through the window and tuned out the voices in the car. The winding road up the mountain led them through beautiful lush country and pristine air, and when they pulled to a stop at the lookout and alighted, she breathed in that fresh cool air and slowly exhaled. "Wow."

"Wow is definitely the word for it," Sherri said

from beside her. She wrapped her coat tighter and made sure her gloves were tucked into her sleeves to keep out the chill. "We *so* need to post this view to social media."

"Fully charged and ready to go." Bethany waved her iPhone at them and proceeded to take a shot of the view. "It's so beautiful," she said and then stuck her face in her phone and uploaded it to Instagram.

"Can't you kids stay off those things and just enjoy the view?" Martina asked as she laid out the blankets on the ground in a sunny spot. "We're here for a picnic and a leisurely day before going home tomorrow."

Marcus set the food hamper beside her and went back for the last one.

"But what are we meant to do?" Seb asked. "It's kinda boring even if it is beautiful." He took some pictures, but didn't post them to social media.

"Well, at least you understand its beauty," Martina said. "Places like Eagle Ridge are still fairly preserved thanks to keeping the towns small and not having a lot of tourists. Everything's been kept pristine..." She gazed over the view and saw the town and camp grounds. "It is so beautiful."

"At least you can't see any cities from here." Marcus set the last hamper down. "Clear blue skies all the way. No other town, no other city, no congestion."

"No." Martina took photos using her *actual* camera. "I can see why Chatan paints up here. "I'm glad I bought that painting."

"Is it lunchtime yet?" Casey asked. "Or do we

have time for a walk?"

Marcus checked his watch. "We have an hour or so. Go film your social videos if you need to."

"Dad," Flynn complained. "You know *nothing* about social media." He traipsed off with Seb and Jarrett, while Casey, Sherri and Bethany went in the opposite direction.

"Be back in an hour, and be careful," Martina called. "I don't want to have to rescue you from a cliff top or crevice." She turned to Marcus. "Why do I get the feeling they'll be longer than an hour?"

Marcus laughed. "Because you're right. Once they get on social media they will be."

They were indeed longer than an hour as the girls were busy doing videos and taking pictures, except for Casey who basically tagged along and sat and watched as she was too busy thinking about everything and staring at the view straight down the mountain to the boulder Chatan had pointed out. Oh… She was in the direct path to the spot in the middle of the lake. Her phone buzzed, and glancing at it, saw it was her mother. She giggled. "Mum wants us back for lunch. It's already one."

They hurried back and found lunch spread out on the blankets ready to be eaten.

"Yum." Casey sat down next to her mother and dug into the chicken, tomato and lettuce sandwiches. The girls sat beside her and the boys joined them a few moments later. They ate in relative silence for a while, munching on potato crisps with their sandwiches, washing it down with cold soda, and eating chocolate brownies for dessert. They watched the sun move through the sky and listened to the birds chirp in the trees above them.

"Now, since it's Halloween and none of you will be trick or treating this year, I thought I'd bring these." Martina pulled six ghoulish containers in the shapes of Frankenstein's monster, Dracula, a werewolf, a pumpkin, a zombie, and a ghost out of a hamper. "Happy Halloween." She handed them over and grinned in delight at the smiles on their faces as they accepted their treat and searched through them to see what they had. Lollipops, jelly snakes and spiders, chocolates, whizz fizz and gumballs, all with a Halloween theme.

"Cool, thanks, Mum." Casey popped a chocolate Dracula into her mouth.

"You're welcome, sweetie."

"Thanks, Ms York," Sherri and Bethany said, and the boys followed suit except for Flynn who left it at *thanks.*

As they munched on their goodies, Jarrett pulled a rock from his pocket and held it up for everyone to see. "Look what I found. We were way down that away," he pointed to their left, "when I tripped on some dirt and found this. Don't know what it is, but it looks cool."

Casey trained her gaze on it and asked to see it. When Jarrett handed it over, she studied it the way her father had taught her, and then handed it to her mother for a look.

Martina took one look at it, smiled, and handed it

back to Casey.

"You know it's not a rock," Casey told Jarrett, and gave it back to him.

Jarrett scowled. "Of course it is. I know a cool rock when I see one."

"Do you know a cool *fossil* when you see one?" Casey asked. Everyone looked at her in surprise as she went on. "That there looks like a dinosaur fossil. They technically don't leave their bones when they die. The body is covered by sediment, and eventually, after millions of years, a stony replica is left behind. You struck it rich, Jarrett."

Jarrett's eyes had not only widened, but his brows had risen in shock. "You're kidding? How do you know?"

Casey rolled her eyes. "*How many times* have I mentioned my father was a palaeontologist? I grew up on dig sites and learned what a fossil was. Where did you find it? Let's go see what else there is."

"Yeah," Jarrett yelled. "I found me a dinosaur." He jumped up and raced off with the other teens following and led them down the hill until they reached a patchy area of whitish rock. "Here. I tripped here and found it near my feet." He pointed to a spot.

Casey kneeled down and scanned the ground, but not seeing anything of interest, stood up and carefully gazed across the rest of the patchy soil until something caught her eye. "Ha! Look at that." She hurried over to the rock-like structure and started brushing the dirt away with her hands. The others crowded around and watched in awe as she revealed a bony smooth patch.

"What is that?" Bethany asked, looking at the gaping holes of dirt and not seeing much else.

"*That* is a freakin' dinosaur head!" Casey declared excitedly and stood back. "Get your cameras out because *that* is the find of the century, and we're gonna get our names in magazines and on TV."

"What!" Jarrett exclaimed and pulled his phone from his pocket. "Someone take my picture with it. I'm gonna be famous."

"Hang on." Flynn stopped him. "How the hell do you see a dinosaur head?" he asked Casey. Looking at the dirt mound, he didn't see anything.

Casey rolled her eyes and kneeled down in front of the head. "Here's where its eye would have been. This is the top of his head down to his snout. His teeth would have been here." She'd run her hands over the skull as she spoke, lovingly stroking it with respect as she'd been taught to do when it came to preserving animals long gone. "It's a real find, Jarrett. You'll be famous."

"Yes!" Jarrett fist pumped and high-fived with Seb. "And a freakin' millionaire."

After everyone took photos of themselves with the skull, and spending hours searching for more fossils, they traipsed back up the hill and sat down to post to Instagram and look up news media outlets.

Except for Flynn, who sat silently. He still wasn't sure about his father dating a teacher, although he did concede, as he saw them dancing in each other's arms, that his dad seemed happy again. Marcus had been gutted when his wife left, and more so when the divorce papers turned up. But the moment he met Martina at the parent-teacher night, he'd been besotted, and Flynn *hated* it. Looking at his dad now, though, he saw the wide smile on his face as he slow danced with Martina.

Not a lot I can say to that is there, he thought. *Dad's happy, but I'm not. What the hell?* He leaned back on his hands and watched. *Why am I not happy with my father dating again? Sleeping with another woman who is not my mother. But then, Mum's with some other guy, probably married now, too. To a used car salesman, for God's sake.*

He scowled, drew his knees up and wrapped his arms around them. He saw Casey off with the girls taking selfies and laughing and having fun. *She doesn't seem too cut up about her mother dating another man. Maybe she doesn't care?* He plunged his hand into his Dracula container and pulled out a jelly killer python and ripped the head off with his teeth. As he chewed, he thought everything through and decided he just didn't like any of it.

"I think it's time to start packing up," Martina murmured against Marcus's face. She was wrapped in his arms and enjoying dancing, so didn't want the moment to end.

"Already? We just got here. And aren't we having tea here as well?" Marcus sighed, happy after a year of torture. He still wanted to propose, but just didn't know if it was the right time. He moved his head back to look down into her smiling face. "I love you."

It wasn't the first time he'd said it, but her smile brightened as if it was.

"I love you, too." He was the only man she'd said it to since the death of her husband more than three years ago. Planting her lips on his, she wrapped her arms around his neck as the kiss deepened.

"For God's sake, you two. I'd tell you to get a room, but we're out in the middle of nowhere," Flynn said snidely and rolled his eyes.

Marcus let go of Martina and turned to his son. "And just for that attitude, you can pack up and load the car after we eat tea."

Flynn's scowl got him extra duty.

"You can also go and get the others." Marcus aimed a pointed look at him.

It took them half an hour to eat the leftovers before they started packing up the hampers and the car, and the kids were collected and strapped in.

"It's seven o'clock. We were supposed to be back now so we were in the cabin when the moon came out," Casey said.

"The moon won't be out for a while," Martina said. "It's daylight savings, remember. The sun's still up."

"I know. But I want to be back by then," Casey replied, waiting for Marcus to start the car. All she heard was silence. "Mr Jefferson, we can go now."

"I wish we could, Casey, but the car won't start. I think the battery's dead."

CHAPTER NINE

"What do you mean the car won't start?" Casey fretted. "Why won't it start? It needs to start. It *has* to start. We need to get home."

"Casey!" Marcus said firmly and looked at her over his shoulder. "It's okay. I'll get out and check it." He pulled the bonnet lever and climbed out of the car. "Martina, can you get in the driver's seat and start the engine? I'll check what's going on," he asked through the open door.

She got out and ran around to the other side while he hefted the bonnet and started looking for what was wrong.

"I don't like this," Sherri muttered. "It's Halloween. The dead's going to rise and we're stuck out here in the middle of nowhere." She glanced fearfully at her friends who looked just as worried as she felt.

Jarrett playfully wiggled his fingers in Sherri's hair to scare her.

She screamed and batted at the back of her neck, spinning around, fury burning in her eyes. "How dare you, Jarrett Powell. Stop scaring me. My nerves are already on edge. I don't need you scaring me."

"Enough, all of you," Martina said sharply. "We need quiet and cool heads, so calm down." She peered into the rear-view, looking at all six teens.

"Try it again," Marcus called, and stepped back from the engine.

Martina turned the ignition, but nothing happened.

"Okay. I have no idea why the battery would be flat," Marcus muttered. "Flynn, get me the tool box from the back and come and help."

Flynn rolled his eyes and left the van, found the tools in the back, and walked to the front, noticing the sun sinking beyond the horizon fast. "Can we hurry this up? The sun's setting."

"Not you, too!" Marcus grinned and dug around for a cloth. "Pull out the spark plugs and start cleaning them. I'll check the battery." Handing the cloth to his son, he pulled out the small battery checker and found the battery to be charged. "Okay, so that's not it."

"Sparkies all done." Flynn stepped back. "Is there dirt somewhere?" He and his dad often spent time cleaning and doing up cars. It was one of the things they did together, especially after his mum had left, so both knew the ins and outs of a car engine.

"I don't think so, and I hope not." Marcus checked a few other things. "Give it a crank," he called to Martina.

She turned the key and the engine grumbled, but didn't spring to life.

"It must be something," Marcus muttered, and went back to tinkering.

Flynn glanced at the horizon. The sun was setting below the tree tops and he was growing uneasy about being out when the moon came up. "Ah, Dad, maybe we could do a rolling start. We need to get going."

"I'm not sure a rolling star would work, especially if it won't start while stationary." Marcus scratched his head. "Maybe we need to call a tow truck."

"*No one* will come if we do," Flynn told him. "Everyone's locked up tight, or out of town, and *we* need to get going."

"Oh, for God's sake, you're still not on about that zombie thing, are you?" Marcus glanced at his son, a grin on his face. "There's no such thing. I know it's Halloween, but still, zombies do not exist."

"Do you really want to take that chance?" Flynn asked, looking around to see if anyone or anything had risen. "Once the sun disappears we're screwed if we're not back in time, and quite frankly, I don't want to have to deal with the undead if they're actually undead."

Marcus chuckled and checked a few more things under the bonnet before stepping back and calling out, "Crank it up."

Martina turned the ignition, but got a spluttering cough.

"Okay, I guess a rolling start is the only way to do it," Marcus conceded, glad they had a manual gearbox. He made sure everything was back in its place. "Let's get this packed up and we'll give it a push."

Flynn grabbed the tool box, ran to the back of the car, and threw it in. Slamming the door, he saw the sun's reflection in the glass as it sank beyond the trees and the yellow glow slipped away. He also saw the scared faces of his friends and was sure his own face had the exact same expression.

"Right, boys." Marcus stopped at the back door. "You'll need to get out and push. Martina, do the lights work?"

She switched them on and they illuminated the car park in front of them.

"Okay, good. At least we have light. Put the car in drive, let the brake off, and we'll push it until we're on the road and heading downhill. Ready?"

"Ready," she called. "Girls, got your seatbelts on?"

"Yes."

"Good, let's do this." Marcus went to the back of the van and lined up with the boys. "On three. One, two, three." They dug their heels in and started pushing, managing to move the car. As it gained momentum, they moved faster and faster until they were out of the car park and on the road where the incline started. They kept pushing and soon the car was rolling by itself and they had reached the first curve of the road.

Martina slowly hit the brake. "Get in," she yelled. "I don't want to lose the momentum."

"Okay, boys." Marcus put his arms out to corral the boys and looked back up the road. "Hey, there's someone there. Maybe they can give us a push. Hey." He waved at the slowly moving man as Seb and Jarrett piled into the back seat.

Flynn looked back. "Ah, I don't think that's a

person, Dad. Get in the car."

"What do you mean, it's not a person? Are we back on that zombie thing again?"

"Dad, it's dark, and the moon's about to come out, get in and let's go."

"Marcus, hurry, I'm losing force," Martina called.

"Okay." Marcus saw that the person was still too far away to help, so he shut the back door and turned for the front passenger seat. That's when the shaking started.

"Is that an earthquake?" Martina asked, feeling the vibration through the car seat.

"We don't get earthquakes here; it must be something else." Marcus watched as rubble rolled down the mountain. He saw the person on the road drop to the ground, and trees were felled in the turmoil. "What the hell?"

All of the kids turned around in their seats to look out the back window as the ground behind them opened up and rose higher than the top of the mountain.

"What the bloody…" Flynn muttered, staring in awe as the T.rex skeleton rose from its burial site and let rip with an eardrum shattering roar.

"Holy shit! Marcus, get in," Martina screeched, not believing what she was seeing. She released the brake and the car rolled.

Marcus tore his eyes from the skeletal beast and ran after the car. He grabbed the door with his left hand and the inside hand strap with his right, and pushed the car to gain momentum. After ten steps he jumped in and slammed the door. "I didn't believe in Chatan's fairy tales before, but I certainly do now."

Martina hit the door lock button. "Tighten your seatbelts, kids, it's gonna be a long ride." She manoeuvred her way to the second curve and the car bounced. Checking the rear-view, she saw Rex pounding down the mountain behind them. "Okay, looks like Rex wants to play chasy." She deftly drove around the next curve.

"Are you going to be okay with driving?" Marcus asked, completely blown away at what he was in the middle of.

Martina grinned, despite the circumstances. "Didn't I tell you about the time I raced across the Egyptian desert in an old Rolls Royce Silver Ghost against Lawrence of Arabia himself, Peter O'Toole? He lost, I won. But then, what did he expect? I grew up with three older brothers and a father who raced cars. I know full well how to drive around a racetrack." She kept her eyes on the road and her foot lightly on the brake.

"This isn't a racetrack, love," Marcus reminded her. "It's a mountain. A steep one at that." He kept glancing behind them. "And we have a freakin' dinosaur chasing us."

Martina's smile grew grim. "I know. But I know what I'm doing." She braked as she came around the sharp curve that led them down the other side of the mountain and turned the ignition. At sixty kilometres an hour, it kicked in, and just in time as Rex decided to surf down the side of the mountain, sending boulders flying onto the road in front of them which they swerved around as Rex came tumble-turning across the road and down the rest of the mountain. The girls screamed, as did Seb and Jarrett, and even Flynn let out a few unidentifiable sounds.

"Quiet!" Martina commanded, expertly handling the wheel as she drove across the back of the mountain. When they came around the final curve of the road that led down into the outskirts of town, she put her foot on the accelerator. She'd seen Rex come bounding towards them and needed to get out of there.

Casey looked out the window and saw the moon. "Oh, no, the moon." With her hand pressed against the glass, the teen stared out at the blood orange ball in the sky.

"Crap!" Flynn muttered, feeling the pounding footsteps as they bounced the car on the road. He glanced out the back window. "Ah, he's getting closer."

Casey's gaze moved to her hand and she flashed back to that afternoon when they'd found the skull of the creature chasing them. "Crap!" Her eyes closed. "He's got my scent. And he thinks we're a plaything."

"*What do you mean* he's got your scent?" Flynn leaned forward in his seat, anger on his face.

Casey turned her head and saw his fiery blue eyes. "This afternoon when I uncovered it. I ran my hands over his head. He has my scent."

Flynn scoffed and sat back in his seat; arms crossed. "Yeah, like that's even possible."

"How do you explain that then?" Casey nodded at the dinosaur.

A sigh escaped Flynn. "I can't."

"Unless it's a blood moon on Halloween, the dead will rise every hundred years or so thing," Casey said and turned her head to watch the moon.

"Incoming," Martina yelled as Rex nudged the back of the van with his nose. "Everyone all right?" she asked after the screams died down.

"F-f-fine," Sherri stuttered and clutched at Bethany and Casey. "I want to go home. I've had enough of Halloween, and enough of zombies. I never want to trick or treat again."

"Here he comes," Martina yelled and the car was lifted and thrust forward. She dealt with the landing and skidded onto the main road leading into town.

Rex skidded on the same loose gravel and went tumbling towards the lake where he landed face first. Getting to his feet, he stopped to have a drink.

Martina slowed to the speed limit and came around the curve into the main street where she hit the brakes. "Shit!"

"What?" Flynn asked and the teens looked out the front window to see the dead had risen and gathered in the street.

"What the…? What do I do?" Martina watched them turn towards the van.

"Drive slowly," Marcus suggested. "And try to go around them."

Nodding, Martina lifted her foot from the brake and let the car slowly roll along the street.

"So the old man was right," Flynn muttered, shying away from his window as the undead moved for the car. "Bloody hell, this is freaky."

The girls huddled together in the middle of the seat, leaning as far away from their windows as possible.

"Keep it slow," Marcus murmured as he stared at all of the beings around them. Old tatty dirt covered clothes, piercing blue eyes, flesh rotted from bone, teeth fallen from mouths. They truly were dead. Sort of.

"May not be possible, I'm afraid." Martina saw Rex on the road behind them and he let out a roar.

The undead surrounded the car, oblivious to the dinosaur racing towards them, because all they wanted was brains and flesh and humans.

"Time for speed." Martina hit the accelerator and knocked down all the undead in her way like ten pins. "Sorry, sorry, sorry," she muttered to each one.

Rex raced up behind them, stomping on the undead as if they were bugs.

Martina put on speed, but Rex was still faster and nudged the car, flinging it forward. Martina kept control of it even though Rex couldn't keep control of itself. She raced around the corner for the road to the campground, but it was another ten minutes away.

Suddenly, they were flying, rolling through the air after being blindsided by Rex who had come at them from the side.

Screams littered the air, as did anything that

wasn't tied down, and when they came to a crash landing, they continued to roll, right into a tree. And only then, did they come to an actual stop.

So did Rex, for the Sioux protection symbol was all around them painted on the trees and there was one particularly large one on the tree against which the van had stopped. Roaring, he turned and trotted back to town to play skittles with the undead.

CHAPTER TEN

Chatan had watched it all through his third eye. Cross-legged on the floor of the campground office, he came out of his dream state and breathed. Time was killing everything, and time was nearly up. He rose and proceeded into the attached garage where he closed the door and climbed up into the driver's side of his black GMC van. It had painted symbols on every door and window and he knew what he needed to do. He hit the garage door button and watched as it silently rose. Waiting a moment before slowly driving out, he stopped for the door to come back down and saw the bright lights and waving flags around the totem pole way over to the right of the grounds to keep the undead's attention if they made it to the campsite. The rest of the lights were off, but it still looked as bright as day. He saw a small group around the totem and slowly drove out of the campground.

When he arrived at the van he did a u-turn and pulled up alongside as close as he could get and put the car in park, but left it running. He climbed into the back and slid the side door open.

The girls were starting to stir, as were the boys, and he silently woke each one up and pulled them out until they were in the van. Noticing that Casey and Flynn were gone, he stood on the driver's side door of the tilted van and gently slapped Martina's face. Her eyes flickered open and he put his hand over her mouth and puckered his lips into a silent shh.

Nodding, she managed to climb out with his help and into the van. "Marcus," she murmured, looking back at her partner.

Chatan shone a small torch into the car to see Marcus unconscious and with a broken left arm. He quickly gathered a splint and straps and climbed down into the car. After assessing the damage, he cut Marcus from the seatbelt and pulled him forward so he could strap his arm to his body.

Marcus mumbled as he came to, pain exploding in his arm and body.

"Shhh," Chatan whispered. "You've busted your arm, but I need to get you out." He slapped Marcus gently and helped him wake up. "Come." He slowly backed out of the car and pulled Marcus, while Marcus tried to climb his way out, and managed, with a lot of help, to get out through the broken window and into the van. He slumped into the front passenger seat and sighed. "Ow."

Chatan slid the door shut and leaned between Marcus and Martina. "This is what you must do. You need to drive back to the campgrounds and into the garage attached to the office. This is the door remote." He held it in front of her face. "It will open and close it. Once the garage door's closed, you can go inside the office. There is food and drink, medical supplies, a bathroom, and a couple of couches to rest on. Make sure everything is locked behind you. It's protected by the symbol."

"Where's Casey?" Martina finally noticed her daughter wasn't in the car. "Casey?" Her voice rose and panic set in. "Casey?"

"Shh," Chatan quieted her. "I will find Casey. She was flung from the van and is okay. I will find her. Flynn too."

"Flynn?" Marcus perked up from his dazed state. "My son's not here?" He looked into the back to see two of the kids gone. "Where is he?"

"Quiet!" Chatan commanded in a harsh whisper. "I will go and get them. You must go back to camp and lock yourselves away. Once you get there, turn off the headlights as they will only attract them. Do as I say and everything will be all right."

"*Nothing* about this is all right," Martina spat and turned in her seat. "Got your belts on kids?"

Seeing her no nonsense attitude, Chatan nodded and slipped out the side door, quietly closing it behind him. He stood on the wrecked van and watched them drive off, heard the mumblings to his left and saw the undead coming. Jumping lightly to the ground, he raised his hands, palm side up, and started slowly walking towards them. They stopped and shuffled on the spot as he dashed into the woods in search of Casey and Flynn. He was safe, as he'd painted the symbol on his forehead, throat, chest and back of his neck; four areas that were vulnerable. The symbols were also on his palms.

He raced down the forest incline and finally found them, unconscious, Casey face down, Flynn on his back. He went to Casey first and carefully rolled her over. She murmured, but didn't wake, so he went to work. Pulling a small vial from his pocket, he opened it and dabbed his finger on the opening. It was paint made of blood and bone and he painted the symbol on Casey's forehead. When he was done, he moved over to Flynn who was waking.

"Ugh…what are you doing?" Flynn swatted his hand away and tried to sit up.

"Rest a moment." Chatan stopped him with a hand to the chest. "Casey has not yet woken." He moved back to her and gently rubbed her wrists to get her pulse going. With a gentle slap on both cheeks, she came to. "Come, Casey, you have work to do."

Breathing slowly, she sat up with his help and saw Flynn crawling over to them. "What happened?"

"You were flung from the van," Chatan said. "Rest a moment, because you have work to do. You are safe for now."

They rested for ten minutes before getting to their feet. "Come, I will lead the way." He took her arm and helped her up the incline.

"Where's everyone else?" she asked, her wits coming back even though her head pounded and her body ached.

"Safely back at camp," Chatan whispered and led

them through the forest parallel with the road. "I sent them back in my van. They're in the office and are safe."

They exited onto the road and dashed across it.

"Come," Chatan said. "It is nearly midnight. Do you have the box?"

"No, it's in my bag in the cabin." She stepped over a fallen tree, but stumbled.

Chatan grabbed one arm, Flynn the other, and they righted her on her feet.

"You must get it; you need it. Do not go to the office. You must go to your cabin and get it. Then get to the middle of the lake. Do you understand? We're not far now. You can see the light around the totem pole in the distance. Stay away from it. Head for the road entrance and cut across behind the office to your cabin. It's the only way."

"Why is it the only way?" Flynn asked as they stumbled through the forest.

"Because I can no longer help you," Chatan said and pulled the amulet from his neck. "It is time, Casey."

"Time for what?" she asked as the ground gave way beneath him. He reached out with his left hand and grabbed a branch so he was hanging. The ground broke away and a dinosaur head snaked up through the hole.

"Chatan," Casey screamed and bent down to pull him up.

"Casey." Flynn's hand thrust out and grabbed her left hand while she reached down with her right.

"Chatan," tore from her throat and she saw him

smiling up at her while a diplodocus lazily wandered out of the ground.

"Take it, Casey. It is yours now." He reached up his right hand and she grabbed his hand, and the amulet, before he disappeared into the black hole.

"Chatan," she screamed. "Chatan!"

"Casey, come on," Flynn yelled and pulled her back, dragging her away from the gaping chasm. He looked at her hand and saw the amulet. "Put that thing around your neck or in a pocket because you'll lose it if you don't." He watched her dazedly shove it into her coat pocket and zip it up. "Come on, let's go." He took her hand, and they bolted through the forest to the campground road, ran across it and behind the main office, and on to their cabin.

"The bathroom window's still open," he whispered. "The door is locked so we can't go in that way. I'll have to boost you up." He saw her freaked out expression and held his hands together. "It has to be done."

She nodded and lifted her leg. Getting a boost up, she crawled through the window into the bathroom. Once in, she tiptoed across the hall to her room and found the box in her bag. Holding it, a warmth rushed through her, and she rushed back into the bathroom where she felt the urge, so stopped to take a bathroom break and wash her hands. Peering in the mirror, she saw how scratched and banged up she was, and saw the symbol on her forehead. Drying off her hands, she climbed back up and stuck her head out the window. "Pst."

Flynn looked up and reached out for her as she

slid out. "Got it?" he asked when she was down.

"Got it." She waved it in his face. "What now?"

"What now is we run at a diagonal angle from the cabin to the lake and try not to let any zombies get in the way." He pointed at the box. "You might want to tuck that into your coat, just in case."

She unzipped her jacket and shoved the box in, then zipped it up and made sure the belt was secure.

"Okay, let's go." He took her hand and they ran, cutting diagonally across from the corner of the cabin, bolting down to the lake and into the boat Chatan had left them.

"They're coming," Casey gasped.

Flynn untied the rope and glanced up to see the undead heading in their direction. "Time to go." He pulled the cord and gunned the engine, then headed out into the lake. "Where to?"

"The middle," Casey yelled over her shoulder. "Between that tree and that boulder." She pointed left and right. "But also *that* tree and the totem pole." Looking back, she saw it surrounded by the light. "Slow down."

Flynn had been gazing around and noticed a strange occurrence. "I don't think we have much of a choice," he yelled as the boat come to a soggy stop.

The water had drained from the lake.

"What the hell?" Casey looked over the side of the boat. "What happened?"

"Don't know. But we aren't close enough. We'll have to walk." Flynn stepped over the side and sank into sludge up to his knees.

"Ugh." Casey took the hand he offered and did the same, shivering as she sank. "Yuck."

"How far?" Flynn managed to move through it as the water seeped out and the sludge became drier and lower. "Come on." He slid his arm through hers and helped her to the middle of the lake.

Rex roared into the night as the blood moon neared its peak.

Casey shivered. "This is freaking me out." A cacophony of sounds littered the air and she had to eyeball the distance between the tree and boulder. "I think we're almost there." They moved on, even when Rex bounded onto the boulder and skeletal hands pushed up through the ground to meet them.

"I think this is it." Flynn looked down. "We're on dry land and it's not sucking us in."

Casey pulled the box from her coat and the amulet from her pocket. Under the light of the blood moon, she ripped the chain from the pendant and slotted it into the indent of the box.

Nothing happened.

"What's wrong with it?" Flynn noticed Rex take a leap into the now dry lake. "You might want to fix it now. There's a dinosaur coming."

Puzzled, Casey glanced at all four markers then down at the box and saw the pendant wasn't straight. Turning it to the right, she heard a click.

Her hands thrust skyward as bright light came pouring from it, and then from her eyes and mouth. She saw her ancestors, the tale of all time, and finally, her father.

"I love you, honey." He smiled. "That's my girl. You can do this."

"Daddy…" she murmured.

Flynn clung to her in surprise, watching as the undead flew into a tornado of light, swirling above them to be sucked into the vortex that disappeared into the box. When it was all gone, the box snapped shut and fell from Casey's hands as she collapsed.

"Hey." Flynn caught her and watched the box sink into the mud back to its ancestral burial ground. Water started seeping back up. "Okay, gotta go." He hauled her towards the boat, the water making it harder. It came up to his knees, then his thighs, and making it to the boat, he hefted Casey into it. She slid in, and with the water at waist height, Flynn threw himself up and over the side and slid in beside her. He lay panting while the water rose back to normal and then sat up. It was all gone.

Rex. The box. The amulet. The undead. All gone.

Gunning the engine, he took them back to the dock.

*****

As the world had been restored, everyone met them there. Chatan tied the boat up, Marcus helped Flynn lift Casey out and into her mother's arms and up to the cabin. Once they were cleaned up and put to bed they slept until midday when they woke to a hearty lunch. When they were finished, they packed up and left.

Chatan waved from the cabin porch and watched

them leave. The van was as good as new, and so was he. When the dead were taken all wrongs had been righted. And knowing he might never see Casey again, he'd tucked his information into her bag before they left, hoping to one day get a call or email.

Marcus, his arm magically restored, drove through the main street seeing it come alive with the residents who'd stayed and those returning. They passed the *Welcome to Eagle Ridge* sign, passed the *Thank You for Coming* sign, and headed for home with Casey staring out the window silent and numb.

EPILOGUE

"I now pronounce you, husband and wife. You may kiss the bride."

Marcus turned to Martina and gently kissed her rosebud lips.

She smiled and they turned to the crowd on their wedding day, gathering up their six month old daughter who had been sitting on Martina's mother's lap.

After two years of dating, not only had they had a child, they were now married and happy after the demise of both their past relationships.

Casey smiled at her mother and baby sister. Moana they had decided to call her. Moana Jefferson. As bridesmaid, she hadn't been all that happy having Flynn Jefferson for a stepbrother. But looking across the aisle at him in his best man's tux, she knew that since they were both going off to separate universities, she wouldn't see him for another four years at least, although there were holidays, while she studied palaeontology and Native American studies. *But damn, did he look hot in that tux.* She took the arm he extended to her and pursed her lips into a smile as they walked behind their parents. "Flynn."

"Stepsister," he teased, seeing how beautiful she looked, and tried to forget the crush he'd developed on her two years ago that was yet to wane. Now at six foot and almost eighteen, he hadn't liked the news of being a big brother, or a stepkid, or having a stepmother. But since his own mother hadn't cared, even after he'd contacted her two years ago, he knew he had to give up on his family getting back together. So, with therapy, he'd worked through his issues and was going to Uni to study ancient history and psychology.

"Ugh, don't call me that, stepbrother." Casey glowed under the church lights and knew she'd become quite a stunner in the last two years. And damn it, so had Flynn. But now, it was time to put her crush aside and begin her studies into her past, while also finding her future.

THE BONES OF WRATH: HORRORS

BLOOD DONORS WANTED

"Oh, Igor, I am looking positively pasty." Dr Acula pulled his whiter than white cheeks down to look into his bloodshot eyes. He turned this way and that, eyeing his pale features, and finally, spun around to his assistant. "Oh, I can't see anything in that mirror, Igor, the lighting is horrible. Tell me, how do I look? Be honest, now." He thrust his face towards him. "How do I look?"

Igor, the ever faithful companion, said, "Just as you always do, Master. Pristine white." He had no reason to lie. Dr Acula had saved his life and in turn he was a loyal servant.

"Oh, Igor, you always know what to say to calm me down." Dr Acula patted him on the shoulder, and silently swished over to his desk. Standing behind it, he stared out the expansive window and over the scene laid out before him. With rich green forests, mountain ranges capped with white snowy peaks, crystal clear lakes that reflected the blue from the sky, it was a peaceful scene. Calm and serene, it made him quite relaxed. He turned back to his desk and sat down. "Igor, I think we need to change how we do things." Clasping his hands, he slowly steepled his fingers together until his forefingers rested against his blood-red lips. "I am a doctor. I should be able to come up with a solution."

"A solution to what, Master?" Igor sat his hunched four foot figure into the chair opposite and swung his legs. His toes never reached the floor, never would unless he grew a good few inches, but he didn't mind. Being short got him into places.

"A solution to the blood shortage, of course." Dr Acula narrowed his eyes and thought. "We need fresh blood, new blood, out of town blood. Blood we haven't seen before blood. I just don't know what to do, Igor. We need fresh specimens, but there just doesn't seem to be enough in the local neighbourhood. We need to come up with new ideas. We can't keep going the way we have been, stocks are too low, and for some reason, they keep dying on me. Half the town has been buried now, so we need new people to bring new specimens to life. How do we do this, Igor? How, how? Tell me. Have you figured something out, yet?" Dr Acula leaned back in his seat and sighed. "What are we going to do, Igor? I don't want to starve."

"We just have to think, Master," Igor said, drumming his thick meaty fingers on the chair arm. "It's almost the end of October, the weather is getting colder by the day, the days are getting shorter, people are staying in earlier and locking up their houses. You barely catch them on the street anymore." He thought about the five towns in the local area within a five mile radius of each other. The good doctor had already been through them and stocks were indeed low, so unless new people moved into those towns, or they went farther afield, there was no way they would be able to replenish what they had in the fridge downstairs. He would have to use it sparingly.

"If only there was a way to get what we needed without me taking it," Dr Acula murmured. "Winter's almost here and I hate being out in the cold. It freezes my teeth and puts them on edge." His fingertip lightly brushed across his very sharp incisor and he felt a tiny jab. "Oh, bugger! I've pricked my finger again." Looking to see how bad it was, he eagerly sucked the meagre drop of blood. Not that it was of any benefit. If he didn't replenish the stock regularly, his own went down dramatically.

Reminiscing about the varying types of blood he'd tried, he racked his brain to come up with ideas. The only way he'd done it for a millennia was the way it had always been. He'd stalk the streets at night, come across anyone on their way home, and decide to shout them to a drink. Free for him, paid in full by them. It didn't matter if they were male, female, young or old, a drink was a drink. Nevertheless, he'd realised long ago that young, virginal women tasted far better than men, young or old. Less of a metallic taste and more of a sweet, untouched one, perfect and ripe for the picking. In more ways than one. But there were very few virginal women around these days, and he needed to think further afield. They either moved out of the neighbourhood so he had more towns to troll through, or they somehow brought people to the area. Most people in the local towns knew him and wanted nothing to do with him, and always made sure they were locked up tight before midnight…

He frowned. Midnight…they were always locked up tight before midnight. But there were several nights when they stayed out late. Christmas and New Years were two, Halloween was another, and wasn't it Halloween in a week or two…

"I've got it!" Igor snapped his uncoordinated fingers. "If we can't go to them, and they won't come to us, we'll go to each other."

Dr Acula frowned at his servant. "None of that made sense."

Igor had been thinking long and hard, using what limited brain power he had to figure out how they could restock their supply. "The local towns know what *the monster* does and what time it strikes, but they don't know it's you, or what you look like, or where you live. So…if we go to towns farther away, then we can make them come to us."

"And just how do we do that?" Dr Acula sighed his displeasure, not liking travelling too far from home, especially in colder months.

"You're a *doctor*," Igor reminded him. "In the local towns, people do not know that. In towns farther away, people do not know that. So we can use that to our benefit."

Dr Acula steepled his fingers and tapped his forefingers against his lips. "Yesss," he drawled. "But what does that have to do with the price of blood?"

Igor shook his head and wondered why he was sometimes smarter than his boss. "You are a *doctor*," he stressed. "What do doctors do with patients when they are sick?"

"Well…" Dr Acula thought about it. "We take their temperature, listen to their heartbeat, check their pulse, look in their mouths, take their blood…" The blood drained from his face in shock. "We take their blood…" His insides quivered and he excitedly leaned forward. "What was your plan, Igor?"

"What do doctors do with that blood?" Igor asked. "What happens to it? What's it used for?" He tried to push his master along on the thought process.

"Well, we test it for diseases and infections, and throw it out when we're done. We don't really use it for anything, although transfusions have been medically looked into in some countries and have become all the rage." Dr Acula still didn't quite see where Igor was going, but the light was beginning to dawn.

"And *how* are the transfusions performed?" Igor pushed on. "*How* do you get the other donor blood to be transfused?"

"Well, usually from families. So it's the same DNA. We stick a needle in them with a tube and let it drain into a vial, or bottle, or some such. Where *are* you going with this, Igor?" he asked, perplexed by the whole line of questioning.

"And what is it used for *outside* of that? How would you store it?"

"Well, it's not used for anything *other* than that. And it would be stored in the containers it's put in. But I really don't see where you're going."

"What if people were asked to *donate* blood?" Igor went on, willing his master to get the point. "How would you store it for later?"

"Later when?" Dr Acula frowned and the light finally dawned. "Oh…Igor…my friend…how fascinating is your brain, that you thought of that and not me, and *I'm* the doctor." Dr Acula sat back. "Well, well, well. We could ask them to donate blood and store it ourselves."

"That way," Igor went on, "stocks would never get low from people dying, and you could suggest they could donate once every three or six months. Use the excuse that it's for their health, there are benefits to giving blood, it will make them healthier, it will help people in other counties who are in need of a transfusion…"

"Like me!" Dr Acula's blood-red lips curled into an arrogant smile. "I need it on a daily basis. Igor, your plan is brilliant, but how will we execute it?"

Igor swung his legs and tapped his fingers together in glee. It wasn't often he came up with an idea worthy of execution, and he was quite excited. "Well, one idea is to set up a shop, or doctor's surgery specifically asking for blood donations. The other, was that we go to them. Get a horse and cart, deck it out like a doctor's office with a small room at the back that you can hide in and store the blood, and you can either do the transfusions yourself, or hire someone to do it. A lure, perhaps. A young buxom lady would get the men in, and an attractive young man would get the women in. They can take their blood, or keep them calm while you do it. Imagine how many bags of blood we could get from one town. Hundreds—"

"And if we go town to town, thousands…" Dr Acula finished off. He spun around in his chair to stare out the window. "Excellent suggestion, Igor. How long do you think it will take to complete?"

"A week or so, to get the horse and cart and do it up. If you want to hire help, we can do it in the same amount of time, or it may take longer to find the right person."

"Yes, hire the help when you buy the horse and cart. Buy two carts, one for the office, one to sleep in. I cannot be seen in daylight, it's too harsh on my skin." His fingers trailed down his pale cheek onto his neck. "Hire a young man or woman, maybe a doctor or nurse. Impressionable young people who will do what they're told for a small wage a week."

"How much?" Igor slid off the chair to his feet.

"A silver coin a week. Put beds in the second cart. We'll sleep in those to save money. Yes, Igor, this is a very good plan indeed." He steepled his fingers and peered out into the encroaching night.

*****

The next day, Igor went to the farthest town in the area and bought two plain square gypsy-style wagons and four horses. He filled the wagons with lumber, nuts and bolts, an old dentist's chair, and boxes of medical supplies. He managed to hire a young man in need of work, who drove the second wagon back to their stone house on the mountain.

Igor drove his wagon into the large workshop, unhitched the horses, and led them into the stables off to the side. He instructed the young man to do the same.

"Say, who lives here, anyway?" Vladimir, the young man, asked. He'd heard stories in town, but was never sure of who, or what, was being talked about. No one knew if it was a person or beast, or where they lived or came from. But rumours about the strange place carved into the mountain had spread far and wide. "Doesn't some whack job live here?" He unhitched the horses and led them to the stable. "There are rumours, you know."

"Of which none are true," Igor snapped and shuffled over to the cart. "We are paying you to drive the cart and help collect donations. But for now, you'll help me renovate the interiors. Come, we'll start working." He stabilised the first wagon, set a ladder up to the back, and climbed up.

"What! Tonight?" Vladimir asked, looking up at Igor with disdain. "Do I not get to eat, to sleep?" Placing his hands on his hips he grew a little indignant. "For a piece of silver a week, I didn't expect to be working around the clock. It's after five. That's knock-off time."

"Not around here, it isn't." Igor held out a hammer

to him. "You'll get board, if you want it. Otherwise, stay at your place in town and get yourself to and from work. You'll be expected to be on time and do as your boss says. Understood?" He waited impatiently, disliking the young man who was tall and good looking, unlike himself. There were times he hated humans and the way they looked. Better than him. Making him feel inferior in looks, stature and abilities. That's why he was the faithful servant to Dr Acula who'd saved him decades ago as a small boy being ridiculed and bullied by the local children. Those children had long been adults, and long been dead as he'd offered them to the slaughter by the doctor. Yes, he'd had no issue doing that, had served his master well in gratitude, but now, when they needed extra help, they'd had to hire someone to do it. And he resented it.

Vlad's eyes shifted from the hammer to the look of scorn on the man's face. At least, he thought he was a man. He hadn't been quite sure when he'd seen the deformed person before him asking for help for a silver coin a week. He'd overheard, and his ears had pricked up. He needed work and a silver coin was more than he received from the odd job about town that he was doing. So, he'd followed him around, watching him be turned down time after time, people laugh at him and shun him every time he asked, and eventually had felt sorry for him, and, in desperate need of money, had approached and offered his services. If only he'd known what he was getting himself into. Silently, he took the hammer and climbed the stairs.

*****

They spent the next three days renovating and decorating the carts, making small rooms at the back, windows on the sides, and bunk beds attached by chains to the wall. They bolted the dentist's chair to the floor in one and attached shelves and fold down tables to work on. On the fourth day they started painting and wrote *Dr Acula's Blood Bank. Blood Donations Wanted.* on the side in bright blood-red.

Igor stood back and nodded. It was perfect. And after sending Vladimir home for the night he went and found his boss. "The carts are ready, Master. Do you want to come and see?"

"Of course." Dr Acula excitedly flew from his place beside the fire and followed Igor down to the garage. "Is that young man still here?"

"No. I sent him home." Igor opened the door and led his master to the newly renovated carts. He stood proudly, waiting for his boss to examine his hard work.

Dr Acula slowly walked around each, went inside and had a look at the placement of everything, walked back out and stood on the small deck Igor had added. "Very good work, Igor. You will be greatly rewarded for this. When do we start?"

Thrilled to have pleased his master, Igor was embarrassed but secretly warmed by the praise.

"Whenever you want, Master. As you saw, the back room is for you and has plenty of home comforts. We have chests to store the blood, and lots of bags to drain it into. We can get more supplies in each town."

Dr Acula nodded and carefully stepped down to stand before him. "And what about me flitting from cabin to cabin? I cannot see the sun, Igor."

Igor rushed over to one cart and started turning a handle. A shade blind unfurled from the side and stretched across to the other cart. "A sun shade, Master. We can also park them close, side by side in the shade of a building, or so the sun is behind us and you can move from one to the other with no problem."

"Very good, Igor." Dr Acula was incredibly impressed and nodded his assent. "Let's start tomorrow."

*****

The following day, when Vladimir arrived for work, he finally met the good doctor who informed him that they would be setting off to gather donations. He was handed a piece of paper. "What's this?"

"Your spiel," Dr Acula told him and carried his bag into their sleeping quarters.

Vladimir read it, nodding his head slightly. "Okay. We're selling the idea of better health by giving blood. Do I say this in every town?"

"Every town we go to." Igor carried his own bag

up the stairs and placed it just inside the cabin door.

"And what will we do with the blood once we have it?" Vlad asked, and looked up at Igor who was staring disdainfully down at him.

"We store it." Dr Acula's voice was soft behind him, making Vlad spin around.

"Argh, where'd you come from?" Vlad's head spun left and right. "I just watched you go into the cabin. You didn't come out."

"Didn't I?" Dr Acula's lips slowly spread into their usual evil position. "I'm very quiet, and you were busy reading. Now, shall we go? You can drive the medical cart and learn your lines while you're at it."

Vlad eyed the good doctor. He was at least six feet tall, with a full head of jet-black hair parted on the side and slicked back, piercing blue eyes, full, blood-red lips, the palest of skin he'd ever seen, and he was well fitted in a black suit, shirt and tie. A matching cape swung from his shoulders to his feet. "So, uh, yeah…you're who?"

"Dr Acula, Vladimir." The doctor stepped closer to the tall, good looking young man with ruffled brown hair and big brown eyes. He was muscular and manly. "And I expect all of the women will come swooning over you. So, know your lines well; you'll need to charm the ladies while I take their blood." He silently stepped into the cart and Igor deftly closed the door, attached the small ladder to the deck and nodded to the other cart. "That one's yours. Let's get them out of here."

Igor backed the horses out of the garage and waited for Vlad to do the same before locking the door tight. He hit the alarm system and climbed into the seat of his cart. Slapping the reins, they set off for the first town on the map, making it by afternoon and parking against the setting sun so the doctor could exit safely.

After unleashing the horses and setting up, they got to work.

"Step right up, ladies and gentlemen," Vlad started, looking at all of the intrigued faces that had stopped to look. "And learn about the miracle benefits of bloodletting. Would you be generous in helping out a fellow human with life-saving treatment?"

He went on to tell them about blood donations and how poor, unhealthy souls were in desperate need of the help. He quickly explained about the technique, that it was quick and painless, and done in minutes, and that bloodletting was also beneficial for one's health and wellbeing. He charmed the men with his words, and the women, especially the young buxom ones, with his good looks, and soon, had a line of people not only prepared to give a donation of blood for their health, but for the poor souls who needed help. He escorted each person into the medical cart, sat them down in the chair and spoke to them while the doctor did his thing. "This is Dr Acula. He'll be taking your blood."

"Good evening," Dr Acula drawled. "I just need your arm." His good looks made the women swoon, and with his light touch, they were putty in his hands. He spoke softly to each. "I'm just going to clean your inner elbow so no infection occurs. And then I will insert a small needle with a tube attached. It will only hurt for a moment, and then your delicious blood will drain down the tube and into the bag. We will give you a sweet treat on the way out so your sugar levels rise back up, and then you'll be fine."

"Oh, thank you, doctor," the buxom young blonde murmured, batting her lashes at the good looking doctor and his silky smooth fingers with their magic touch. She rested back in the chair, her eyes half closed, marvelling at the good looking men on either side of her. She hoped both, or at least one, might be single and in need of a virginal young woman. And if the good doctor was single and had money… Her gaze slowly drifted to the doctor and took in his features in the lamplight which was low to keep the donors calm. She noticed how pale his skin was, how dilated his pupils were as he gazed down at the blood slowly sliding down the tube and into the bag. Noticed his full lips were curled into a small smile, and his tongue eagerly licked them left to right and right to left. Noticed how sharp his incisors were and how healthy his teeth looked. *Mmm,* she thought, *he's definitely kept himself in shape.*

"And we're done." Dr Acula removed the needle and laid the bag and tube on the tray to finish draining. He wiped her arm and placed a piece of cotton over it and swiftly applied a small bandage. "You can go now, and thank you for your delicious donation." His tongue slid over his lips as he eyed the buxom body of the young woman. It's not that he didn't desire the female flesh, he just had no need for it in that way. His incisors extended and his pupils dilated more, making the blue of his eyes more piercing.

Vlad noticed and said, "Why don't I help you outside, miss." He held out his hands to her, and drunk on lust, she noticed and extended her hands to him.

"What's the hurry?" Dr Acula asked, his eyes pinpointed on Vlad. "This young lady is quite charming. She can stay."

Vlad helped her from her seat and glanced at the doctor, a bad feeling rising in his gut. "I'll help her out, you deal with the blood." He escorted the young lady out of the cabin and down the stairs where he offered her a sweet treat and some fresh orange juice. "It will get your blood sugar back up. You'll feel a little weak and woozy for a few minutes."

"Oh, thank you," she murmured, gazing seductively up at him and over the rim of the cup. "The doctor's very good looking. Is he single?"

"Um…" Vlad frowned and glanced back into the cabin to see the doctor was gone. *Probably in the back dealing with the blood,* he thought. "Wait here a moment and I'll walk you home," he told her and ascended the steps and quietly went inside.

Sidestepping the chair and tray, and picking up the lamp, he quickly opened the door and thrust the lamp into the room.

There was Dr Acula, blood bag in hand, fangs out, feeding from it with blood all over his mouth and chin.

The doctor glanced up in surprise, caught completely unawares. He hadn't been able to help himself. He'd sensed her virginal blood the moment she'd walked into the cart and now he'd been caught feasting on it.

"Oh…my…God…you're that…that monster everyone talks about. I'm working *for you?* Oh, my God." Vlad, disgusted by the turn of events, held the lamp to the doctor's face. "I'm going to stop you."

Dr Acula lashed out, knocking the lamp from Vlad's hands, scratching him in the process.

Vlad slammed the door and made a dash for it, but Dr Acula was on him like a flash, planting his teeth into the soft flesh between his neck and shoulder. Vlad shook him off and landed a hard right punch to his face, knocking him back. He ran, but tripped over the chair and broke his fall with one of the small tray tables.

"Argh," Dr Acula screamed. "Igor, Igor, help me."

Vlad turned his head to see the doctor's cape going up in flames, along with the front of the cart.

Igor climbed into the cart. "Master, Master, oh, what shall I do?"

"Help me, Igor, help me." Dr Acula flapped his wings to rid them of the fire, but they only fanned the flames and Igor flapped at the fire, unsure of what to do.

Vlad rose to his feet, determined to stop this

monster once and for all. His fingers curled around a slice of wood from the tray table, and without thinking, he surged forward and rammed it into the doctor's chest, making the doctor scream, making Igor scream, making the young woman outside scream.

Vlad glanced over his shoulder and saw her standing on the deck watching, horror on her wide-eyed face. "Get out, get out now." He felt a blow to his stomach and looked down to see Igor pummelling him with both fists. The doctor's body dissolved into dust, and shocked, Vlad took a moment before hefting Igor up with his left hand and stabbing him with the stake.

Igor's breath left him, his eyes widened, and he was dropped where his master had died.

Vlad ran out the door, slammed it shut and locked it, and grabbing the girl by the arm, he rushed her down the stairs and a safe distance away. They stood watching as the second cart caught on fire and burned. He'd never killed anyone before, never thought he'd need to, never thought it would be a monster if he did. He felt the anger and power of the kill surge around his body, and heat burned his skin, but it wasn't from the raging fire.

"Oh, thank you, you saved me." The doe-eyed girl was staring dutifully into his big brown eyes.

He studied her intently, her features, her face and body. Felt the surge of anger and power around his own, and in the heat of the flames closed his eyes and breathed. Slowly, calmly, he had done what no one else had been able to do, and now he vowed to hunt down more monsters like the doctor. From now on, he'd be known as Vlad the Impaler.

His eyelids rose and his piercing blue eyes stared coldly into the night.

DANCE NIGHT FRIGHT

"Oh, I can't wait for the Halloween dance. I have the coolest costume. It's pink and frilly and I'll look absolutely drop dead gorgeous in it," Brooke Bonefield babbled to her clique in the schoolyard Monday afternoon.

"You know it's a week away," Maisie Heartford reminded her. "It's not until Saturday. Are you saying it's already done?" While a part of Brooke's clique, she certainly wasn't best friends with her and sometimes found her painfully egotistical. All she ever did was talk about herself.

"Of course it's done," Brooke said almost snidely. "It's been done since last year."

That caused the other girls around her to frown.

"What do you mean it's been done since last year?" Madeleine Westwood asked. As Brooke's best friend, she knew nothing of this. "Why didn't you tell me?"

Brooke preened a little, relishing the attention. At sixteen, she was the most popular girl in school in Westwood High, a high school that was named after

Madeleine's great-grandfather who had paid for it to be built. And while many thought she was the snobbiest, she knew that her popularity year after year ruled that out. She always won Halloween Queen, or, at least, had for the last four years in a row. Since the whole school got to vote, it was clear that her victory showed how popular she was. Even though she had been accused of rigging the competition. "Why would I?" she finally said. "You already know I start right after each Halloween on next year's costume. Why did I need to tell you?" She went back to nibbling delicately on her crustless cucumber and cheese sandwiches that the family chef made her every day. Wholemeal, not white, no butter or margarine, and dairy-free cheese which she didn't even know existed.

"So that *I* don't end up with the same costume." Madeleine rolled her eyes. There were times Brooke was so brainless she seemed to walk through life like a zombie. Either that, or she was just extremely egotistical.

"Oh, we won't," Brooke said confidently and finished her drink before wrapping up her rubbish into her lunch box. "I always make sure to have a costume no one else could possibly think of."

"You've been a princess or queen every year that we've had the party," Claire Restile told her. Another member of the clique, she was getting over Brooke's ego pretty quickly. "So we know it will be another version of something like that."

"Doesn't mean I will be wearing the same thing

this year." Brooke didn't believe she had to defend herself.

"You said it was pink and frilly and you'll look drop dead gorgeous in it," Claire reminded her. "Other than a princess or queen, what other costume would require pink frills?"

"Well," Brooke huffed. "Goes to show how much you know. It's going to be completely different this year. Just you wait and see." She put her lunch box into her bag, brushed her school blazer off, and flipped her long blonde hair over her shoulder. "But regardless, I'll be voted Halloween Queen again. After all, who *wouldn't* vote for me?" Standing carefully, she surveyed the ten or so girls around her. "And I know you'll all vote for me as my best friends. After all, why *wouldn't* you? Let's go, girls. The bell's about to ring." As she sauntered off, the girls slowly followed, rolling their eyes behind her back, trading glances with each other, and shaking their heads.

"I somehow don't think I'll be voting for her and her ego this year," Claire murmured to Madeleine and Rebecca Aldorn, another classmate and member of the Bonefield Clique. "Isn't it time someone else was voted for and selected?"

"Yeah," Rebecca mumbled, and slung her bag over her shoulder. "Not that it matters, she still wins by majority. Not that I've ever voted for her."

Claire suppressed her laughter. "You too? I never have," she whispered, and let the laughter pour forth with Rebecca joining in.

Brooke turned around and eyed them critically.

"Girls, we do not act like hyenas in the schoolyard. Have some decorum if you're going to be a member of this clique." Her perfectly plucked eyebrow rose and she turned to walk on.

Claire, Rebecca and Maisie rolled their eyes and burst out laughing.

"And here's the snobby clique." Bradford Jennings stopped in front of Brooke. At five foot ten with dark brown hair and sparkling green eyes, he was the hottest boy in school.

"Move out of our way, Bradford, like a good little boy," Brooke chastised, secretly thrilled that he and his friends had just stopped them. She also couldn't wait for him to be voted Halloween King as he had been every year she'd been queen. He was the hottest boy in school, and also the smartest jock.

"Like a good little boy?" Bradford repeated, his lips turning into a sneer. "I'm no little boy, Brookey Wookey. But you do very much act like a childish brat at times. I really don't know why people bother voting for you each year for Halloween Queen." He leaned in close and peered into her big innocent wide eyes with his sparkling mischievous ones. "I personally can't wait for someone else to be picked so I can have a change of queen. In fact," he watched her eyes grow wider as they looked over his shoulder at his own clique of friends, "I've told the boys, that once again, we'll be voting for someone *other* than you. It's time for your reign to end, Your Majesty, Queen Brookey Wookey." He bowed before her and then moved on past with his friends following.

"Girls." He nodded to her friends and they all giggled and blushed.

Once clear of Brooke and her clique on the other side of the building, Bradford turned to his friends. "I want *any*one other than Brooke to be Halloween Queen. Tell everyone you know, boys *and* girls, to vote for the next person on the ballot. *No one,* and *I mean, no one,*" he warned his friends, "is to vote for Brooke. You got it!"

His friends nodded and trailed after him until they reached the classroom.

"You know," Chance Billington drawled. "Anyone would think you've got a crush on Brooke." He heard his friends guffaw. "You do get to be Halloween King and Queen each year."

"I bet there's a whole bunch of boys willing to be king to her queen," Rinniford Von Batten teased. "Hell, even I'd consider being king just for her to be my queen." At sixteen, he was potentially the richest heir in school with Von Batten money going way back. He was also smart to go with being rich, but far from the hottest, or most good looking, kid in school. With flaming red hair and freckles, he knew he only got to hang out in Bradford's clique because of his money and status. But he didn't care.

"*You!*" Charles Fenetta declared. "Why would *you* want to be king? Why would *you* think you'd be voted for? Why do *you* think you'd even win over Bradford?"

"*Besides* being the richest *and* the smartest?" Rinniford dropped his bag by his feet and scornfully looked at Charles. "Because I can rig the vote to do so, that's bloody why," he told his friends, a smirk firmly in place. "How do you think li'l old Bradford here's been winning all these years? How do you think *Brooke's* been winning all these years? Because it was so freakin' hilarious to put them together." Rinniford glanced at each friend's face, seeing a range of shock and surprise. He grinned at Bradford. "You and Brookey Wookey looked so perfect up there on stage together. She fawns over you and you stand there like a zombie's eaten your brains. It's hilarious." He sat in his chair and leaned back until he could cross his feet on his desk without falling, a trick he'd practised for months. "The look on your face every year. Tsk, tsk, priceless." He pretended to take photos of Bradford, but Bradford knocked his feet from the table, making his chair topple backwards with a thud on the floor.

Bradford crouched over him and pointed his finger in his face. "How bloody dare you, you sodding bugger? Have you done it every year?"

Rinniford arched a brow, clamped his fear down, and stared Bradford straight in the eye. "Yes. Every year. *Because I can!*"

"Argh!" Bradford growled and curled his fists into balls, stomping in circles. Anyone watching would have thought he was a child throwing a tantrum. He moved back into Rinniford's face. "Then you can bloody well rig it so she *doesn't* win. You understand me?" His spit flew out of his mouth and hit Rinniford in the face.

But Rinniford just stared back. He'd grown up

accustomed to bullies as his two older brothers had done the same to him.

"You make it so Brooke Bonefield *does not* win Halloween Queen. Do you hear me?"

"How about I make it so *neither* of you wins?" Rinniford asked and climbed to his feet. He stood so he was eye to eye with Bradford. "How about if *someone else* is king and queen instead of the same old same old every year?"

Bradford flinched. As much as he couldn't stand being king to Brooke's queen, he still liked being king and the attention he received from it.

"How about, I make *myself* Halloween King," Rinniford pushed on. "I can do that. I can make *any of us* king and queen and no one ever figures it out. Would you like a break this year, Bradford?" He stared into his enemy's green eyes. "I can *make you* take a break, or," his brows rose, "I can do nothing with the votes and let everyone dictate for themselves." He spread his hands. "Which they already think they do. So, what's it gonna be, Bradford?" His gaze never left Bradford's and he saw something other than fear flicker through them.

Finally, Bradford stepped back and scowled. "I don't care what you do, Rin Tin Tin," he said, using his degrading nickname for Rinniford. "Just make sure Brooke doesn't win."

*****

On Saturday, at the West Cheston Cemetery, old

man Fred wandered through the gravesites picking up rubbish, getting rid of dead flowers, and doing the daily tidy up as he always did. But today, of all days, was Halloween, and he didn't like being in the cemetery on Halloween, especially at night. So, every year he got to work when the sun was up and made sure he left before the sun even hit the horizon. Made sure everything was locked up tighter than a drum. The doors to the main office, the main crypt, the gates. He didn't like it when kids thought they could scavenge through the gravestones for whatever they could find to show their mates or scare them with.

Walking along, he found patches of grass on some graves had been disturbed, pulled at or dug up. "Mmm…" He reached down with his rubbish stick and poked at the grass, trying to push it back in. It didn't do the job as well as he'd hoped, so he kneeled down and pushed the grass back into place with his fingers. Glancing up, he saw the date on the headstone. The person buried there had only died last Halloween. "Mmm, one year ago today. Well, I am very sorry, Ms Mildred Peaceright. You've been gone for one year. Many respects to you."

He stood and brushed off his hands and noticed that the grave beside it also had upturned grass. He checked the name and date and found that Miss Petulia Greyson had been buried the Halloween two years ago. "Miss Petulia, just straightening up your covers. Don't mind me." He tidied the grass and went on his way, finding more grass had been uprooted on other graves. Noticed that they too had died on a Halloween in the past. Noticed they were all relatively the same age. Noticed no husbands' or wives' names on the gravestones. Assumed the deceased were all single. No children, or other family was mentioned either.

"Mmm…" Fred finished off the last grave, brushed himself off, and held up a hand to shield his eyes. The sun was slowly descending to the tops of the trees in the distance and he looked at his watch. "Yep, four on the dot. Better get back and lock up." Collecting the rubbish cart he'd been pushing all day, he rolled it back up the hill and into the garage located behind the main office building. Tying up the bag of rubbish, he threw it into the dumpster and rolled down the door, padlocking it tight. "Better make sure I padlock everything tonight," he murmured. "Don't want anyone getting in, let alone getting out. It's the big Halloween party tonight." Chuckling to himself, he thought it was funny that on every gravestone of every person who'd died on Halloween said they loved to dance and have a good party. "Well, they'll certainly have one tonight, won't they."

*****

At seven-thirty that night, Brooke entered the high school gymnasium, hoping to have the spotlight on her. And she did, as she'd already charmed Alfredo, the school nerd who was managing the lights for the night, to make sure it swung around to her when she entered precisely at seven-thirty. There she was in all of her ethereal beauty as Glinda the Good Witch from *The Wizard Of Oz*. Her blonde hair was curled to perfection, her pink frilly gown sparkled in the spotlight, and the crown she wore on her head dazzled in all of its fakeness. At least, until she had the Halloween Queen crown on her head.

All eyes turned to her, to admire, to congratulate, and then turned away.

"Wait, why aren't you looking?" she demanded, and stomped her foot. She strode over to her friends who huddled together as they danced. "Why is no one looking at my costume?" Pulling at her friends' arms, she forced them to face her.

"Because it's nothing new," Madeleine told her. "It's the same style dress you've worn year after year, with every other costume." She surveyed the gown. "It's pretty and all, but nothing new."

"Besides," Claire added, "why should we give *you* more attention? Everyone here deserves the spotlight on them when they enter." She glanced around and saw hundreds of kids wearing all kinds of costumes, including some zombies, witches, and Draculas. She turned back to Brooke. "Why would we make *your* head bigger by giving *you* attention?" Shrugging, she walked away and was followed by several other girls.

"*What* is going on?" Brooke asked Madeleine. "Seriously, *what* is going on?"

Madeleine shrugged. "It's Halloween, makes people weird."

*****

Since none of the boys had driver's licences and all of them lived within a one mile radius of each other, they'd all gone to Bradford's house to change into their costumes. And since Bradford lived the closest to the school, they were going to walk to the party.

"Okay, let's go. We're going to take a short cut through the cemetery." Bradford rounded them all up.

"Ah, no way in the entire universe," Chance declared. "I am *not* walking through that place at night, *especially* Halloween night. Are you nuts?"

Bradford gave his friend the raised brow and narrowed eye expression he used when he was annoyed with someone. He'd learned it from his father and grandfather. "It will be quicker, Chance, and I know a way over the fence so we can cut diagonally across it, otherwise, we'll have to walk all the way around it. So stop being scaredy cats and be grown men."

Rinniford raised an objectionable finger. "You do know we aren't men?"

"Ugh," Bradford growled and headed out the door.

The others followed him down the block until they came to the street with the cemetery. Because of the way the town had originally been built, the cemetery was now surrounded by housing developments and had the school on the next block.

Rushing across the road, Bradford clambered up the tree on the street, hitched a leg over the fence, and jumped down. Getting to his feet, he stared at his friends through the iron-gated fence. "Come on, you pussies. I dare you to do it."

With unsure glances at each other, they climbed the tree one by one and jumped down. Once all the boys were in, Bradford led them across the huge two-block-sized cemetery.

"Do you know where you're going?" Gregory Planton asked. He'd been a part of the clique for a year since his family moved to Cheston.

"*Of course* I do. I walk through every morning," Bradford sneered. "How do you think I get to school so fast?" He was led by the light of the full moon beaming down and they hit the grassy area of the cemetery and hurried over graves.

"Ah, dude, no. I'm not walking on a dead person's grave." Nicholas Broughton hopped over a tombstone and tried to find the path between. "Dude, we should *not* be doing this."

"Quit yer yammering," Bradford demanded and led the way. "We're barely halfway. Let's go." He didn't bother watching where he was going, so when something grabbed his ankle, he face planted on the grass. "What the hell?"

The boys hustled to help him and he looked down at his ankle. "What is that? A tree branch?"

Rinniford pulled his torch from his pocket and turned it on, directing the light to Bradford's ankle, and the whitish yellow roots that encased his friend's foot. "No, unless it's really old. I'll try and pull it off. It might be a tree root instead." His hand was reaching for the white root-like structure when it moved. "Whoa." He lurched back onto his butt.

"What?" Bradford demanded and grabbed at the branch. "What is it?"

Rinniford aimed the torch at Bradford's foot and watched as the branch curled and uncurled, forced its way up and clicked its fingers.

"Argh!" The boys scurried back in ten different directions, and Rinniford kept his torchlight trained on the grave. They all watched in horror as that arm was joined by a second, and then a head, and then a body.

"Argh!" Charles lurched sideways. "It's got me, it's got me." He brushed wildly at whatever was grabbing him and Rinniford swung his torch around to see Charles being mauled by a body.

"Argh! What are they?" Quentin Brockmeyer stumbled to his feet and looked around in a panic. "Argh, there's more of them. Look, zombies. We're gonna be eaten by zombies. Argh!" All ten boys spun every which way to see countless dead rising from their graves.

"Run for it," Bradford yelled, and took off across the cemetery in the direction of the school, the boys hot on his trail. They bolted over the fence, down the street, onto the school grounds, and finally into the gymnasium. Slamming the doors behind them, they slid the locks into place and stood huffing, trying to catch their breath. When they did, they saw the whole school, including the teachers, staring at them.

"Boys, what is the meaning of this?" Mrs Mitabne,

the school's principal, asked. She stood with her arms crossed and a scowl on her face.

"Zombies," the boys yelled.

*****

The cemetery's residents ambled along to the sound of the music, following the melodic tone wafting on the air.

"So different to the music of my day," Mildred told her companion. "But music is music, and a dance is a dance."

"Oh, absolutely," Petulia agreed. "I wore my best outfit for the occasion." She glanced down at her pink party dress and satin heels. "So nice of my friend to pick this out for me to wear."

"It's very pretty." Mildred nodded to the others who joined them. "Evening Stu, Fred, Peter, Mary. How are you?"

"Fine thanks, Mildred," Fred replied. "You're looking very nice this evening."

"Oh," Mildred giggled girlishly. "Thank you, Fred."

"Save me a dance for later?" he asked and doffed his hat.

"Oh, I just might, if I'm not dancing with anyone else," she said, and led the way through the fence and down the street.

*****

"What do you *mean* zombies?" Mrs Mitabne demanded of the boys. "Unless you're talking about the kids' or adults' costumes, you know full well there is no such thing. Have you been drinking?" She frowned, noticed the pale faces and wild eyes, and stepped closer to the boys. "Or smoking pot?"

"No, miss, no," Bradford babbled. "We were cutting through the cemetery when I fell over. I thought it was a branch, but when Rin Tin Tin put his torch on, we saw it was a hand. A skeletal hand, and then we saw them all rising from their graves and ran."

"We ran," Chance gasped. "It had us. *They* had us. They all had us. Quick, call the police, call the National Guard, call the air force, the zombies are out. They're coming, they're coming."

The boys all babbled at once trying to convince the principal to do something.

"Good grief, what *have* they been inhaling?" Claire murmured. The girls were all huddled together and started a running commentary on the boys who were bedraggled and acting as though ghosts were after them.

"Still want Bradford for Halloween King?" Madeleine asked Brooke.

"They all look like they did more than run through a cemetery," Rebecca muttered.

"They have to be on *something* to spout that rubbish," Maisie said, eyeing off Chance on whom she had a huge crush.

"Or they're just trying to get one over on us,"

Brooke spat. "How *dare they* take the limelight away from me." She crossed her arms and her brow furrowed. "And *no,* Madeleine, I don't want him for king if he's going to spout that rubbish."

Madeleine glanced over her shoulder at their friends and rolled her eyes. Brooke had to make everything about her.

"Well, *I,* for one, want to get back to dancing," Michaela declared and checked the clock on the wall. "Only ten minutes to go until king and queen are crowned." She couldn't wait to see who did get the vote since she'd helped Rinniford rig them so any votes for Brooke and Bradford were evenly spread among the other nominees. That meant Brooke and Bradford would receive no votes at all.

"Now, boys." Mrs Mitabne tried to calm them down along with the other teachers who were there. "I have no idea what you're on, drank, or smoked, but I will have none of that here at Westwood High. Empty your pockets." She realised their costumes may not have any. "The ones under your costumes, if you have any."

Dazed, the boys emptied the pockets of their shorts or pants under their costumes to show they had nothing on them except their phones.

"See!" Bradford exclaimed. "We're not on anything. Zombies are *really* coming."

Bang, bang, bang!

"Argh!" The boys jumped away from the double doors. "Don't open them!"

"Oh, for goodness sake. Stand aside; it's probably

the police coming to look for all of you. Stand back."

"No, miss, no," Chance pleaded, backing up with the rest of his friends. "No one open that door."

"Boys, stop!" the principal demanded sternly and eyed them up and down. "You're being ridiculous." She unlocked the bolts and swung open the doors. "Yes, can I…he…lp…you…" Her eyes widened, her mouth dropped, and her hands let go of the doors.

"Hello, dearie, we've just come for a dance," Mildred told her and proceeded into the gym.

"T-told you!" Bradford stuttered, and made a run for it.

Screams and cries echoed around the gym as the kids saw the zombies and scattered for other exits, running one another over, knocking each other down in the frenzy to get out and away from the herd of the undead.

"Ow, my crown," Brooke cried as it flew from her head and she was flattened beneath other kids. "Get off me."

The undead walked to the middle of the gym, stood under the bright lights, and started dancing. As couples, they swished around the floor, as singles, they danced in groups of three or four, and regardless of what song was playing, they did it anyway because they loved dancing and weren't about to let death stop them from enjoying themselves.

The teachers looked on in horror and shock, and as for the kids who were still waiting to get out of the gym, they stopped and watched, realising the undead weren't after them at all.

And that's when Brooke noticed that her crown had somehow managed to find its way into the crowd of zombies. Torn between getting out and retrieving her crown, Brooke hesitated, and saw Petulia awkwardly pick it up and place it on her head. "Hey, that's mine!" she yelled.

Petulia turned and took a few steps in Brooke's direction.

"Doesn't matter, you can have it," Brooke called, and gathering the frilly skirt of her dress, she hightailed it out of the gym.

DON'T SCREAM IT'S OVER

They tore through the forest, running as fast as they could, not stopping, not looking back. They ran on, dodging trees and bushes, and rocks and animals, the only other stupid beings that were out late at night.

"Argh." She fell face first and scored a mouthful of dirt and leaves.

"Come on," he panted, grabbing her hand and helping her up. "We have to keep going." They ran on, but she soon stopped.

"I can't," she gasped, trying to catch her breath. "I can't breathe anymore. Everything hurts, and my lungs are burning."

"We must," he urged her on. "Or we are dead. Come." Holding hands, they ran on, hearing them come in the distance.

She stopped again. "I cannot. Everything hurts." Bending, she leaned on her knees and gulped in air. "I would rather they kill me."

"Don't say, that," he begged. "Come on." He dragged her, moving on, albeit at a slower pace, until they came to the bridge. "Come, we must hurry across." They started over, trying to keep their footsteps quiet and trying not to look down at the hundred foot drop to the water below. "Quickly, they're coming."

The screams tore through the forest behind them, after them, haunting them. Echoing through the night, reverberating off everything around it.

"Come, quickly." They raced across the bridge and made it to the shadows of the other side before the creatures made it to the bridge.

The screaming stopped.

"Now where have they gone?" Clarissa clenched her fists by her side. "I thought we had them."

"So did I." Violet looked down at the water below. "Did they fall?"

"I don't think so." Poppy looked at both of her sisters. "I think they made it across the bridge."

The sisters stared across the river and into the dark forest.

"Well, we're not about to find them now." Clarissa sighed. "And we can't cross over because it's not our territory, so it's off limits. How did they get away?"

The sisters turned to go back when they saw Eugenie slowly floating towards them.

"What happened?" Clarissa demanded. "They could have only got away if you let them. You were the one guarding that side."

"I know, and I'm sorry," Eugenie wailed, her voice croaky. "But it's my throat. You know it's been bad lately."

"Oh, for God's sake." Violet rolled her eyes.

"You're a *banshee*; you *can't* have a bad throat. It's not part of the job description."

"I know, I know." Eugenie wrung her hands. "I don't know what's going on. I've never had a bad throat in all of my days. Yet for some reason, it's been funny lately." She rubbed her throat to emphasis her words.

"Funny how?" Poppy asked. As the youngest, she always cared about her sisters and their wellbeing. "Funny sore, funny burn, funny weird?"

"Not its usual self," Eugenie told her. "I've had all of that. Some burning, some pain. I can't scream as I used to. At least, like a couple of weeks ago. I was fine *then*. So what's happened now?"

"Have you been drinking tea with honey?" Clarissa asked as they floated towards home. "Tea with lemon?"

"I've tried those," Eugenie croaked, feeling the burning pain down the side of her throat. "Maybe I have an allergy."

"Oh, don't be ridiculous," Clarissa chastised. "You've never had allergies in your life, and you're one hundred and three. Neither have I, or Violet, or Poppy, for that matter. There must be something else wrong."

"Why can't I have allergies?" Eugenie asked. "There's a first time for everything, and this is the first time I've had a bad throat," she paused, "well, the last few weeks, anyway."

"Maybe you should see the doctor." Poppy floated back and forth in front of her sisters, bringing them to a halt. "Have you tried Mama's remedies?"

"They didn't work," Eugenie told her.

"So then, you need to see a doctor." Poppy shrugged and they moved on. "You should make an appointment for tomorrow. Doctor Ghoulash is wonderful. He helped my friend with her headaches. Said she needed to stop letting her husband drill holes in her head. And my friend, Melany…" She stopped them again. "She was having issues with her children."

"Which one?" Violet asked.

"All of them," Poppy went on. "Those pesky little buggers refused to be toilet trained and kept peeing against the furniture."

"That's what happens when you're half werewolf," Clarissa murmured. "You have to toilet train puppies before children."

They arrived home to find their parents reading in front of the fire. "Hello Mama, hello Papa." They kissed their parents' cheeks and warmed themselves in front of the fireplace.

"And how did tonight go?" Persimmon asked. She was currently the head Banshess of the community and was seen as a role model and mentor for other young banshees in the area.

"It would have worked out great had Eugenie not spoiled everything," Clarissa complained. "She let them get away."

"I didn't let them get away," Eugenie fretted. "It's my throat. It's still playing up and I couldn't scream like I normally can. So while I was having a coughing fit—"

"She let them get away," Clarissa finished for her. "Pathetic!"

"Clarissa," her father chastised. "We do not criticise our kin. We respect and defend." Vardaark, a seer of the highest order, was the current leader of the community. Blinded from the womb, he always knew what his life would be and how it would turn out. The fact he could not see like normal people, helped him have no preconceptions of appearance and personality. That was why he'd fallen in love with a banshee.

"Yes, Papa," Clarissa murmured, thoroughly chastised. "Sorry, Eugenie."

"Go suck a lemon, Clarissa. My throat's killing me," Eugenie wailed softly.

"Eugenie," Persimmon chided. "Be nice. She apologised."

"Only because Papa told her off," Eugenie said. "None of your methods have worked, Mama. My throat's still bad and I can't scream. What am I going to do?"

"I suggested she see Doctor Ghoulash tomorrow," Poppy interjected. "She should, shouldn't she, Mama?" As the youngest, she always wanted her mama to know she was helpful.

"Yes, Poppy, she should." Persimmon stared from one daughter to the other. "Since my methods haven't worked, maybe he has something new for you to try. Why don't you go over there first thing in the morning and see if he can fit you in? It could just be a cold or flu since it's nearly winter. It is getting cold earlier and you girls are always out late. Are you wearing enough warm clothes?"

"Yes, Mama," they chorused.

"Maybe you should drink a hot lemon water with honey before you go to bed each night just to be on the safe side. It will keep your throats soothed. A good steam would help too. A nice hot shower, or a bucket of boiling water and you hold your head over it with a towel over your head. A good steaming can do wonders for opening up the larynx and pharynx. Try it before you go to bed and see how you are in the morning."

"Okay, Mama. I'll do that now." Eugenie kissed her cheek. "Goodnight. Goodnight Papa." She kissed him and floated upstairs with her sisters.

"How did we have four such boisterous daughters?" Vardaark asked, going back to his Braille book.

"Because we couldn't have boys for some reason," Persimmon murmured and remembered back to the four baby boys she had given birth to. Due to extensive deformities, they had not survived past a few hours.

"I know, my love." Vardaark tilted his head in her direction. "I know it was hard, and I know they were not meant to be. But we have our girls."

Persimmon smiled sadly. Reaching out for her husband's hand, she squeezed it and added softly, "and each other."

*****

After a good steaming and a cup of lemon and honey

tea, Eugenie had gone to bed with high expectations. But in the morning when she went downstairs to wish her parents good morning, her voice came out in a croak. "Oh no, what's happened now?"

"Oh, dear." Persimmon checked her daughter's throat, feeling for swollen glands. "I think you've finally come down with something."

"What!" Eugenie's voice cracked. "What have I come down with? How can I come down with it? I can't come down with anything. I'm a banshee; I need my voice."

"Then you'd better get your throat over to Doctor Ghoulash because I have no idea what else to do." Persimmon checked her other daughters. "Sore throats?"

"No."

"No swollen glands, either," she said. "Off you go, Eugenie. See if you can get in sooner rather than later."

"Okay," Eugenie managed in a small voice and floated over to the coat rack by the door. She morosely donned and buttoned her coat up before going out into the chilly air, and closing the door behind her. She floated down the street and across the field to the doctor's house which had an office on one side of the building. Entering, she heard a little bell above the door chime, and the three patients in the waiting room looked up, along with Epiphany, the receptionist.

"Hi, Eugenie, what are *you* doing here?" Epiphany asked. The whole town knew the family and revered the parents.

"I have a bad throat," Eugenie said. "Is there a chance I can see the doctor?"

"Ooh, that sounds bad." Epiphany screwed up her face. "Not good for a banshee. Let me check." She looked through that day's schedule. "You can pop in after Mister Wolf." She pointed to the gentleman with the big ears, nose and mouth. "All three will be in front of you."

"Okay. I'll wait. Book me in." Eugenie morosely floated over to a seat and sat down; waiting the half an hour it took before she could get in.

The doctor opened this door and bade goodbye to Mister Wolf. "Eugenie, you're next." He watched her enter his office and closed the door after her. She sat down and he whipped out her file from behind his desk. "Ah, empty. You've never been to me before."

"No," she croaked. "Never been sick before." Staring forlornly at him, she waited for the bad news.

"Ah, now that sounds bad. Not good for a banshee," Dr Ghoulash said. "Have your mother's remedies not helped?" He walked around the desk and pointed to the exam table. "Hop up on the bed and I'll examine you."

"No," Eugenie said. "I've tried all manner of remedies, and even she's surprised they haven't worked." She settled in a seated position on the table and waited.

The doctor dug his fingers into her neck and played it like a piano. His eyes closed, he felt her collarbone to her shoulders, then over her shoulders to her back ,and back to her neck. Making note of her bones and spinal discs, he opened his eyes and made notes on her file for a few moments, and then grabbed a stick and told her to open wide.

"Open what wide?" she asked, having never been to him before she had no idea what he was doing, but hoped *he* knew what he was doing.

Smiling, he nudged his wire-framed glasses up the bridge of his nose with his forefinger knuckle. "Open your mouth wide. I need to take a look inside."

"Oh." She blushed and opened wide.

Picking up his torch, he shined it into her mouth while poking the stick inside. "Say ah."

"Ah," she repeated.

"Mmm…" He leaned closer and poked the stick farther. "And again."

"And again," she managed around the stick.

Dr Ghoulash chuckled. "Say, ah, again."

"Oh, ah." Embarrassed, she kept her gaze on the ceiling.

"Mmm." He directed his torch closer and poked the back of her throat with the stick. "Once more, and make it a long one."

"Aaaaaahhhhhhhh…"

The doctor retreated, threw the stick in the bin, and set the torch down. "You, young lady, have a very serious problem."

"What!" Eugenie croaked in shock. "What? What's wrong with me? Am I really sick and dying? Oh, my God, I'm dying, aren't I? Oh, my God, I'm dying."

She started to wail, but with her throat as bad as it was, she couldn't even get to one one-hundredth of her normal shriek.

"No, no, calm down," the doctor placated her. "Come and sit down and I'll tell you what the problem is." He waited for her to be seated before seating himself and making notes in her file.

"Well, if I'm not dying, what's the problem?" Eugenie asked, wringing her hands.

"You're losing your voice," Ghoulash told her and made some more notes.

"What!" she tried to shriek, but it came out in a croak. "*What do you mean* I'm losing my voice? I can't lose my voice, it's my lifeline, in my blood, it's what I do, what I'm made to do, I can't lose my voice. I'll, I'll, I'll…" Running out of words, she burst into tears and fled the surgery. Flying home, she flew into her house and threw herself at her parents' feet. "I'm dying."

"Hardly, Eugenie." Her father laid his hand on her head. "You didn't listen to the doctor, did you?"

"I did, Papa. I did," she wailed.

"He did not say you were dying, did he?" Vardaark continued, using his inner sight to see through her eyes.

"N-n-no," she stuttered through her tears and looked up at him.

"What did he *actually* say, Eugenie?" he asked.

She sobbed. "That I'm losing my voice."

"Oh," Persimmon gasped and pulled her daughter to her feet. "Exactly what did he say? Tell me." She grasped her firmly by the arms and made her daughter look at her.

"That I was losing my voice," Eugenie repeated.

"And what else?" her mother persisted. For one of her daughters to lose their voice, oh, would bring shame to the family.

"I don't think so, my dear." Vardaark turned his head to his wife. "There will be no shame because our daughter is *not* losing her voice. She ran out before the doctor could tell her more. So, I suggest you take her back and find out *in full* what's going on. Run along now, while he has no other patients."

Persimmon, glad for her husband's sight and abilities, took her daughter by the arm and flew her back to the surgery.

"He's waiting," Epiphany said and waved them into his office.

"Ah," Dr Ghoulash said. "I figured you'd bring her back. She flew out of here before I could finish explaining."

"Then please do, Doctor." Persimmon seated Eugenie and then herself. "Because the way my daughter tells it, she's losing her voice, and we can't have that." She took note of the lack of wedding ring and the good looks of the handsome doctor, and silently debated which daughter to try and marry him off to.

"As I was trying to explain to your daughter before she flew out of here," Ghoulash chuckled, "she *is* losing her voice due to the serious infection she's contracted. The rawness of the throat, the swelling of the glands, I'd say she has multiple infections, and *will* require surgery."

"What!" Persimmon's eyes widened. "What sort of infection would require that?"

"Tonsillitis, for a start." Ghoulash picked up his notes and read the list off. "From the look of it, it's more extensive. Potential pharyngitis and laryngitis, which is what will result in the loss of voice. We remove the infected tonsils and you won't have that problem anymore. But, due to the current infection, it's attacked the whole throat and voice box, so, you won't be able to talk for quite some time. Shriek, either."

"But I'm a banshee," Eugenie croaked. "It's what I do."

"Not anymore, you won't. And if you try it while your throat is that bad, then you could do more damage to your voice box and destroy it completely. You don't want to lose your voice completely, do you?" The doctor looked at her with concern and noticed the mother eyeing him off. Not that it was the first time a mother had tried pairing off her daughter with him.

"N-no," Eugenie whimpered and frantically turned to her mother, clinging to her hands.

"Then you'll have to stop talking." The doctor wrote out a script for painkillers and pulled out a packet of throat lozenges from his desk drawer. "These have antiseptic in them. *Three a day* only." He handed them over and escorted them out to reception. "Epiphany will schedule your surgery for the day after tomorrow. I'll see you then." He laid a hand on Eugenie's arm. "And remember, no talking." Smiling, he bade them goodbye and escorted the next patient into his office.

"Okay, let's see, we can fit you in at three p.m. how does that sound?" Epiphany glanced up from the calendar.

"That's fine, thank you," Persimmon told her and took the appointment card she was handed. "Let's go, sweetie, we have to let your sisters know." They flew home and prepared dinner, and once the family was gathered, she told her other daughters. "So, there will be no scares in the next few weeks. Not while Eugenie can't shriek. She'll need to rest after surgery, and then do vocal scales before going out again."

"Oh, how awful," Poppy murmured. "You can't speak at all?" She watched her sister sadly shake her head and morosely nibble on her food.

"You will be fine, my child," her father told her. "You will be back to shrieking on Halloween just as usual. Do not worry about it; it's just a temporary setback." He reached out and squeezed her hand.

She squeezed back and tried to finish her dinner.

After washing the dishes and putting them away, the four girls sat down for a chat before bed. But Eugenie, feeling sorry for herself at being unable to talk, left them and went up to bed early. The day after tomorrow could not come fast enough. Nor could the day the pain in her throat stopped. The pills didn't help the pain, but the lozenges took the painful edge off, and the swelling was still there and made swallowing hard. Punching her pillow and rolling onto her side, she stared out the window and prayed for the day after tomorrow to come.

*****

Two days later, Persimmon and Poppy escorted Eugenie back to the doctor's office for surgery. They were going to wait so they could see her after.

Nurse Ghoulash, the doctor's sister, called Eugenie's name. "This way, please." She escorted Eugenie to a small room and picked up a white object. "Please change into this gown and I'll come and get you in a few minutes." She smiled and laid a reassuring hand on Eugenie's arm. "Don't worry. It won't take long and you'll be home tomorrow." She left, and Eugenie quickly changed.

Ten minutes later, she was on the bed in the operating theatre with a blanket over her and a bright light above her.

"Don't worry, Eugenie, it will all be over soon. You just sleep." Dr Ghoulash placed a face mask over her mouth and she breathed in…

*****

"Eugenie, sweetie? It's Mama. Are you okay?" Persimmon brushed her daughter's hair back and saw her eyes slowly open. "Eugenie?"

Breathing in, Eugenie opened her eyes to see her mother and Poppy and opened her mouth.

"No speaking, now." The doctor looked over her. "The surgery is over. It went well. I removed both tonsils and have given you something for the bleeding and swelling. We'll keep you in overnight, and tomorrow, you can go home."

"When can she shriek again?" Poppy asked, eyeing off the good doctor's physique.

"She may not be able to for a month or so. Definitely no talking for at least a week. Lots of bed rest, lots of cool herbal tea and chicken soup. The rest of the infection will slowly heal from the antibiotics we're giving her, but won't fully be gone for a couple of weeks, I'm afraid. So again, lots of bed rest, tea and soup. You need to fight off a nasty infection." He glanced at Persimmon. "You can have another couple of minutes, and then you need to go."

"Of course, Doctor, and thank you." Persimmon kissed her daughter's forehead. "We'll go now, sweetie, and pick you up tomorrow. You rest. We'll see you then."

"Bye, Eugenie." Poppy kissed her cheek and followed her mother out the door.

Eugenie breathed in…

*****

The next day, Eugenie was picked up and taken home, tucked into bed and given lots of herbal tea and chicken soup. It continued that way day after day, with visits to the doctor and quiet talking.

Eugenie could talk softly as to not strain her voice box, but Halloween was fast approaching and she was panicking. Every Halloween they always went out to scare the trick or treating children in the nearby villages. But if she couldn't this year, well… bugger!

*****

Four weeks in, and the day of All Hallows' Eve came with Eugenie meeting with the doctor.

He examined her neck and shoulders, playing them like a piano as he had all those weeks ago. He examined her throat in the same manner, and declared her fit for duty. "I don't know about shrieking, but I'd say you were pretty close to being one hundred percent healed and ready to go."

"Oh, thank you, Doctor." Eugenie impulsively grabbed him by the face and kissed his cheek. "It's Hallows' Eve and I must fly. My sisters are already out there chasing children down." Glancing at the wall clock, she fled the surgery, mainly to join her sisters, but also because she was embarrassed at having kissed the doctor. Flying home, she started her vocal scales and ran through them with her mother for a good fifteen minutes.

"Come on, Mama," she whined. "I need to go; the girls are already out there having fun."

"Patience, child," her mother said. "After what you've been through, if we don't do it right you'll do *more* damage. Another fifteen minutes. And again."

Annoyed, Eugenie continued the scales until she could shatter glass. "Sorry. Can I go now?"

"Well, I see you're at your peak." Persimmon glanced at the glass. "Off you go. Your sisters are over near *Timber Falls*. It will take you about fifteen minutes—"

"I'll speed," Eugenie butted in and kissed her parents. "See you later." On leaving home, she flew straight up and sped off for *Timber Falls*, the fancy resort-style town that was newly built for humans who liked to ski and hunt. Hearing her sisters in the distance, she put on a burst of speed and raced towards them until she could see them circling a spot in the distance. Noticing which positions there were in, she knew exactly which manoeuvre they were trying to execute. With a clap of thunder, she increased her momentum and when she was close enough, opened her mouth, breathed in, and let out a shriek that could burst eardrums and explode heads. Her sisters heard her, saw her coming, and went into a dive bomb.

She was back, baby!

DON'T FEED AFTER MIDNIGHT

"So, dude, what are you going to buy with your birthday money?" Billy Mumford asked his friend, Ryan Lennon as they cruised the mall on a Saturday afternoon. They'd met up with their friends Coby Smears and Teddy Dartford to try and find Ryan something to blow his money on.

"I have no idea," Ryan replied. "And this money's burning a hole in my pocket."

"How much did you get?" Coby asked, envious that Ryan had received money for his birthday when all he'd received was socks and jocks. 'Cause a teenage boy *really* wanted *those* for his birthday.

"A hundred." Ryan pulled his wallet from his pocket, attached by a chain to his belt, and opened it to flash five twenty dollar notes. "But that's from everyone in the family. My parents, both sets of grandparents, and my aunt and uncle all dipped in twenty so it would add up. I was after that new telescope I saw a couple of months ago, but I don't know if I want it now." He shoved his wallet back into his pocket and they kept on walking. "I don't know what I want anymore. I don't really need anything, and nothing really interests me. So…" Shrugging, he stopped and looked around the mall. Sports stores, clothing stores, music shops. None of them held any interest. "Maybe I should just keep it until I do find something. Ask for money for Christmas as well and then buy something mega awesome."

"Do you really want to wait that long?" Teddy shoved his hands in his jeans pockets and tried to look cool, despite his name. "Christmas *is* four months away."

"Yeah…" Ryan glanced up and down the mall. "I have no idea what I want to buy *now*, so I may as well keep it."

"Have we checked the side streets? We haven't checked out the side streets yet," Billy babbled. "There's all sorts of stores off the mall. You might find something in one of them. Let's go down one side and up the other. Then it will be time to head home."

They headed off down the mall and into the first side street, finding a couple of knick-knack shops for tourists. Moving on, they scoured side street after side street until they ended up in the last one at the end of the mall. Coming across nothing of interest, they grabbed food from the burger shop on the corner and quickly ate it.

"Well, that was a bust," Ryan complained. "Nothing. Zip, zilch, nada. Guess I'll be saving my money for Christmas after all."

Teddy had been staring out the window. The

burger shop was just down the mall from the last street, but had a view of the square that was behind the mall. He noticed the small stores around the square and said, "We didn't check out those stores."

The others looked in the direction he was pointing and turned to each other, their excitement renewed.

"Come on," Billy cried and hastily dumped his rubbish in the bin.

The others did the same and followed him across the street and down to the small square that backed up against the mall.

"There's the last street we went down." Billy stopped to look at the wall that cut off the lane and then glanced around the small green square. Tiny shops spread around two sides of it while the main road butted against the fourth. "Let's start at the beginning and we'll head home when we're done." He led them to the first store, a small art and craft shop selling paintings, jewellery, and decorative handmade goods.

Moving on, they found Ryan a few interesting trinkets for a few dollars, and bought some things for themselves. When they came to the end of one side, they stopped and peered down the tiny little alley poking into the corner of two streets.

"Nothing there," Ryan mumbled and walked on.

But Teddy had been peering down the alley in the late afternoon shadows and spied a small double-sided whiteboard outside what looked to be a door. "Wait," he called. "There's a shop down there."

The others turned back and hurried over to him, looking to where he was pointing.

"Let's check it out, at least," Teddy encouraged, and wandered off towards the shop.

Coming to a stop outside the door, they read the white billboard. "Canonfire Toys and Terrors, where play turns to nightmare. Enter if you dare."

"Sounds cool," Billy said. "Let's go in." He shoved the door open and heard the bell tinkle above his head. The shop was cluttered with rows of shelves filled with all manner of toys and tidbits, but the dim lighting made it hard to tell with a glance. They slowly made their way down aisle after aisle, found trinkets of interest, and multiple smaller rooms down a hall off the main one.

"Blech, look at this." Teddy held up a tub of cosmic jelly that was black with spider legs poking out of it. "Gross."

"Googly eyeglasses, whoopee cushions, glow in the dark stuff, pretty much everything you can get in most shops now," Billy complained, and added a tub of cosmic jelly to his growing list of things he was buying.

"Yeah, but there's other cool stuff too." Coby held up a tub of sea monkeys. "You don't get these in normal shops."

"True," Billy agreed and kept on moving.

"Are we back in the hallway? Which way do we go?" Teddy asked, noticing the same poster. "I think we've been here. Which way now?"

They found themselves back in the main shop

and looked around.

"Are there any more rooms off this one? I feel like we went round and round in circles." Ryan scratched his head and looked around. "And there's no shopkeeper. You guys see anyone else in here?"

"Nope." Teddy felt a gust of air behind him and spun around to find a short, grey-haired old man in a dusty grey cardigan, brown pants, and old man slippers.

He pushed his gold-rimmed spectacles up his nose and eyed the boys up and down. "Can I help you boys with something?"

"Argh." The rest of the boys spun around and stared at the old man.

"Ah, just ah," Ryan stumbled on his words. "Wondering if we'd finished looking, or if there are more rooms."

"Oh…I think you've seen everything," the old man said and shuffled behind the counter. "Do you want to pay now?"

"Um, yeah. I will." Teddy stepped up to the counter and laid his items on it.

Billy and Coby crowded around him, but Ryan stood back. He hadn't found anything to buy and still had over eighty dollars in his wallet. While he waited, his gaze wandered around the store and found a half open door he didn't think they'd gone through. Curious, he walked over to it and peered through the gap, seeing shelves and shelves of small plastic aquariums and containers. They looked empty.

"Don't go in there," the old man snapped and

hurried over. "That room is off limits." He shut the door and stared at the boy in front of him. "Only people who know what they're doing can go into that room." Moving Ryan away from the door, he went back behind the counter.

"What they're doing with what?" Ryan asked. "All I saw was empty plastic fish tanks and containers on shelves. Who needs to know what about them?"

"They're not empty," the man said, and closed the till after the last sale. "They have very special creatures in them that need to be taken care of, and not by hooligan teens like you."

"Hey!" Ryan protested. "You certainly didn't mind taking my friends' money and yet you call us hooligan teens. That's a bit rich."

"Yes, well..." The old man drew his cardigan around him. "The items in that room are not toys and need very particular care. Besides, you couldn't afford them and would probably let them die."

"And that's an assumption based on what?" Coby asked. "You just took our money and yet you keep insulting us. That's not fair. What's in the room?" He moved towards it, but the old man stepped in front of him.

Ryan took that moment to rush over to the door and into the room.

"No," the old man cried, his arms extending towards Ryan. "Get out of there." He rushed after him and found the boy peering into the tanks curiously. "Get out. Get out now, this instant."

The other boys had rushed in after them and

stood wide-eyed in the room. Every wall had shelves from floor-to-ceiling filled with empty tanks.

"There's nothing in them," Coby muttered. "What's the big deal?"

"The big deal is there are animals in those tanks. Very special animals that need very special care and attention from people who will understand the rules and follow them to the letter. Unlike you hooligan boys who have already shown that you can't be trusted by bursting into a room I said was off limits. You've already shown you're untrustworthy. Now get out." He pushed his spectacles up the bridge of his nose. "You've already proved I was right."

Billy, Coby and Teddy turned around and headed out the door, but Ryan had been intently peering into the tanks and reading the care instructions on the side. "Do not feed after midnight, do not get wet, do not let out into sunlight." He came across an African plains scene with tiny hills, logs and trees, and a river that sparkled. Tiny plastic animals covered the ground. "They're plastic!" He spun around to face the old man and his friends who'd stopped and turned around at the sound of his voice. "They're just tiny little plastic toys. They're not real. So why would you need to feed them or not get them wet? That's just stupid."

"It's not stupid," the old man barked. "They're magical animals that need to be looked after by adults who have the respect to follow the rules. *Unlike you.* So you would not make a good owner. Get out."

Ryan ignored him and kept looking, amused and

bewildered by the toys in the tanks. "What happens if you *do* feed them after midnight, or get them wet, or take them out into the sun? Do they die, multiply, turn into Gremlins?" He'd seen the old *Gremlins* movies many times and was finding the situation very similar to this.

"This is not the movies, young man," the old man spat. "Now get out. Or I'll—"

"You'll what?" Ryan dared him and found one of prehistoric times. Tiny dinosaurs, spiders and snakes roamed a green field. It was similar to Jurassic Park, and he'd noticed that many scenes in the tanks were similar to movies, if not straight out of movies. And loving movies as he did, he pointed to the dinosaur tank. "I'll take this one."

"You won't take any," the man said, and grabbed him by the arm, dragging him out of the room.

Ryan managed to grab a hold of the tank's handle and allowed the man to pull him out, holding it behind his back so no one saw it.

The old man shut and locked the door, unaware of what had happened. "If one of those tanks so much as leaves the room, we are all doomed," he muttered and turned around.

"Like this one?" Ryan held up the tank and watched the old man go as grey as his dusty cardigan. "One of those tanks *has* left the room. Why are we all doomed?"

The old man could barely breathe. "How…dare… you…" Gasping, he crossed himself and pulled out the gold cross pendant from under his shirt. Kissing it, he motioned another cross. "What have you done? You have no idea what you've done."

"What I've done is pull a tank out of that room and I want to buy it." Ryan looked for a price tag, but couldn't find one. "How much?"

"They're not for sale and cannot leave that room, let alone the store." The old man hastened behind the counter to put distance between himself and the tank.

Ryan pulled out his wallet and counted. "I have $83.55. Here." He put all of the money on the counter. "It's all I've got, so I'm taking it." Holding up the tank, he stared into the tiny Jurassic scene. "Don't worry, if they're like sea monkeys, they won't grow, but I'll follow the instructions to a T. Thanks for a cool birthday present." He led the boys outside and held up the tank for them to see before walking off down the street.

The old man chuckled to himself and pocketed the money. "Ah, that old routine gets them every time."

*****

The boys arrived back at Ryan's late that afternoon and Ryan cleared off a shelf on the bookcase next to his desk and sat the fish tank on it. He stared at the scene inside it and wondered why he'd wanted it so badly.

"I *cannot* believe you bought that thing," Billy muttered. He crossed his arms and stood staring at it. "It's just tiny little plastic figurines and foam to look like Jurassic Park or something. *Why* would you buy that?"

"*Why* would you pay $83.55 for a fish tank? I wouldn't fork out money like that. Hell, I never even *have* money like that," Teddy added, envious that Ryan had so much money. He was lucky if he got *twenty* dollars for his birthday.

"I don't know," Ryan said slowly and stroked his chin in thought. "There's just something about it, something about the way the old man acted, made it all mysterious and a secret. Like it was some big secret no one should know about."

"Yeah, I get that. But $83.55 for it," Billy said. "*Way* too much. Was there even a price on it?"

Ryan turned the tank around, looked on the bottom and top, but found no price tag. He settled the tank back with the instructions facing out. "Only feed grass cuttings and dead ants between 6 a.m. and 6 p.m. each day, and do not feed after midnight. Do not get wet, do not take out into the sun. After a week you should see growth. Animals will grow no higher than one inch, *unless* rules are disobeyed. *These are not sea monkeys.*"

"No, they're not," Coby murmured. "You do realise that dinosaurs ate each other and I have no idea why spiders and snakes are in there. The current species are not from the Jurassic era."

"*So what!*" Ryan turned to his friends. "I think it's cool."

"What? A plastic fish tank full of tiny plastic

dinosaurs that are supposed to grow to an inch in height is cool? You know if there's a T.rex in there he'll eat the others. And the whole, feed them grass cuttings and dead ants thing, that's just weird," Coby said.

"Yeah, it's all weird. But something made me want it, and yes, I should've got a price instead of just dumping my money on the counter. It may not have been as much as $83.55, but I wasn't taking no for an answer, and he was telling me no."

"And he made $83.55 out of you," Billy retorted. "He fooled you."

"Maybe, maybe not. It's after six now so they can't be fed for today. I'll feed them tomorrow, and then next week we'll see how much they've grown."

"Okay, but I still say you've been duped," Billy replied.

*****

Every day for the next week, Ryan diligently fed the plastic animals grass cuttings and dead ants, by placing them in the tank each day, and each day he found them missing. He obeyed the rules, and didn't feed after 6 p.m. or midnight, didn't get them wet, and kept them out of the sunlight. And every day he took a picture of the scenes in the tank, but didn't notice much difference. Since the food disappeared, he was curious as to what was going on, and set up a camera that he aimed at the tank on Friday night.

On Saturday, the boys huddled around the tank

and peered at the Jurassic land, trying to figure out if they'd grown.

"It's certainly not an inch, so that was a lie," Billy said while they waited for Ryan to put the photos and film on his laptop.

"No, definitely not an inch," Teddy added. "But something seems different. I just can't put my finger on it."

"That's the feeling I got," Ryan told him. "I sensed there was something different, but couldn't figure it out, so I took the pictures. Here we go." He brought up the first one on the screen and carefully forwarded through the week's worth of photos. The boys leaned in close to stare at the screen.

"Can't see any difference," Coby said and then thrust his arm forward, his finger pointing at the screen. "Go back."

"To where?" Ryan asked and clicked the back button.

"Those." Coby eagerly leaned closer to the screen. "Set up another screen so we can compare them side by side." He waited and leaned even closer. "There. They've moved. Did you move them?"

The other boys leaned in to look at what he was pointing to and noticed that the tiny plastic toys had indeed moved from their original spots to another. They had also grown, but not by much.

"They could have just moved every time he moved the tank to feed them," Billy argued. "It's probably normal movement."

"No." Ryan shook his head and looked at his

friend. "I'm very careful and put it on my desk. I slide the vent across and drop the grass and ants in, slide the vent back, take the picture, and then put the tank back. They don't move. Nothing moves."

"Well, they *certainly have* moved," Coby pointed out. "And have only grown, what, half a centimetre?"

"Maybe I'm not feeding them enough," Ryan murmured. "Maybe they need more food. Let's watch the video." He clicked on the file and up it came.

"Whoa!" Four sets of eyes widened and they leaned closer to see the tiny plastic animals moving and chasing each other around the tank.

"That…can't…be…" Ryan's gaze was glued to the screen as tiny dinosaurs moved around the tanks. "Oh…my…"

"*That cannot be real!*" Billy straightened and stared wide-eyed from the screen to the tank and back. "It just can't be. You playing tricks on us, Ryan?"

"No, dude, I swear I'm not." Ryan put his hands up in protest. "I only set the camera up last night and let it run until I got up when I stopped it. That's all."

They continued watching as T.rex chased all the dinosaurs, the diplodocus ate from the tiny trees, the triceratops fought with each other, and the snake slithered over the whole tank.

"This…is just…unreal…" Ryan muttered and inhaled a deep breath, holding it in a moment before releasing it. "They're real."

Teddy scratched his head in bewilderment and stared at the footage. "I cannot believe I'm watching this. They're just little plastic figures glued to foam dirt and mountains and grass. They *can't* be real."

"They have to be because they're moving," Ryan argued and shook his head. "They have to be and I've got real dinosaurs." He swung around in his gas lift desk chair to face his friends. "I've got real dinosaurs," he crowed. "For $83.55 I've got a tank of real dinosaurs. Yes!" He double fist pumped and swung back around to the laptop screen. "Yes."

Billy, Teddy and Coby traded glances behind his back and then moved their gaze to the tank on Ryan's shelf. Sea monkeys were weird enough and weren't actually real, but to have a plastic fish tank full of real live dinosaurs seemed all too *unreal*, too ridiculous, too fantastical, and way too unbelievable. There had to be something else going on and maybe they should go back to the shop.

Ryan shut down the file and sat staring at the tank. "Maybe we should wait another week to see if they grow to an inch, and if not, maybe I need to feed them differently."

✳✳✳✳✳

For the next week, Ryan added more grass clippings and dead ants to the tank, took pictures every day, and set the camera up to catch the live footage.

And once again, the feed was eaten; the plastic figurines grew and ran around the tank in the middle of the night.

Come Saturday, the boys gathered around Ryan's

desk and stared down into the tank, looking at the toys which now stood one inch in height.

"Okay…" Billy murmured. "It took *two weeks* to grow to that height. So that was a lie."

"But they *did* grow," Ryan said, resting his crossed arms on the desk and looking in the tank. Every figurine was more noticeable now it was bigger. You could see the markings on fur and flesh, the tips of the armour, the claws, even the teeth of the T.rex you could see clearly. And it was all too surreal for Ryan.

"I think I should feed them even more and see if they grow bigger," he said.

"If they get any bigger, you won't be able to control them in the tank," Coby told him. "You'll have actual man-eating dinosaurs on your hands."

"I doubt they'd get much bigger," Ryan argued. "It's already taken double the time than it said for them to reach an inch in height. They may grow to two inches, or three—"

"Or three feet or four feet, or ten or twenty," Billy argued back. "Yes, they've grown, and yes, they move, so yes there's clearly something going on with them, but you have absolutely no idea how big they could grow and why would you want to find out? Why can't you just be happy with them the way they are? If they grow big enough to hurt animals, or even humans, they'll either be killed, or taken away from you. Do you want that?"

"Of course not," Ryan told him. "But I also didn't believe two weeks ago that any of this was real. We all thought it was a joke."

"We did and I have to wonder what's going on," Teddy said. "Maybe we should go back to that shop and ask the old dude for more information on them."

"No, don't bother," Ryan mumbled. "I googled and couldn't find anything. I doubt he could tell us more."

"Considering he sold it to you, he probably could," Coby added. "And you're just being stubborn or stupid. Which is it?"

"Don't know, but I've got a plan…" Ryan replied.

The boys stayed for a sleepover, and later that night when the others were asleep, Ryan set his alarm for twelve-thirty and hid it under his pillow. When the time came, he managed to quickly turn it off without waking the boys and silently slipped out of bed. He grabbed the tank and set it on his desk, and using a small flashlight to see by, he slid the vent back and dumped a pile of grass cuttings and dead ants into the tank. He also poured water into the river to see what would happen. He shut the vent, replaced the tank on his shelf, and slipped back into bed.

*****

Something nudged him awake.

Probably the sliver of sunlight coming in around the blind and curtain and hitting him in the eye. He breathed in, smelled something foul, and sensed something was wrong. Turning his head, he came face to face with the T.rex. He blinked. So did Rex.

He opened his mouth. So did Rex. He screamed. So did Rex.

So did the other boys when they woke up and saw all of the dinosaurs from the tank in the room.

Ryan rolled left out of bed and landed on the floor between it and the window. He rolled under his bed as Rex jumped on it and roared. He heard his friends scream and was grabbed by the ankles and pulled out from under the bed just before the triceratops stuck his horn under it and threw the bed, and Rex, against the wall.

Ryan kicked out at what had him and managed to roll over to see the gigantic tarantula on the wall ready to reel him in. He kicked at it and rolled to the right towards his friends who were trying to dodge the dinosaurs all around the room. Managing to get to his feet, he was faced with a pterodactyl flapping its wings in the middle of the room, sitting atop the head of a diplodocus.

The boys huddled together and yelled, screamed as the dinosaurs crowded around them, suffocated them, ate them…

"Oh, for heaven's sake, *what is going on?*" Mrs Lennon said from the doorway. She flicked the light on and saw the creatures. "Ryan, where did you get these balloons from? No wonder you had nightmares. You would have thought you were being eaten." She noticed the spider and grimaced. "Ugh, can you get rid of that thing, please. You know I hate spiders."

Ryan managed to glance at his friends who were beside him on the floor and sat up. "Balloons?" He pushed one up and managed to stand between a stegosaurus and a velociraptor. Staring at every single one, he finally realised he'd been dudded. "Naw, man! They're just balloons. Bugger!" Fighting his way to the window, he pulled back the curtains and flipped up the blind.

The early morning sun hit T.rex and into a puff of air he burst. The spider, pterodactyl and triceratops followed as the sun hit them. The boys stood and shook their heads.

"Yeah, you got dudded, all right," Teddy said and shoved a diplodocus aside. "All you got was a bunch of lousy balloons, and the old dude got your $83.55."

WHO'S YOUR WEREPUPPY?

"And this is the fourth Lord Bantleroy who built the village square and surrounding buildings of the council offices, police and fire stations, the court rooms, jail, and the royal theatre," the butler, and current tour guide, Jeeves, droned.

Randy Bantleroy and his friends hovered in the doorway off the hall and watched as Jeeves took the small group of tourists on a tour of *Bantleroy Castle*. At four hundred years old, it was falling apart and in need of repairs, and since they didn't have the money, the only thing to do was offer tours to make it.

"How much are you earning out of all this?" Seth Codsworth asked his friend. They'd known each other their entire lives, well, fifteen years, eleven months and three weeks, anyway, as they'd grown up together because their families were neighbours and the kids went to the same posh school. He stuck his head into the hallway to see the group being led into the section that included the tower chamber and basement.

Randy sighed and leaned back against the wall,

his arms crossed in front of his chest. At fifteen, he was in line to be the ninth Lord Bantleroy upon his father's death, but that didn't thrill him since he'd seen how much the lifestyle cost. Not only financially, but emotionally and physically. It was wearing his parents out and the family was not a happy one at the moment. Looking up at the cracks in the hallway ceiling, he replied, "About five hundred a day."

"Whoa!" Michael Windsor's eyes widened. "And you run them six days a week, that's…three grand a week!" He attended the same posh local school as the boys but lived a county over.

"You could do a lot with that," Harrison Levi added. As the fourth member of the group, he lived on the other side of Seth and attended the school as well.

"Yeah, but with taxes and costs, what's left goes on the bills for repairs," Randy told them and cocked his head into the hallway. When he saw the coast was clear, he waved his friends on. "Come on, let's get out of here." They made their way down the main hallway, into the private quarters cut off from the tour, and up to his bedroom. Flinging himself on his bed face first, he dangled his arms and head over the side. "It's taking its toll."

"It would be." Seth shut the door and turned on the radio to their favourite rock station.

"Not too loud," Randy warned, looking up. "They'll hear. So we need to keep the noise to a minimum."

"Can they hear a radio from here?" Seth asked and turned it down.

"Travels through the vents." Randy rolled over and stared at the ceiling. The private quarters had been overhauled first as they weren't so damaged by age and wear and tear. They'd had the money for that, but not the rest of the house. And even though the local historical council was pitching in to preserve the castle, it was still going to take a lot of money and time to repair and renovate.

"What's the timeline for this then?" Harrison asked. "My olds are looking into doing up our place. We may need to sell off some land to help."

"That's what my olds are doing." Randy bent his legs and cocked one over the other, swinging it casually. "We've just sold some land to the west and are waiting for the payment to come through. Dad said it will help a lot, but not pay for it all."

"What about the Bantleroy fortune?" Michael lounged in an easy chair by the huge window that overlooked the east garden and green fields.

Randy snorted. "What fortune? It's all hearsay and no one's ever found it."

"But from the way Jeeves is going on about it on the tours, you'd think it really existed." Harrison picked up a car magazine from the floor, flipped through it, and then flung it down.

"That's the main point of the tour." Randy rolled over and sat up. "The Bantleroy fortune, the hidden treasure, money hidden in walls and wells, and jewels and gems. Apparently, it's all they want to know about."

"Which is good, because it earns you three grand

a week," Michael reminded him. "Who knows, maybe with all the renovations, you'll find it."

Snorting, Randy rolled off the other side of the bed and headed for the door. "Follow me." The boys followed him into the hallway and to one end where he stood under the first portrait of his ancestors. "Augustus Bantleroy, 1545, was dirt poor as was all of his descendants until," he walked to the opposite side of the hall, "Michael Bantleroy, 1754. Almost two hundred years plus of poverty and hard times." He walked down the hall pointing at each portrait. "He supposedly made his fortune from bootlegging, murder, torture, etc. etc. and passed it down to his son, grandson, etc. until we get to the lordship of Peter Bantleroy, the first Lord of the Bantleroy family in 1879. *He's* the one who supposedly had the fortune even though his ancestors were rich." Randy shook his head. "It's weird. We don't have money even though Dad's the eighth lord and I'll be the ninth. You'd expect if there *was* a fortune we would've had some, but Dad said by the time *his* father inherited the title, there was nothing left in the coffers and they struggled to make ends meet. He says no fortune exists, but it had to've at some point for our ancestors to build this damn castle in the first place." Shrugging, he added, "I dunno, but there is talk of another family secret that no one's telling me."

"What is it?" Michael asked, always fascinated by other people's family histories.

"I *just said*, no one's telling me." Randy rolled his eyes. "Don't you listen?"

"I thought you might've overheard something." Michael shrugged. "Just because they don't tell you doesn't mean you may not've heard anything. You said before that sound travels through the vents."

Randy pondered that a moment. "True, but no, I haven't heard any conversations, just lots of heated arguments between my olds, and I don't know if it's about the fortune, or this big secret, but it's about money. All. The. Time. So, probably more about the repairs than anything."

"What could the secret be, other than the fortune?" Harrison asked as they walked back into Randy's room.

"I dunno; they were bootleggers, but we already know that," Randy replied and stood at the window staring out.

"They were pirates," Michael offered.

"They pillaged local villages?" Seth shrugged. "What else could it be?"

"They were Dracula." Harrison snorted with laughter.

"Doctor Frankenstein," Michael added.

"Werewolves." Seth scored a filthy look from Randy for that.

"With the way *I* look, as all of my *ancestors* looked, you all think we were vampires and werewolves?" Randy questioned with a raised brow. The glowing red hair, pale complexion with freckles, and green eyes looked nothing like what Dracula or werewolves was supposed to look like.

"You never know," Seth said and threw himself onto the bed laughing hysterically. "Maybe Drac was a red-headed dude of English Irish decent."

"Blood wouldn't look out of place on you," Michael added. "Since it's red."

"And I can't really see a red-headed werewolf." Harrison grasped his sides they hurt so much. "Wouldn't know whether to laugh or cry, or run away."

Randy shook his head. "Laugh all you like, but I seriously doubt anything exists anymore, especially a treasure." Seeing that his friends weren't stopping, he added, "And we're not bloody werewolves either."

*****

October 31st, and Halloween, and the tours of *Bantleroy Castle* were extra special. The basement had finally been structurally secured under the rest of the castle, and secret passageways were added to the tour to spice things up. However, Randy witnessed something strange; his dad locking off the tower and its basement room.

Ducking behind a heavy curtain, he watched his father nervously pocket the key and head for their private quarters. "Now, what's he up to?" Randy muttered and waited for his father's footsteps to fade away before emerging from behind the curtain. He silently ran over to the door and tried it just in case. It didn't budge. "Why would he...?" Curious as to why the best part of the tour would be locked off, he decided to follow the tours for the rest of the day.

That night, his friends came over and joined in.

"So what's happened today?" Michael asked as they trailed after the five o'clock tour group. Each tour lasted two hours with a half hour break in between. They followed at a distance, listening to Jeeves drone on about the history of the castle and all of the Bantleroys.

"Not much." Randy kept his voice low. "We've added the rest of the basement and some secret passageways, but get this, Dad locked off the tower room and its basement. So we aren't going in there."

"How come?" Harrison asked as they followed the group down into the basement via a secret passage.

"Don't know. But I know he and Mum haven't been fighting today, so…" Randy shrugged. "I have no idea."

They wandered along for the rest of the tour until it was over, but took their leave while the group was escorted into the atrium at the back of the house for refreshments so they didn't collide with the next group. The boys casually and quietly wandered through the house looking for anything that would give them an idea about what was happening. Not finding anything, they waited for the next tour and found that to be uneventful as well.

It was what happened at 9:45, though, that changed the course of the evening.

Randy and his friends had freshened up in his ensuite and were on their way down for the next tour when they heard his parents talking in hushed tones. Randy quickly pulled his friends against the wall and put a finger to his lips to quieten them.

"I don't like it any more than you, Violette," Lord Randford Bantleroy the fourth murmured to his wife. "But you know this only happens on a full moon Halloween, and no other. It cannot be helped, it cannot be stopped, and one day, Randy will have to deal with this himself."

That made Randy frown and carefully peer around the corner. He saw his father wringing his hands and his mother looking pale against the darkness of the hall.

"I *know*, Randford," she fiercely whispered. "But of all nights for it to happen. Right when we're conducting a tour to bring money in for the renovations. If only that damn family of yours hadn't squandered it all we'd have the money for repairs and wouldn't have to have people through." She started pacing, two steps one way, three the other, a pattern she continued while talking. "Are you *sure* you've been over every last patch of ground *in* the castle, *on* the grounds, *in* the walls, the ceiling, the roof?"

"That's what these renovations are for," Randford told her. "Well, partly to fix the place and partly to find the treasure. We don't have the map for no reason. We just need to figure it out. But from what I can tell, it's definitely under the house."

"Then how do we find it?" Violette asked. "Why don't we tell Randy and he and his friends may be able to help."

Randford considered, for a millisecond. "You know we can't do that, especially tonight."

"No, I guess not," Violette murmured and glanced

at the clock on the wall. "Five minutes before the next tour starts. You'd better go up."

"Yes. I don't want to be here when it happens. I've avoided the moonlight all night." He pulled the key from his pocket and unlocked the door to the tower and its basement. "I'll take the map with me and try and figure it out until it happens. Lock the door behind me and keep the key safe. I'll see you tomorrow. I love you."

Randy watched his parents kiss passionately and then his dad go into the tower and his mum lock the door. She laid a hand on it, and then pocketed the key and walked away. "That was bloody strange," he murmured and left the stairwell to walk over to the tower door. He quietly turned the knob, but it didn't open. "Now, why would Dad be locked in the tower? Halloween of all nights. A full moon especially."

"Maybe he's setting something up for the next tour. Something extra scary," Seth suggested. "That was weird."

"Weird ain't the word for it." Randy turned to his friends. "We need to get that key and get into the tower. Dad's got the treasure map and says it exists. We need to see it."

"And how do we do that when your mum locked your dad in and put the key in her pocket?" Michael asked. "What's in the tower, anyway?"

"Just a room with a desk and bed. Lots of scratches on the walls. Dad said it was where they locked up the crazies in the family and that it's haunted, so it's always locked off, except for the tours, so it gives people a fright."

"And the basement?" Harrison didn't know particulars as he'd refused to set foot in it and had just stood in the doorway. Something about it had creeped him out.

"Nothing, except for a treasure exhibit," Randy told him. "But I always get a sense there was more to the whole tower than that. Something Dad never told me. Now may be the chance to find out. We just have to get in."

"The tower's not on tour tonight, so they won't come this way, will they?" Seth inquired. "We'd have time to pick the lock if we can't get the key from your mum."

"We'd better get that key then," Randy muttered and came up with a way. He snapped his fingers. "Got it! Let's go." He rushed off for the kitchen where he knew his mother would be, and quickly found her getting everything ready for the next group of tourists, and clearing up after the last group who were being escorted out.

"Hello, darling, we're a little busy right now. Did you want something? Are you boys going on the tour?" Violette placed clean cups and saucers onto trays.

"Not yet. I've been on them all day and since I know the history of the castle..." He shrugged nonchalantly. "Then I don't need to hear Jeeves drone on about it again."

Violette smiled. "It's his job, Randford, that's what he's paid to do." She loaded the dishwasher and turned it on.

"Yeah, but if the treasure is real we wouldn't need to do useless tours. Did we ever find anything?" He leaned on the island bench. "Have we ever found a coin, a jewel, a note, or anything to say it's real? Is there a book, or map, or something that would tell us where it is?" Randy had tried to remain calm through the whole conversation, but had seen his mother bristle at the word *map.*

"No, nothing, darling. Why? Plan on treasure hunting?" She kept her tone light as she passed biscuits around for the boys. "Why don't you go and join the tour anyway; it might be fun since it's close to midnight."

"Is something going to happen at midnight?" Randy asked and took a biscuit. "I see the tower's been locked off all day and isn't on the tour. But the basement and secret passageways are."

"Just thought we'd make it different for Halloween, is all." Violette removed bottles of water from the fridge. "Here, go and join the tour. Who knows, something might happen."

Putting his plan into action, Randy impulsively hugged his mother. "Thanks, Mum."

"Oh," she cried in shock, and responded in kind. "You're welcome, darling, now run along."

"Okay, come on, boys." He waved on his friends, but a spine-chilling howl stopped them in their tracks. Ears pricked and hair standing up on the back of his neck, Randy looked up in fright and then at his friends. "What was that?"

"Part of the tour," his mother said shakily behind him, making him turn to see her whiter than white complexion. "Part of the tour," she repeated softly. "Run along, boys." She ushered them towards the great hall. "Go join the tour."

The boys had barely taken five steps into the hallway off the kitchen when another howl tore through the castle and into the night.

"What *is* that?" Harrison asked and huddled closer to his friends.

"A part of the tour, Mum said," Randy replied. "But I don't see how a dog's howl would have anything to do with *Bantleroy Castle*. Come on, let's hurry." He rushed them down the hall, avoiding the tour group, and through the door to their private quarters, locking it behind him. "Right, up to the tower we go."

"You get the key?" Seth asked and saw it in his friend's hand when he held it aloft. "How?"

"When I hugged her. Stuck my hand in her pocket." Randy ran down the grey stone hall and into the hallway where the tower door was. Inserting the key, he turned it but his hand slipped from it.

"Wait," Michael whispered. "Are there lights in the tower? Do we need torches?"

Randy wiped his sweaty hand on his pants. "Good idea. Run up and get the two torches from my desk drawer. Hurry." He and Seth watched Michael and Harrison run off and waited in the scarily quiet hallway at the side of the castle. No one ever came back there, or hadn't until they'd had to move in and play tour guide to all the tourists. Chills rolled up and down his spine, the hairs on his arms stood on end, and he rubbed them until they settled and the other boys came back.

"Come on, let's go," he whispered and took the torch. Aiming it at the door, he turned the knob as quietly as he could and slowly opened it until they clearly saw the staircase going up to the tower room. Randy shone his light around and saw the stairs leading down to the basement. "Come on." He urged the others through the door, removed the key, and closed it behind him. "Let's go up first." He led the way up the old stone stairs, stepping quietly onto each, and made his way up to the room at the top to find the door locked.

"Try the key," Harrison whispered, and watched Randy slide the key in and turn it.

It clicked, and Randy turned the handle with ease and swung the door in, flashing his light everywhere. He knew what was in there already; a bed on the mezzanine above them, and a desk under the window. The walls were covered in scratch marks from all of his ancestors going bat shit crazy.

"Where's your dad?" Michael whispered, looking around.

"He must've gone down to the basement," Randy murmured, not seeing his dad. But he did see an old piece of parchment on the desk under the window illuminated by the full moon. Moving over to it, he aimed his light at the paper and saw it was the map his dad must have been talking about. "It's a treasure map," he whispered excitedly, his finger tracing the pictures on it. "Here's the castle, the tower, the land, and…" He peered closely at the tower. "What's that?"

"X marks the spot?" Harrison joked and leaned over his shoulder. "Is that a dog?"

"It can't be!" Michael leaned over Randy's other shoulder and stared at the map. "Maybe it's a symbol we have to look for," he whispered, his eyes taking in all of the details. "Was there ever a guard dog here before? Maybe he was guarding the treasure."

"Maybe." Randy shrugged. "But either way, it doesn't really tell us where the treasure is."

Seth had been staring at the wall under the mezzanine, looking at the scratch marks on the stones and bricks. His hand absentmindedly moved to one that looked like a hand, but its nail marks were narrower, deeper, longer.

Drip.

He felt the droplet on his head and moved his hand up to investigate. His eyes didn't take themselves from the wall. His brain thought there was a leak in the roof and the rain must be coming in. Except…it wasn't raining, it was clear and bright with a full moon shining in the windows. His head shifted and he looked up at his hand as more water dripped onto it, but the farther up his gaze travelled, the farther up he saw the marks, all the way to the mezzanine where there stood a hairy beast looking down at him, eyes flaming red, teeth bared and dripping saliva onto him.

"Oh," came out in a high-pitched squeak and the

other boys turned to look at him, saw him looking up, and looked up themselves to see the giant red-furred wolf snarling down on them, fangs bared.

"Ah, ah, what is that?" Harrison squealed and stumbled sideways along the wall, trying to get to the door, but stopped when the beast let out an almighty growl.

"Argh!" All four boys stumbled back against the wall and the beast turned the growl into a howl.

"Th-that was what we heard before," Michael stuttered, plastered against the wall next to Seth who'd stumbled back. "What do we do?"

Randy was flinging his arms around in fright, and Seth was doing the same from nerves, his arm shaking so badly the light bobbed all over the room, and when the animal saw it, he changed from a fang-baring werewolf into a puppy dog in seconds.

"Arh-arh," he huffed and bounded down to the floor to chase the bobbing light around the room. "Arh-arh." Like a young pup in a playground, he had energy to burn.

"Oh, my God, are you seeing this?" Randy asked. "He's playing with the light. Seth, keep doing it and we'll run for it. Aim it up high." He shoved Seth's arms up and the beam flew to the ceiling above the mezzanine. The wolf bounded up to it and the boys made a run for it.

"Argh!" they yelled all the way down to the ground floor. The puppy, having lost its plaything, turned back into the wolf and chased them down the winding steps.

"Hurry," Seth cried as Randy tried unlocking the door. It wouldn't budge. "Did you lock it? I don't think you locked it before which means you've locked it *now*." The growl sounded behind them and they turned to see the werewolf and his bare fangs. "Argh!"

"The basement," Randy yelled and bolted through the door and down the winding steps to the basement level. He'd hoped to get away from the beast, but the beast had followed and pounded through the closed door at the bottom of the steps landing on the children huddled in the middle of the room.

The floor collapsed beneath them.

Down, down, down.

One floor, two floors, three floors, four.

They landed in a cloud of dust and dirt and rotted wood. Coughing, they rolled over and crawled to their knees, waving the air with their hands to clear it, covering their mouths with their t-shirts.

"How did we…?" Harrison coughed. "Where are we…?"

Randy saw a sliver of light shining through a pile of rubble and found his torch underneath. He dug it out and aimed it at his friends, seeing they were as dirt-covered as he was.

"Is that the map?" Michael pointed to the half covered parchment.

Randy shone his light on it and picked it up, glad it was still intact except for a rip on one side that could be repaired. "We must have fallen through so far. How many floors?"

"Four?"

Randy turned to see his father gasping in the ruins. "Dad." He crawled over to him and pushed off the rubble. "You were down here. There's a beast, a creature, like a werewolf, but he acted like a puppy, he chased us, we have to get out of here." He helped his dad sit and his beam caught the glint of metal. "What's that?" Pointing the torch's beam over to the far side of the room, they saw rows and rows of chests and bags, silver goblets and golden crowns, gems and jewels and treasure galore. "Whoa…the treasure."

"It really does exist," Randford murmured. "I could just never find it. Do you have the map?"

Randy swung his torch back to his father and held the map under the light. They examined the tower and the notes, and the drawings over it and around it. "I don't get what the dog means," Randy said. "Was there a guard dog here at one point?"

Randford realised the meaning instantly and his memory flew back across everything he'd been told, everything he knew, and he started chuckling. That chuckle turned into a rolling laugh until he choked on the dust. "Yes. Yes, there was, and still is. I just didn't know I had to dig deeper."

"You mean that thing upstairs?" Randy waved his torch around, but didn't see the beast. "It was the weirdest thing. The moment he saw Seth's torch he was like a puppy bounding after it. Weird, I tell you. I didn't know we had wolves in the area."

"Not in the area." Randford coughed and pointed at the map. "Just in the family."

"Whoa, bet this'll cost a pretty penny." Seth held up a rock. But it wasn't just any rock. It was a glittering emerald green rock.

*****

After the rescue happened, and the treasure was retrieved, the Bantleroys sat their son down and told him the truth about the family secret. And while they hoped it stopped with Randford, it was entirely possible that Randy would have to deal with it. And two years later, on his 18th birthday, which, coincidentally, was also a full moon, Randford Bantleroy the fifth carried forth the Bantleroy legacy of turning into a werewolf upon his entry into manhood. His father had locked the two of them in the tower and stayed with his son during the transition. And the only way to calm a newborn werepuppy was to play games by throwing sticks and bobbing a light around. And once he'd howled a few times, Randford the fifth, known as Randy to his friends, settled down to sleep in his brand-new doggy bed.

ABOUT THE AUTHOR

T.K. is a children's TV show veteran who loves watching disaster and creature/zombie movies and TV shows, but not at night.

T.K. started writing many a year ago back in primary school, but only started her author career in 2015 with the release of her first three stories and anthology. She will write and release stories until there are twelve *Bones* books and a special edition numbered 13...

T.K. lives in Australia, loves extra cheesy cheeseburgers and chocolate, and gets a kick out of watching funny dog and cat videos.

T.K. Wrathbone is the kid's/tween pen name for author Tiara King. You can find more about Tiara on her website; follow her on social media, or visit her publishing house, Royal Star Publishing.

SOCIALS

tkwrathbone.com

tiaraking.com.au

royalstarpublishing.com.au

Sign up for *Tiara's* Newsletter…

Make sure you're always in the know and never miss free exclusives, the latest news, book updates, and so much more with newsletters from…

tiaraking.com.au

HAVE YOU READ THESE?

Next Top Mannequin
Cinderfella and Princess Charming: Witch Hunters
www.badluck-youredead.com
The Bones of Wrath: Changes
One Bone: Anthology 1

The Orphanage
Hantel and Gresel: Food Critics
Mirror, Mirror On The Wall
The Bones of Wrath: Haunted
Two Bone: Anthology 2

The Howler
Shadow Walkers
Faded
The Bones of Wrath: Ghosts
Three Bone: Anthology 3

I Spy With My Little Eye
Knock, Knock…Who's Dead?
It Creeped At Midnight
The Bones of Wrath: Monsters
Four: Anthology 4

OR THESE?

Trick Or Treat
All Hallows Possession
They Rise On A Blood Moon
The Bones of Wrath: Horrors
Five Bone: Anthology 5

All Clowns Must Die!
The Demon Resides
Infestation
The Bones of Wrath: Terrors
Six Bone: Anthology 6